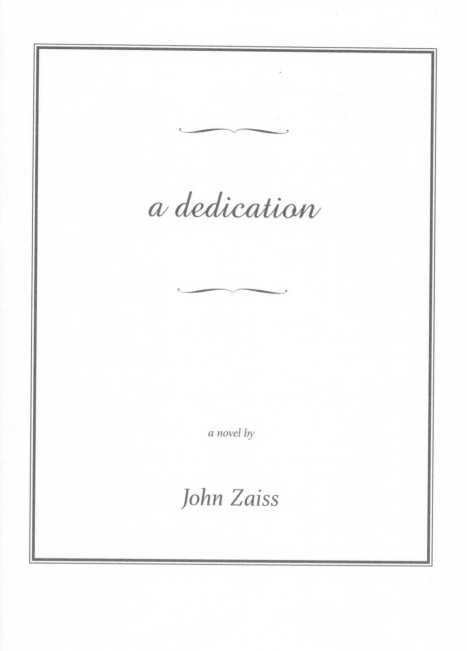

a dedication

a novel by

John Zaiss

Synergy Books

Austin, TX

Publisher's Cataloging-in-Publication
(Provided by Quality Books, Inc.)

Zaiss, John.
      A dedication : a novel / by John Zaiss. -- 1st ed.
      p. cm.
      ISBN 0-9755922-3-8
      1. Maturation (Psychology)--Fiction. 2. Family--
  Fiction. 3. Vietnamese Conflict, 1961-1975--Fiction.
  I. Title.
  PS3626.A6255D44 2005   813'.6
                      QBI04-800129

Published by:

 Synergy Books

FIRST EDITION

10 9 8 7 6 5 4 3 2 1

For my children Mike, Steve, and Becky ...

I love you.

a dedication

one

It doesn't seem so long ago that I reveled in being labeled a loner, a troubled teenager, and I wore that badge with an angry pride, willing to challenge and ready to dismiss any type of authority. I believed solitude and loneliness were inseparable companions, that being different meant being ostracized, and that individuality precluded fitting in. Sadly, perhaps predictably, I was willing to pay the price.

But my life changed.

Some might argue maturity arrived—losing the attitude, gaining perspective, the transformation of boy to man—but that's too simple, like it's assumed and not special. I think it was more. I believe one of life's secret windows momentarily opened, and that I was invited to take a peek. Even though looking through that window complicated my world, it's when life became fulfilling and truly my own.

When I look back to that time in my life, when I sift through memories and recall events, I can't help but think of the teachers who guided me, the people who played both major and minor roles that made a difference. They took me to different vantage points of that window with their unique perspective, and each helped me define, or at least hone in on, who I am.

And then there was Joe Toscano. A retired warrior, gifted artist, and perpetual student, he was the person who, despite grappling with his own demons, somehow connected and kept me from the destructive path I was so bent on following. Joe's lessons—owning choices, defining my own success, accepting that even good people make mistakes—aren't difficult to remember, though they can be hard to follow. They've stayed with me through a gently persistent inner voice when day-to-day challenges become too difficult.

I'm sure there were books that dispensed equivalent doses of counsel, the self-help gurus with their formulaic programs and cute slogans, but they didn't know me. And besides, books don't offer Marie Callender's pie or blinking eyes or knowing smiles that pave the way for wisdom that can sometimes be too hard to swallow. Those belong to Joe.

Although I am now quietly confident with whatever tomorrow brings, it wasn't always so.

two

It didn't take much. A hot chat room, flipping through TV channels with the remote until something grabbed me, imagining circumstances that would transform my mostly geek status to popular, tapping a pencil or foot to a song I liked. They were distractions, basic tools for a procrastinator, and I was using them instead of writing a paper for my Contemporary American History class. I told myself I'd start in just a few more minutes, but I knew if I bounced back and forth long enough, it would be too late to work on the assignment that night. It was an unproductive habit that suited me well.

Discuss whether FDR allowed a Japanese attack on Pearl Harbor in order to thrust America into World War II.

Right. I was seventeen years old and basically didn't give a shit.

I suppose I wasn't all that different from other kids my age; I played loud music, wore baggy pants that threatened to fall off with every step, and I'd perfected that perpetual scowl, the one hovering somewhere between distant and dangerous. Still, I wasn't an extreme version—no tattoos or piercings, and I didn't do drugs—but that didn't seem to matter to most adults.

Rationalizations work better with larger numbers, so I think they lumped all of us together for the sake of convenience.

I knew my mom would be checking in soon. Her routine was annoying. She would knock on my bedroom door, walk in without being invited, and ask whether my homework was done. She'd list every subject—American Lit, Chemistry, Spanish, History, Pre-Calculus—and watch for any hesitation when I answered. I never hesitated. I was always caught up with my homework, or at least that's what I'd tell her before turning my music louder and flipping a page of whatever book happened to be open. She'd perform this ritual twice a night, three times if she was feeling particularly out of control, and then stomp off in a dramatic display of self-pity and frustration.

My dad jumped into the rotation every now and then. He was an airline pilot so he was out of town quite a bit, and I used that to my advantage. It was a big enough challenge for him to know what classes I was taking, so asking about homework just didn't happen. It seemed like all he cared about were my grades, anyway. What did I think I had so far? Could I get it to an A? I guess you'd call him a bottom-line type of guy.

My parents never asked about my other class. Mom didn't care whether the homework was done, and Dad never queried about the grade. Photography didn't count as a real class with them. Capturing images of joy and despair and pain and innocence just didn't compare to solving logarithms as far as they were concerned. Maybe they had a point. I spent three hours working math problems and deducing word analogies when I took the SAT. The damned thing never asked one question about photography.

My name is Quinnlan Marshall, but everyone calls me Quinn. Quinnlan is a family name from some guy in the Revolutionary War who led a battle against the British and got himself killed. I used to joke that he was the extent of heroes in our family, but what was really funny is that no one even knew how the guy was related; they just liked his name. I didn't. It wasn't cool having a weird first name at seventeen—just something else to be ragged about—so when I heard the name Quinnlan, I never turned around. It was either someone I didn't know or didn't like, or I was in trouble.

We lived in Louisville, Colorado, a suburb between Denver and Boulder, and I was a junior at Monarch High School. I was tall, almost six-foot-two, and I weighed one hundred and forty pounds. I tried not being self-conscious about being skinny, but that didn't work. The truth was simple and painful: I felt awkward and clumsy when I wasn't in my room—which is why I quit playing sports. Falling down in front of spectators sucked.

When I looked in the mirror, if I was being really honest, I had to admit to being good looking. It was the blue eyes. A lot of people have blue eyes but not many have pitch-black hair and blue eyes. It's what everyone noticed—that and being skinny. Of course I was pretty good at disguising nature's statistical quirk; hit-or-miss personal hygiene, scruffy clothes, and less-than-disciplined hair sent a message that I didn't care what others thought. Unfortunately, I did.

I was locked in a kind of no-man's land at school; not cool enough to be popular and not dorky enough to be a loser. There were others in the same caste as me, but I kept my distance. They mostly imitated the cool kids and dreamed of being one of them. They were the wannabes. Me? I dreamt of the day when I'd figure out who I was, and that would be good enough.

Despite an appearance and attitude suggesting otherwise, I hadn't always been so cynical. I used to care about a lot of things besides blaring music and hanging out online. I played sports, joined a couple of clubs at school, even had a pretty good grade point average at one time. That must be why they kept me in honors classes—that and an IQ somewhere north of one-fifty. Like that mattered. Being cursed by intelligence was just another reason I didn't fit in, and I did my best to bury the evidence. Sloppy homework, unread chapters, and careless tests kept me unremarkable and discreetly comfortable, though deep down I knew I was still smart. But I also knew there hadn't been a reason to show it lately.

The predictable rap on my bedroom door came during a temporary stereo silence, and my mom entered. "How's the homework coming?" she asked just as an angry electric guitar jolted the room with a new song. Of course I couldn't really hear her words, but the mannerisms and expression told me what I needed to know. I never asked, "What did you say?" That would have admitted the music was too loud.

"Still writing the history paper." With an effortless dexterity reserved for you-didn't-catch-me moments, I lowered the volume, moved the cursor on the computer and clicked on the article I'd already downloaded off the Internet. The article argued that FDR had advance knowledge of Japanese intentions because U.S. Navy codebreakers had intercepted and decoded several radio transmissions warning of the attack on Pearl Harbor. Sounded good to me.

Mom gave my room the once-over. Actually, it would have been correctly labeled the twice-over since she'd already made the rounds earlier that night. She noticed that the various piles of clothes scattered around my room still hadn't moved, but she didn't broach the subject. I was surprised by her lack of comment, but then again I thought maybe her battle-picking skills had improved a bit recently.

"How can you possibly concentrate with the music blaring like that?" she asked before looking at the images flashing across the television on my dresser. She sighed. Mom never liked *South Park*, not even the reruns.

"I'm writing a term paper," I said with just enough edge. "I already know the material, and I'm gathering my thoughts. Are you complaining because I like to feel comfortable when I study?"

"Comfortable is a lot different than being distracted." She scowled at the collection of sheets and blankets twisted across my bed.

"Oh my God." I raised my tone and rolled my eyes. "I have a B, and it's an honors class. In fact, I have a B average in all my classes. Isn't that good enough for you?" I held my eyes steady, hoping she wouldn't tabulate the homework, tests and quizzes for each class. The truth was, except for Photography, I had C's across the board. Okay, so maybe a D in Pre-Calc, but there were still three weeks until the quarter ended. I could have argued that I'd probably have B's.

The tiny muscles tightened around my mother's jaw as she debated whether to answer. Maybe she was counting to ten. "It's not the grades, Quinn," she finally said. "If B's and C's were the best you could do, then your father and I would be happy. The problem is we know you're capable of so much more. You get decent grades without even trying. Imagine what you could achieve if you really focused."

Of course I knew my mom meant well. She was always trying to do the right thing: timely thank-you notes, checking in on friends with problems, volunteering at church. Doing the right thing was an image Mom liked, but that she meant well didn't matter to me. I only heard her telling me what to do.

"I get the same lecture over and over," I snapped. "Can't you come up with something original? And how do you know I'm not focused? Maybe grades aren't as important to me as they are to you and Dad." I had a winnable argument. Whose life was it, anyway?

"Getting good grades translates into being accepted at the best colleges. We've had this discussion before, Quinn," she said, folding her arms across her chest.

Mom was a forty-five-year-old homemaker and looked the part. Always precise makeup and appropriately outfitted before breakfast; her brown hair was cut short and painted by the hairdresser every month to keep the correct shade. She was average height and always talked about the five pounds she needed to lose. I thought it was closer to fifteen.

"Argue all you want about the standard, but the coldhearted fact won't change. Topnotch colleges demand good grades. You don't get in without them." Her tone was not encouraging or motivating.

"Bill Gates didn't graduate from college, and Warren Buffett went to the University of Nebraska," I fired back, wondering if she'd recognize the names. "The two richest men in America didn't need topnotch schools to be successful, now did they?" Needless to say, *my* battle-picking skills needed serious work. I never backed down from arguments.

Mom's eyes wandered through my room again, seeking confirmation that her only son was hopeless. The can of Mountain Dew and bag of potato chips with crumbs strewn across my nightstand did the trick. "Just get your homework done." She sighed again and abruptly left the room.

I turned the music louder, but not as loud as before. Despite my combative nature, I just wasn't in the mood to press the skirmish. Besides, deep down I got the party line that my parents provided for my sister and me, and that they only wanted the best for us. But "what's best" came prepackaged. It only fit their terms.

I realize now that my never-ending rollercoaster ride of confusion and frustration and anger—unsure which emotion was next in line or when it would kick in—wasn't all that noteworthy, or even distinctive. I was just at that anxious age; too old to blindly believe that my parents knew everything, yet too young to accept their experience. Sure, I knew it wasn't all their fault, and sometimes I even felt guilty when I lashed out at them. Sometimes I even wished we would talk. But that had never worked before. My parents didn't talk, they lectured, and I didn't need to be told how to live my life. I needed someone to listen to how it was going so far.

three

I had decided to go to Eldorado Canyon after school that day in March. It was seventy-one degrees, the sky was startlingly blue, and the sun had taken an unforgiving attitude toward winter's surviving snowpacks. It was a Friday so I didn't have to think about doing homework, and Mom wouldn't be home from an airport run until after seven.

I knew I could be there thirty minutes after leaving the school parking lot, which would leave more than two hours to wander through nature's antidote for snippy teachers, the latest made-for-teenage-girl music I heard playing down the hall, and a pathetic Pre-Calc test. I needed a strong B to offset a litany of careless mistakes on previous tests, and a sixty-five percent just didn't cut it. About the only good news I could muster was that I didn't have to get worked up over the next exam; a D for the quarter was pretty much a lock, no matter what.

It was five minutes after the final bell and the halls were filled with students jostling to get to their lockers, eager to dump text-books in with candy wrappers and graded papers that just never seemed to make it back into notebooks. Most of us didn't waste a lot of time after the final bell, especially on Fridays. It was like releasing trapped bees from a mayonnaise jar; there was a lot of animated buzzing while we scattered. A few lingered, though. Guys who wore letter jackets huddled in groups testing the limits of horseplay, while the girls who dated them leaned their shoulders against the walls, giggling and gossiping like they couldn't be torn from their protective womb. They were the ones who liked school.

I adjusted the strap of my backpack and fumbled with the combination lock, thinking ahead whether I had time to eat. I was starved but really didn't want to miss any remaining daylight, so I decided on Rudy's Café just this side of Eldorado Springs. Their burgers tasted better than fast-food and if there weren't any traffic problems, I could spare twenty minutes to tame my growling stomach.

Something pressed the locker door against my shoulder as I reached for the camera bag dangling from the coat hook.

"Hey, Quinn." It was Michael Wingate, a sophomore who lived down the street from me. He was a letter jacket guy—the sucker weighed two hundred and forty pounds and played offensive tackle for the varsity football team—but we'd known each other for ten years, and he ignored my status at Monarch.

"Hi, Winnie." The nickname dated to an era when I could pound Michael Wingate just because he was younger than me. Those days were long gone, but the nickname stuck. It was always kinda funny when the football coaches yelled, "Knock 'em on their ass, Winnie."

"Hey, any chance I can catch a ride? My mom took an extra shift at the hospital and I really don't feel like takin' the bus home."

Winnie's mom was a nurse at Boulder Community Hospital and was always working extra shifts. She'd divorced Winnie's dad two years earlier and was determined to make enough money to stay in the neighborhood. Spending less time with family in order to live in a family neighborhood? I was always quick to pinpoint other people's contradictions.

"I'm not headed home," I said, hoping the succinct reply sent the right message. I turned back to my locker and hoisted the camera bag onto my shoulder like the matter was settled.

"Yeah? What's goin' on?"

So Winnie didn't pick up on nuances. What can I say? The guy played offensive tackle, for Christ's sake.

"I'm heading up to Eldorado Canyon with my cameras." I toyed with the idea of sharing my hope of capturing the first hints of spring on film, but decided that green buds popping from branches and animals munching on grassy patches recently freed from a blanket of snow couldn't be translated into terms Winnie would appreciate.

"Dude, I love that place," he said, pursing his lips and shaking his head. "South Boulder Creek, the cliffs? We used to go up there for Cub Scouts, remember?" Winnie stared vacantly down the hall, his mind's eye locked onto memories of rushing streams and adventurous rock climbs.

"Yeah." I didn't admit to remembering Cub Scouts; only guys who weighed two-forty could get away with that in high school.

"My mom's not coming home until late and I got no plans. Mind if I hook up?"

"It's still cold up there, Winnie. The elevation change and all." I cocked an eyebrow, waiting to see resignation from my neighbor. Nothing. "I've got my ski vest, gloves and hiking boots already in the car, and I'm in a hurry to get there. Sorry," I said, and shrugged my shoulders.

"I got a ski jacket and gloves in my locker. I can meet you at your car in two minutes." The idea of communing with nature was gathering steam with Michael Wingate, but then he hesitated. "Hey, it's okay, isn't it?"

"Look, I'm going up there to take pictures, not goof around." I wanted to be bolder, to say what was really on my mind, that I wanted to be by myself, but those words didn't come.

Winnie sensed acquiescence and started trotting down the

hall. "I'll be at your car in two minutes," he yelled back over his shoulder.

It could have been worse, I suppose. Winnie wasn't such a bad guy, and hey, maybe one of the cheerleaders would spot a football player riding in my car. Better yet, maybe some crazed animal scavenging for food would decide he was a meatier proposition. I grunted at both thoughts. I was invisible to cheerleaders, and I'd never heard of a wild animal attack in Eldorado Canyon.

When I flipped the locker shut and twirled the lock, I was startled by someone standing next to me. It was Mr. McCormack, my history teacher.

"Uh, hi Mr. McCormack," I finally managed.

"Quinn." He nodded but didn't smile, and his eyes, cloudy green marbles hiding behind thick wire-rimmed glasses, told me that this was not a passing hello.

Mr. McCormack wasn't old by teenager standards, probably mid-thirties. He was short, squatty and never bothered running a comb through a crop of unruly red hair. But being funny-looking didn't keep the guy from strutting the halls with an open arrogance, like he'd been teaching forever and knew all the tricks. I wasn't fooled, though. Mr. McCormack didn't like teaching, he liked authority.

"Well, have a good weekend," I said with a half-smile, and turned.

"Quinn, we need to talk. Let's go to my classroom."

I strained not to show emotion while turning around. It had been a long time since I'd talked with a teacher and felt good afterward. "What do you want to talk about?" The pitch of my voice, despite considerable effort, rose with each word.

"I think we should talk in private."

My camera bag was slung over one shoulder, my backpack over the other, and it was Friday afternoon. This couldn't be happening. "I really can't, Mr. McCormack. I have a dentist appointment right after school and it's a fifteen-minute drive. I need to hustle if I'm going to make it." Teenagers lie at the slightest provocation, and I admit, it was my preferred weapon.

My history teacher frowned and riveted his eyes to mine, waiting for a hint of weakness, weighing his options. Making a student miss an after-school dental appointment was a tough call; parents got testy when prized time slots were wasted.

In a slow monotone that threatened to call my bluff, he finally said, "I suppose it can wait until Monday morning." Mr. McCormack scribbled on a small notepad and tore off the sheet. "Here. This is a pass from your first-period study hall Monday morning. You be in my classroom. No excuses." He handed me the slip like it was a subpoena.

"I'll be there, Mr. McCormack."

I started walking down the hall, wondering what new violation I'd committed: dress code, chewing gum, disrupting class? I knew I was current with my homework, but I made a mental note to double-check over the weekend, just in case. And then I forgot about it. I wasn't going to let anything ruin my afternoon.

SPRING FEVER WAS CONTAGIOUS at Monarch High School. The remaining snow, shielded from sun by overhanging eaves and brick walls, was losing its battle against higher temperatures. Crunchy powder had turned wet, and students were launching snowballs with gloveless hands and rebellious attitudes. Sweatshirts that began the day covering blouses and T-shirts were now tied around waists, designer sunglasses were perched on noses, and the assault on Louisville's streets began as waves of sixteen- and seventeen-year-old drivers gunned engines, their tires spitting a layer of rock salt behind them.

Winnie stood next to my Ford Explorer, waving acknowledgment of his timely presence when a snowball splattered against his back. It didn't faze him. He pointed to the offender, pretended an unmerciful payback, and laughed. "What a day!" he shouted to me as he ducked from another incoming.

"There will be a lot more snow in the canyon," I said, unlocking the car doors. "You sure you're okay without boots?" I opened the back door, tossed my backpack on the seat, and wedged my camera bag on the floor beneath it.

"No sweat." Winnie plopped into the front passenger seat, latched the seatbelt and flashed a grin.

The guy just got pelted with a snowball, he'd be trudging with frozen feet in an hour, and he was grinning. I'd never kept up with his academic career so I wasn't sure if he was good-natured or just stupid.

"I think we have time for Rudy's if you're hungry."

I wasn't surprised that Winnie's grin widened as he gave a half-nod. I was going to have a couple of burgers and fries, but his intake would surely make the restaurant's week.

"So you're into this photography thing, huh?" he said as we pulled away. "I really like the picture you took of Geezer."

"Thanks, but I'm not sure he did."

Geezer was more formally known as Harold Gendler, our school principal, and his nickname tells you everything you need to know. I had captured one of his private moments, closing his eyes and holding his head during a school band performance, and the school newspaper had printed it the previous week with the caption "O, Lawrence Welk, where art thou?" I didn't have anything to do with selecting the picture or penning the caption, and it wasn't really that good of a shot, but I had accepted the compliments and slaps on the back like I'd planned it all along.

"Ah, he knew it was in fun. So, you like taking pictures of people or nature better?"

Winnie wasn't just making conversation, he was actually interested. He looked across the seat and gave me another sloppy grin.

"I like taking both," I said, somewhat surprised by his question. "The techniques vary a little because of the subject. Nature is beautiful, it's awesome, it's inspiring, even frightening." I cleared my throat and paused, anxious to talk about my passion yet hesitant to reveal myself. "But the pictures I take of people? They tell a story, their story. The eyes, the wrinkles, the scars— the stories are buried in their faces."

"Cool." Winnie scrunched his mouth and nodded. "So you want to be some famous Ansel Adams type of dude? My aunt gives me one of those calendars every Christmas."

"Naw, I just enjoy it." Of course I wanted to be like Ansel Adams! Getting paid to travel the world and take pictures, being famous and drenched with public admiration, Quinn Marshall calendars in every bookstore? Shallow, but I would have taken it. Even brooding teenagers have dreams, and Winnie had poked mine square in the belly.

"I don't do much stuff like that, mostly 'cuz of football and all. I'm hopin' I can play college ball. Coach says I'm probably not done growing, says I might pick up a couple more inches and twenty, maybe thirty pounds before the college scouts get serious next year. Been lifting quite a bit, you know, stayin' in shape during the off-season."

"You're pretty good." I was relieved the subject had changed from photography, but I guess I could have been more complimentary. Very few sophomores at high schools our size made the varsity football team, much less started. I think I'd even read that Winnie was an honorable mention for the all-metro team. But my dark side popped out when I asked, "Do you *like* playing football?"

Winnie paused and stroked his lower lip. "Yeah," he finally said. "I like it okay. My mom says everyone is blessed with different talents, and that it's important not to waste them. I guess

God decided I should push people to the dirt when he gave me this body." Winnie laughed at his own joke, then added, "I gotta be realistic, Quinn. My mom works her butt off to keep the house and put food on the table. I got two younger sisters, so I can't expect her to pay for my college. Not when I can get a scholarship by playing football."

"How are Janice and Laura?" I felt guilty about prying, about losing touch with a friend, about assuming my parents would automatically pay for college.

"They're fine. Pretty good kids, actually. My Grandma picks 'em up and keeps 'em on nights when my mom works." Winnie gave me another one of those smiles. "It's kinda cool being a big brother."

I nodded, but not because I liked being a big brother. Yeah, right. My twelve-year-old sister Elizabeth was a prissy little smart-ass who knew just when to scream for Mom or Dad. I nodded because it was a good time not to talk.

I veered the Explorer onto Highway 170. There was a little more snow as we gained altitude, but the road was mostly clear. The car ahead sprayed a blinding mist onto my windshield as it sped through a wet spot, and I flipped the wiper switch and pumped the dispenser. Even nasty brown slime couldn't dampen my anticipation of a few hours in Eldorado Canyon with my cameras.

Winnie broke the silence. "Ya know, it's hard not to like something you're good at." His eyes didn't blink and he stared through the cleared path on the windshield. "But there's lots of things I like better than playing football."

four

I was satisfied. My stomach was busy searching the deposit from Rudy's for traces of nutrition, and I'd guided the Explorer almost two miles off the main road before deciding the snow hadn't melted enough to press my luck. When I stepped out, my eyes narrowed against a stiff breeze and my cheeks reddened as the crisp air stung my face. It was invigorating, refreshing.

Eldorado Canyon was hidden in the foothills south of Boulder and extended west into the Rocky Mountains. It wasn't really an isolated or out-of-the-way place—students from the University of Colorado had staked out party zones, hiked the trails, and climbed the cliffs for years—but I wasn't expecting much company. College crowds packed the bars, not Eldorado Canyon, on Friday afternoons.

"The snow's not too bad," Winnie said as he zipped his ski jacket. He did a three-sixty, pausing briefly when he recognized a familiar landmark. "There's a basin with a stream running through it, just over that ridge." He pointed and looked to see if I followed. "The football team had an end-of-the-season party there. Cool place, but dude, it was cold!"

I nodded and faked a smile. A bunch of football players chugging beer and making fools of themselves wasn't news. "I've been there. The stream feeds into a little lake about a mile north," I said, fastening the hip-pack stuffed with film around my waist. "You ever see it?"

Winnie shook his head. "I haven't really explored around here much," he admitted.

"I was thinking about either going there or Buffalo Pass this afternoon. Come on, I'll show you the lake. It's closer, and there won't be as much snow."

Winnie's nod settled it, Hideaway Lake it was. Hideaway Lake didn't really have a name; I christened it myself, but I didn't tell Winnie that. And it's more of a pond than a lake. Still, it was one of my favorite spots, and I was willing to share it that afternoon.

WE REACHED THE BASIN AFTER a mostly uphill and silent fifteen-minute hike. Although there were no campgrounds in Eldorado Canyon, the clearing where we stopped was a popular gathering spot; a six-foot circle of bucket-sized rocks surrounded a pile of ashes and the remnants of burned logs, confirming that the site was far enough off the beaten path, but not too far.

Winnie leaned his back against the trunk of a ponderosa pine and took deep gulps of air. "This is where we had the party I told you about." Another grin. "You know Timmy Spahn?"

Who *didn't* know Timmy Spahn? Come on, Mr. Football/ Basketball of Monarch High? The guy every girl in school talked about? With the wavy blond hair? That Timmy Spahn? "Yeah," I said, "I know who he is."

"Well, maybe I shouldn't be tellin' ya this, but that's one crazy dude." Winnie paused but didn't really think about *not* telling me. "That night? We're all hangin' out, staying close enough to the fire to keep warm, talkin' and stuff. There's some beer, but that's about it. Nothin' too extreme. Well, Timmy? We don't see him for awhile, and then somebody asked where he was. Nobody had seen the dude for like a half-hour." Winnie leaned forward and shook his head. "All of a sudden we hear a voice say, 'Are you talking about me?' It was Timmy. Standing right over there on top of that rock."

"So?"

"So he's buck naked. Not a stitch. Not even shoes. Nothin'."

I didn't say anything, just smiled as my brain connected this picture to my newly validated, albeit self-serving, opinion of Timmy Spahn.

"Then," Winnie said, eyes widening, "he does a swan dive right into a big snowdrift. The dude's like buried in five feet of snow. And we're all laughin', thinkin' what an idiot, that he must be freezing, gonna catch pneumonia, stuff like that."

"I can see why you'd think that, Winnie. He *is* an idiot. He must have frozen his balls off," I said.

Winnie's famous grin erupted but he didn't say a word.

"What?" It bothered me that I was even mildly interested in anything having to do with Timmy Spahn.

"He's in that snowdrift for like sixty seconds and nobody can see him. All of a sudden someone screams, 'He's suffocating!' so we all rushed over and started clawing away at the snow, trying to find Timmy."

I knew Timmy survived. I'd seen him at school, so I waited to hear the ending.

"We're all frantic, we gotta find Timmy before he dies, right? Then we heard this unbelievable scream. Agony! Absolute agony!" Winnie's eyes teased me with their dance before he muffled the words under his breath like he was drawing a conspirator into a plot. "Aaron Greenberg accidentally grabbed Timmy's dick when he was diggin' in the snow!" Tears filled the corners of Winnie's eyes. No longer concerned with secrecy, he started laughing uncontrollably, swallowing and struggling, starting and stopping. It took several deep breaths before he could finish the story. "So we find Timmy, he's like gray or blue or somethin'. And he's yellin' at the top of his lungs that somebody broke his dick!" Winnie couldn't hold back and fell to his knees as the tears streamed down his cheeks. "Sure enough," he said, "his cock was blue. And it was bent!"

I couldn't stop laughing either. Timmy Spahn—so cold, in so much pain, and with a broken dick. Yes!

Winnie wiped a glove under each eye and swallowed. "Dude," he said between a last few chuckles, "you can't say anything. We all promised Timmy. Okay?"

"Did he have to go to the hospital?"

"Nah, we just wrapped him in, like, five blankets, and stuck him right next to the fire. He shivered awhile, but then he warmed up. Timmy said he was okay, so everyone hiked back to where we parked, and some of the guys drove him home. The dude didn't even miss any school."

"So how's Greenberg feel about yanking Timmy Spahn's dick?" I asked. Aaron Greenberg was a senior and about the same size as Winnie. He didn't, however, share the same disposition. Actually, he was a pretty nasty SOB.

"That's another good reason not to talk about it."

WE HIKED THROUGH A SAW-TOOTHED pattern of rocks and Rocky Mountain junipers for nearly a mile and nature was quite agreeable, filling our senses with sights and sounds and smells. The sun, still hovering above a canopy of trees, had warmed select patches of earth into spongy combinations of dead leaves and awakening prairie grass, and sweetened the air with the smell of moist pine. Then Winnie and I got lucky. We spotted our first live subject just before crossing an open meadow to the next hill.

The young buck maintained a guarded vigilance as he paused between bites. Nothing seemed out of the ordinary, no other creatures warned of stealthy predators tucked behind trees preparing an attack. He pawed the ground, flinging soft clumps of snow from the straggling grass, and yanked another mouthful. His body was strong and lean. His pedicels were covered with a thin layer of velvet and looked tender, not yet resembling a majestic rack.

I looked at Winnie and held an ungloved finger to my lips. He was crouched behind a wall of willow shrubs twenty feet to my right, and gave me a slight nod before returning his gaze toward our target. I was on both knees, hidden behind a giant rock, and had already attached the 300mm telephoto lens onto my Nikon N90. It was heavy and awkward, so I felt for a depression or edge on the rock with my left elbow, angling for a position that would shift some of the weight and reduce the possibility of camera shake. I'd already adjusted the shutter speed to compensate for any unintentional movement, and was waiting for a gust of wind to mask the noise of my first shot.

I was ready to switch to the Canon EOS 30 hanging around my neck whenever the buck sensed our presence. The Canon automatically adjusted the shutter speed, was preset on moderate zoom, and ready to click continuous frames of the buck's escape; meanwhile, I was eager to record the unhurried and simple pleasures of this creature.

I felt the wind before I heard it rock the branches. My left hand tightened around the base of the camera and my right finger was poised as I took one final sighting. The buck had raised his head and was twitching his nose while the breeze gathered momentum, but the wind was blowing in my face, carrying my scent away from him. He pawed the ground again, and I took the shot.

I was waiting for another pose when a twig snapped, and my gut told me that the sound carried the thirty yards to where the buck stood. The noise came from Winnie's direction, but I'd trained myself not to waste precious seconds; there would be time for reprisals later. Instead, I quickly dangled the Nikon from my neck and raised the Canon in its place.

My gut was right. The buck threw his head back and his body stiffened, looking almost like one of those silly statues cluttering neighborhood backyards. His hesitation, honed by a million-year-old instinct, lasted only an instant. I stood and trained my camera on the fleeing animal and kept the shutter release depressed, hoping my photographic barrage captured the escape. CLICK, CLICK, CLICK, CLICK, CLICK. And then he was gone.

"Shit, Quinn."

Winnie stood and walked toward me shaking his head. It was one of the few times I can remember ever seeing him frown.

"I'm sorry, dude. My foot was fallin' asleep, and ... I must've stepped on a branch or somethin'. I'm real sorry."

I brushed the snow from my knees and, out of habit, checked the film in both cameras. "Don't worry about it. I got plenty of shots. He could have been spooked by anything," I said, but my tone was not convincing.

"I'm real sorry." Winnie's expression told me that he wanted to rework the apology with fancy words and excuses, but then he held a momentary breath and stared at the ground, perhaps deciding he'd said too much already.

I crossed between the trees and started toward the hollow where the buck had been grazing, channeling my frustration into rude, heavy steps. I was good at pouting. Winnie arrived a few seconds later and fell in behind me without speaking, like a little kid tagging along who keeps enough distance out of fear of being told to go home.

When I looked over my shoulder it was obvious that my few seconds of pissed-off silence had exacted a toll. I finally stopped and turned. "It's okay," I said again. "I got some great shots, so let's get to the lake."

"I can't wait to see the pictures." Winnie didn't try to decipher any hidden meaning, his head no longer hung at half-mast, and his smile returned.

That was the thing about Michael Wingate. You just couldn't stay mad at the guy. God, it was frustrating! He screwed up and instead of making some lame excuse, he apologized. And meant it.

We trudged across the meadow and into a dense wall of ponderosa pine and Douglas fir, and began climbing the final bank, grabbing branches and boulders to steady ourselves. The snow was slick and crunchy now, our footing precarious. We paused every twenty-five yards or so, catching our breath and mapping the next leg through the swaying trees and around barren rock outcrops too dangerous to climb. We were at 8,000 feet, not a big deal for a couple of kids used to the mountains, but the steep incline and heavy camera equipment combined to make our journey a physical challenge.

"Whoa!" Winnie forgot he was winded as he took in the view when we reached the summit. He looked down the hill we'd just climbed, verified our steep perch, and then admired the vista again.

Hideaway Lake was not an imposing body of water that stretched forever, or even a man-made reservoir designed to lure campers. It was odd-shaped, like those wooden salad bowls you see in gourmet catalogs, only a quarter-mile long and a hundred yards across, carved between three hills and fed by a stream from the melted snowpack. But its size fit the surroundings and guarded a delicious secret. Hideaway Lake didn't show up on any maps.

I took a couple of deep breaths and felt my heart rate slow as the exertion of the last fifty yards subsided. Part of the reason that more people didn't know about this place was accessibility. It was hard enough getting to where Winnie and I stood; there were no paths and the gentler side of the slope we'd climbed led to a point where the lake was not visible. You had to go straight up or miss it. Those following the stream were met by an impassable thicket and had to retreat, while access from other directions was even less likely. Walls of treacherous cliffs surrounded the lake's perimeter from three sides, and dissuaded all but the most insistent climbers and hikers.

"How'd you find this place?" Winnie asked. "I mean, this is tight!"

"Pure luck. I trailed a fawn last summer, trying to get some close-ups, and this is where I ended up."

I would have liked to say that God directed me there, that I was meant to capture the intensity, the beauty, but I couldn't. I had trouble grappling with the concept of God. For every picture I took of Hideaway Lake, I snapped a homeless man on Market Street in downtown Denver. For every leaf that changed color, for each wildflower, there were dilapidated buildings, polluted skies, and broken people to memorialize. My pictures were extreme and they conflicted, just like my feelings about God.

Winnie and I angled our way down the mountain, sidestepping fallen branches and leaves, keeping quiet just in case there were other animals in the area. I'd been surprised by bursts of wildlife before, and I cradled the Canon in my left hand just in case. Winnie's eyes darted back and forth with each step, undoubtedly hoping to sight a replacement photo opportunity for me.

We were about two-thirds of the way down when a lone cloud temporarily blotted the sun, casting an unusual filter of light through the valley. I tugged Winnie's sleeve and pointed to the effects. The sapphire blue lake had turned an uncertain gray with patches of shiny ripples glinting off the water, while magnified shadows and cold, colorless walls added a layer of intimidation onto the already rugged face of the rocks to the north.

Flickers of sunlight pierced the cloud and shot through an arch formed by two boulders across the lake. I'd snapped pictures of the rock formation from a dozen angles before, but had never seen a ray of light seemingly stab through the opening. I dropped to one knee, focused the telephoto lens, and took the shot. I quickly changed to a wide-angle lens that would include the overhead sky effects, all the time hoping I hadn't made some dumb-ass mistake that would ruin those few seconds of nature's artistry.

"Hey Quinn," whispered Winnie. "Look." He pointed toward a spot two hundred feet below us. "Who's that?"

five

I saw someone standing next to the lake's edge. I couldn't tell if it was a man or a woman, and it looked like there was something resting on a nearby stand. I snapped the telephoto lens back in place and sighted the target. It was a man, an older man, with closely cropped white hair. He was wearing blue jeans and cowboy boots, and a checkered flannel shirt that covered a navy turtleneck. I scanned the area and spotted a coat and gloves on the ground, and an easel with canvas in place, standing on three legs. A palette rested on a backpack next to his feet.

"Some guy's painting," I said to Winnie. "Come on. I want to get some shots of him, artist at work stuff. But *be* quiet."

Purposeful poses just seemed to miss the essence of character I craved, so I'd developed a kind of sixth sense with unsuspecting subjects. I handed the camera bag to Winnie and led the way, straining to duck walk, not slide, down the embankment while the two cameras swayed around my neck. It was a tricky proposition. My calves burned and I felt tightness in my hamstrings as I crept behind shrubs and trees. I saw a fluted rock guarded on both sides by fir saplings just twenty yards from the man, and edged toward it. Winnie copied each of my steps, but I didn't hear them. I heard humming instead. When I gave Winnie a what-the-heck-is-that grimace, he smiled and shrugged.

The sound of music filled the air as we reached the observation point—literally, as in Julie Andrews dancing on an Austrian mountaintop and singing "The hills are alive!" Except Julie wasn't singing. It was the old guy humming, tossing in an occasional lyric just to mix up the monotony. A guy singing *The Sound of Music* ... because he wanted to? Not pretty, but at least it provided background noise.

Winnie and I leaned against the fluted rock and stretched our legs, quietly working out the kinks. I'd already decided to use the Nikon and 300mm lens, hoping to capture triumph or temperament, ready to link a crusty frown or calculating eyes to just one moment of inspiration. I mentally ran through the checklist—caps and settings and knobs—before angling to an opening between the base of the rock and the baby fir trees. I steadied my hands and targeted my subject. I was mostly camouflaged, but my camera wasn't.

My painter was chewing the handle of a brush and twisting his head like he was double-checking, not ready to commit. He turned his face into profile. The brush was still clenched between his teeth as he seemed to ponder the issue further. I didn't wait. It was the perfect shot. My body was rigid, frozen to the ground, when I depressed the shutter once.

The man tightened his face and then grunted. Apparently he'd come to a decision because he whipped the brush from his mouth, bent to the backpack, and dabbed the palette. His epiphany must have been on target. The humming grew louder and his mixing of colors was deliberate. I was ready for him to attack the canvas, to transform concept to reality, but he paused again and the humming stopped. He laid the paintbrush on the palette and walked backward, cupping both hands against the sides of his face, sort of how Tiger Woods wraps the bill of his cap while reading a putt. The painter's steps were slow, almost halting, as he approached our hiding place.

Winnie nudged me and raised an eyebrow, and I withdrew my camera and held my breath. I couldn't see the man now, but I heard ominous footsteps every few seconds, and I felt my heart pound against my chest. *Why am I so uptight? We have as much right to this place as he does, maybe more. I'm the one who named it.* My musings were interrupted when the footsteps stopped.

"The light's not going to stay like that," the man warned himself.

I visualized him shaking his head back and forth, while Winnie looked like he was going to break out laughing. I placed a finger over my lips and threatened him with my eyes.

"Damn it, there's no way I'm going to remember these colors," said the man.

A sigh was followed by several seconds of silence. My painter seemed to be deliberating, torn between staying on task and discerning subtle colors created by a fleeting filter of light, or simply appreciating the moment. And I was desperate to get that shot.

"Well, fuck-a-duck," he said with a salty but graceful resignation to his voice.

I heard footsteps again, crunching twigs and pebbles as he walked away from us. I closed my eyes in relief, then swallowed and remembered to breathe, but I was still locked in that void where ambition and guilt took turns tapping me on the shoulder. I wanted the candid shots, it's what I did best, but I still felt funny about intruding on people's private moments ... even *if* they hummed the *Sound of Music.*

Especially if they hummed the *Sound of Music.*

Winnie's muffled snicker jolted me back to reality. I turned in time to witness the explosion from his mouth, the kind of laugh that's been held behind hands and muted by bitten fingers, yet still manages to escape. It was part cackle, part snort, mostly roar, and it echoed across Hideaway Lake. "Fuck-a-duck?" he blurted.

"What the hell!" boomed the man.

"Aw, jeez," I said, and stood to face him, resigned to explanations and apologies.

The man was surprised but not scared. He was a few feet in front of the easel, knees bent in a cat-like crouch, and he grabbed the paintbrush from the palette and gripped it like a weapon. His eyes were dark and angry, and fiercely focused on me.

"I was taking some pictures." I looked down at the cameras hanging around my neck like they'd vouch for my story, and then latched onto a half-truth. "I didn't want to disturb you."

"What are you doing spying on me?" he growled, shifting his weight in my direction.

The guy had to be at least sixty, and a good five inches shorter than me, but he was thick and muscular, and intimidating as hell.

"I didn't want to bother you." I was about to add an apology, but then Winnie stood. I watched the man's eyes narrow and his body tense as he took in Michael Wingate's physique. His eyes locked onto Winnie's every move and I sensed cold calculations taking place.

Winnie swallowed, trying to suppress another outburst before taming it into a friendly smile. "Hey, we didn't mean nothin'. Like Quinn said, just takin' some pictures, ya know. It's just when you said fuck-a-duck ... well, I got this image of you and this mallard and ... "

The man's body twitched while he labored to breathe through an open mouth. Once-narrowed eyes glazed and stared at us, but they were distant, frozen elsewhere, consumed. His chest heaved in exaggeration, his shoulders arched, and his back stiffened.

I watched for several seconds and debated whether to approach and ask whether he was okay, but I was afraid and mesmerized by the changes taking place.

Then he saw me again. He squeezed the paintbrush handle and snarled, and his eyes bulged like they were going to pop from their sockets. The transformation to unchained fury was complete.

I was terrified when he threw the paintbrush to the ground. "Look," I said, holding my hands in the air, "we didn't mean to bother you. We're here taking pictures, and I wanted to get some shots of you painting. That's all."

The man didn't hear me.

"I'm sorry if we startled you."

My plea for mercy ended when the man charged us, and for a split second I wondered how a guy who sang Julie Andrews songs could be violent. Then I ran.

I looked over my shoulder and was relieved to see that Winnie was smart enough not to beat up an old man; he was running, but not as fast and not as frightened as me, and not in the same direction. That's when I realized that the old man was chasing me, not Winnie. Hell, I suppose I would have picked the one I could have beaten the crap out of, too.

"You good-for-nothing punk."

My attacker lunged and grabbed a handful of ski vest. It ripped when I changed direction and headed back toward his setup area. I saw Winnie waiting halfway up the hill, unsure whether to stay put or intervene, waiting to see whether I'd escape or be captured. From my viewpoint capture was imminent, and I raced around the easel, keeping it between us, hoping for interference, while the two cameras swung wildly around my neck and took turns pounding my back and chest.

I latched onto the easel and used it as a shield. The old man was breathing hard but there was a controlled, almost methodical rhythm to it. He paced himself, gauging my every move, preventing an escape, knowing the right moment would assure a final confrontation. I swung the easel when I switched direction again, and that's when I saw the painting, somehow wedged between my hand and the easel, fall to the ground. I heard a thud, followed by a harsh snap when my hiking boot crushed the canvas.

I instinctively stopped, surprised and concerned about the

painting, but my cameras were still moving in sync with a body racing to escape. The Canon strained against the strap, then jerked back and landed flush on my cheek, sending me sprawling to the ground. I was dazed and didn't feeling anything except adrenaline squirting through my body, and then halfway heard Winnie yelling to check whether I was okay. I shook my head and was trying to focus when I saw the man standing directly over me.

"I was just taking pictures," I managed, while raising my arm to deflect any heavy blows. I peeked through my last-ditch defense and expected to see a towering figure, the victor daring me to stand. Instead, I saw the man's back. He was turned, looking at the painting.

I slid backward, hoping to get a few feet of leeway, but he turned and faced me. I knew he was ready to pounce, flushed with rage and inspired by revenge, but what I knew and what I saw were different. I saw a hunched over white-haired old man, drained of energy. He blinked a couple of times, but there was no moisture in his eyes; the raw ebony circles had lost their intensity and seemed almost vulnerable. I saw a curious mix of sadness, regret, and embarrassment as the painter replaced the fighter.

An awkward hesitancy hung in the air before I quit dragging my butt and flipped over to my hands and knees. I was up and running a second later and didn't look back.

WINNIE FINALLY BROKE THE SILENCE. "So you're pretty pissed off at me, huh?"

He didn't bother looking in my direction, but gripped the armrest instead, trying to mitigate the effects of the Explorer racing forty miles an hour off-road. We fishtailed, and it took several yards and a few seconds of anxiety before the vehicle righted itself.

I didn't say anything, but I wasn't really pissed at Winnie; it hadn't been his idea to sneak up on the guy to take pictures. My feelings were a little more self-centered. I was humiliated by running from an old man, I was self-conscious of the bruise on my cheek that hurt like hell, and I wondered whether I'd lost Hideaway Lake forever. Oh yeah. And there was a twinge of guilt about a crushed canvas.

I slowed enough to avoid flipping the vehicle when I turned onto the dirt road that eventually connected to the highway back to Boulder, and then pressed the accelerator to the floor. I didn't, or maybe I couldn't, let the emotions out. My brain was screaming "Slow down!" no doubt in tandem with Winnie's, but I needed to go faster and faster, I needed to escape.

Escape from what, from whom? I steered to the side of the road and slammed on the brakes.

Winnie stiffened his legs against the floorboard, waiting for the final lunge forward, controlling his fear. He muffled a sigh when we finally stopped.

"Look," I said, "I'm not pissed at you, okay." I took a breath and swallowed hard. I didn't want to share my feelings; opening up was not something I did naturally and I hadn't exactly spent time practicing. But that wasn't fair to Winnie. "I just feel bad about that guy, okay? He wasn't hurting anyone. He was just enjoying nature and painting." My voice trailed off when I looked at Winnie. "I'm the one who messed up, not you."

Winnie nodded, like I finally got around to figuring that out. "Dude, it's just one of those things, ya know? Probably thought we were tryin' to jump him or somethin'. Probably scared, that's all."

"Scared *him*? Christ! I set a new world record for the hundred-yard dash."

"We both ran, but not 'cause we were afraid." Winnie's voice sounded patient, even calm. "We ran so we could avoid a fight with an old man."

I looked in the rearview mirror and touched my face where the red mark on my cheek was swelling. Most boys my age wore their injuries like medals that proudly announced athletic prowess or some conquered physical challenge. Not me. I was mortified by evidence of the confrontation, though I suspected it was providing some measure of consolation to the man gathering his art supplies at Hideaway Lake.

Winnie noticed my uneasiness. "Don't worry about that," he said. "Didn't I *accidentally* elbow you when I lost my footing? Real sorry about that, ya know."

I shook my head, twisting my lips between acceptance and resignation, and started the Explorer back on the road. "So, is this kind of like the Timmy Spahn story? Are you waiting until the next time you come here to recant how some sixty-year-old chased me around until one of my cameras whacked me in the face?" I grinned. It *would* have been a pretty funny addition to Winnie's repertoire.

"Naw, Timmy's a little shithead quarterback. Hardly even gets his uniform dirty. I've been dying to tell someone that story." Winnie cocked an eyebrow. "But you definitely need to go out for the track team. Dude, I never saw skinny legs move so fast."

Skinny legs? That was being kind. A chicken had bigger legs than me, but my physical imperfections, normally a reliable source of distress, weren't a priority. I was focused on matching comebacks, yucking it up with a letter jacket guy, seeing what it was like, whether I fit in.

"Won't have time for track," I said. "All my free time will be spent singing in the chorus. The hills are alive ... with the sound of music." My exaggerated notes were harsh, and I looked across the seat to make sure Winnie appreciated the performance.

He chuckled, but it was polite, almost noiseless. "I haven't heard that song in, like, ten years," Winnie said.

It was a discreet change of subject and it was effective. And I knew, even then, it was appropriate.

"It's too bad about his painting," Winnie added.

six

Sleeping late—one of the perks of being a teenager.

I'd read that sleep provided a setting where your mind could deal with stuff that bugged you; the subconscious chopped up problems your conscious mind wouldn't acknowledge, and then fixed them. Sounded creepy, a little too Freudian. My view was more basic. I would assemble a mishmash of bedcovers into a cozy cocoon where manageable and mostly comforting images came and went. It was a perfect arrangement.

But my last few roll-over-and-go-back-to-sleep efforts the next morning had resulted in dreams a little too taxing, so I hadn't made my normal weekend waking time of noon. I was in the kitchen and I was grouchy. Adding to my irritation was my sister Elizabeth, sitting at the kitchen table, eyeing my every move.

"What do you want?" I poured Cheerios into a bowl and reached for the milk. "Don't you have some Barbie that needs a change of clothes?"

Elizabeth tightened her face into an up-yours smile and said, "So what happened to your face? Did you finally pick on somebody big enough to fight back?"

I hadn't been self-conscious standing in front of my sister in boxer shorts and a T-shirt, but being reminded of the bruise changed that, and I instinctively touched my cheek, wondering how bad it looked to everyone else. I avoided Elizabeth's eyes, dumped sugar onto my breakfast and mumbled, "It's no big deal."

"Oh, really? Well, I guess Mom and Dad will just have to decide whether it's a big deal or not, won't they?" Another venomous smile.

I swear the girl never needed to talk. She had a look for everything and this one screamed *Watch how fast I turn this into a hornets' nest.*

"Whatever."

"Mom and Dad will be back from the store soon. Doesn't leave much time to get your story straight." Elizabeth pushed away from the table and stomped toward the stairway. "And for your information, I don't play with dolls!"

Not a bad exchange. I wasn't up for any question and answer sessions with Mom or Dad, and the little snot knew it. Then again, I hadn't really known she was embarrassed by the Barbie doll collection in her closet. I tucked the revelation into my memory bank and took the bowl of uneaten cereal to the sink. I wasn't that hungry ... and I wanted to be out of the house before my parents returned.

A few seconds later, I turned on the shower and examined my face in the mirror while the hot water kicked in. The bruise, right beneath my left cheekbone, was puffy and had turned a nasty shade of blue. I winced when I touched it, mostly because I realized it was going to be there a while. At least it looked like something Winnie's elbow could do.

NICOLE STRANDLUND WAS ONE reason I never totally panicked about becoming an adult. My description of her in no particular order: forty-two, witty, not fat and dumpy, sensitive, upbeat, chafed at authority figures, ate sushi, and played Jimmy Eat World CDs while she worked. Oh yeah. And she had long, thick hair that was mostly gray. For some reason, I trusted her because of her hair.

Nicki was my photography teacher, and was addicted to taking pictures. I use the term addicted because saying she was an Alfred Eisenstaedt award-winning photographer would miss the point. Nicki shot roll after roll, seemingly without pause or thought or effort, much the same as I imagined Willie Nelson singing or Michael Jordan knocking down jump shots—for pure pleasure. She didn't dismiss the recognition; a certificate acknowledging the "Eisie" hung on a wall in her studio, but you would have had to look carefully to find it among the many appreciation plaques from local charities and pictures of soccer teams she'd coached. In fact, it hung right next to the 1998 team, the one that lost every game that season.

For reasons I didn't really understand, she'd been turning down most freelance assignments offered by the national publications; said she wanted to cherry pick and that she enjoyed passing the baton. I guess that meant teaching high school kids like me.

We were in the darkroom of her studio on Pine Street, a brick storefront that used to be a coffee shop. You could describe the architectural style of Louisville's original downtown as uneventfully rectangular: the buildings in the three-square-block area were mostly single-story, topped with flat roofs and covered with predictable paint. Most, however, sprouted awnings from the top of their windows that provided shade for window-shoppers, and splashed varying degrees of originality and color through the town.

The shops were once occupied by mom-and-pop businesses that catered to a country community, but that was thirty-five years earlier, before Louisville's growth shot in every direction, before real estate developers recognized the trend and grabbed cheap farm acreage. A few restaurants did well (my favorite

Italian restaurant had been around since 1919), but most of the buildings on side streets, like Nicki's studio, were either empty or rented to low-budget tenants straddling the line between quaint and extinct. Meanwhile a jigsaw puzzle of Wal-Mart-type boxes, chain restaurants, and strip malls were ringing up cash registers with their choices, convenience, and congestion just a few miles away.

A part of me liked the old Louisville—maybe because it had character, but mostly because no one else my age did.

"Not used to seeing you so early on Saturday," Nicki said.

"Guess I didn't have too late a night." I shrugged and continued clipping my images across the line to air dry. She'd already asked about my face, and was apparently buying the story about Winnie's elbow.

"I like these," she said. She was a step behind me, evaluating each print I hung. We both knew the shot of the deer eating was passable, but that the only real keeper was when he threw his head back right before bolting. "Oops. Weren't ready for him to take off on you, huh?"

None of my "escape" shots were worth a shit; I'd incorrectly anticipated his direction with the first few, and then overcompensated. "Winnie stepped on a branch and I had the Canon preset. Thought I could get it ready in time," I said, realizing I might have done better taking a chance with the Nikon's shutter speed.

"You did the right thing," she said while still looking at the pictures and apparently reading my mind. "If you'd been lucky enough to have backlighting, either one of these," she said, pointing, "could have been interesting. Hey, better taking a risk for excellence than being safe with adequate."

I'd heard the words before, and in fact had thought of them when I'd reached for the Canon. Crafting illusions, capturing the unique, allowing chance combinations of mood and light and perspective; Nicki had taken me beyond the mechanics and into the philosophy of photography.

"And who is this?" she asked.

I kept working while she studied the picture of my painter chewing the paintbrush handle. "Some guy who was painting up at Hideaway Lake."

"Interesting." She waited for a reaction without looking at me, then said, "Did you talk to him?"

"A little," I said with an uninterested tone.

"So, where's he from? How'd he find the place?" Nicki fitted the glasses hanging around her neck to her nose, and inched closer to the picture.

I pretended to concentrate on my shots of the light shooting through the rock formation, and hoped the inquisition would end soon. "Didn't ask him, just said hello."

"I love the eyes. He doesn't appear to be looking at anything in particular, but there's dramatic intensity, a focus. And the angle—it's perfect. The brush in his teeth, white hair pitched against the gray sky. God, his painting just lurks in the background, like a scorned lover demanding attention. Was he posing? You had to have positioned him."

The yin-yang thing suddenly popped into my mind. The previous day's photo shoot had been a huge success because of one picture—a picture of a man who'd chased me away from Hideaway Lake. Was everything in life a good news/bad news proposition?

"No, he didn't pose. He was just doing his thing and I caught it."

"Where are the rest?"

"The rest of what?"

"The rest of the pictures of this guy! You know, actually painting, mixing his colors, wiping the brush. Come on, Quinn. I get what you obviously saw. His features are wonderful, and the man's got passion written all over him. If you didn't take at least thirty more shots of him, I'm sticking you back in Photography I with a Kodak throwaway."

I looked away from Nicki and sighed. Should I compound the lie—I ran out of film, the others didn't come out, he said only one picture? Nicki wouldn't have bitten on any of that, and she would have resented me for not being straight with her.

"He didn't like me taking pictures of him, so there's just the one shot," I finally said.

"Oh." It wasn't the answer she'd expected.

There was a pause, but I knew Nicki wouldn't let this slide, that the wheels were turning, that uncomfortable questions would be coming my way, so I decided to just get it over with. My words spilled, then surged like a tide finally smashing through sandbags.

"Look. I wanted to get some candid shots, okay, and he went berserk. He must've thought we were stalking him or going to rob him or something. I don't know, some stupid-shit thing like that. He started screaming and yelling about us spying on him, and the next thing I knew he was chasing me around the place. One of my cameras knocked me in the face."

Nicki was quiet for a few seconds, then turned my shoulder so I faced her. She inspected my face for evidence besides the bruise before locking her eyes to mine. "So he hit you?"

"No, he didn't hit me. I pretty much hit myself." I was angry and embarrassed because I had to blink back tears that had no reason to fall. I clenched my eyes through a deep breath.

"Do you want to call the police?" Her voice was solemn and her stare tightened.

"Not unless I'm turning myself in for vandalism. I ruined the guy's painting." I snorted a laugh and tried to dilute Nicki's concern with a half-baked smile. "It was really my fault. We surprised him, he thought we were making fun of him, and ... well, it just got out of hand. He overreacted."

"That doesn't excuse him from chasing you."

"For me it does. I'm calling it even."

Nicki didn't let go of my eyes; she was judging, making sure. Finally she nodded and said, "Keep to the story about Winnie's elbow. It sounds better." She smiled and patted my cheek—the healthy one—and fixed her attention on my painter again. The examination was comprehensive and meticulous, almost as if some return on my investment/injury needed to be salvaged. She reached for a magnifying glass and held it up to the photo. "I'll be damned," she said.

"What?"

"You know that rock formation? The one you've shot a gazillion times?"

"Yeah."

Nicki pressed the magnifying glass closer. "That's what he was painting."

seven

Timing was everything when it came to confrontations, especially when there was little room to backpedal. My mantra when accountability breathed down my neck? Avoid. Postpone. But as I stretched across on my bed, mildly engrossed by a changing shadow of energetic computer screensavers, those preferred techniques seemed pointless. My problem wasn't going away, and it could only be ignored a few more weeks. What was worse was the faint dose of common sense that kept nagging me, whispering advice: Nip it in the bud, face the music, control the problem before it controls you. The Muse of Maturity must have liked clichés and must have known I was susceptible to hearing them.

The problem was my quarter grades, not so much what they'd be, but what they'd be relative to my parents' expectations. Personally? I hadn't given a rat's ass about grades since sophomore year when I got a B- in Advanced Algebra. I had a 96% test average, a 98% on the final exam, and received a final grade of B- because I was given an F for homework. Oh yeah, my homework. All those sheets of paper I'd turned in on time with the right answers? My math teacher said I hadn't followed instructions because I'd skipped steps when solving the problems. That those steps were busywork, or that I could shortcut them hadn't mattered. Anyway, that's when grades and I parted ways. But my parents had a different take. And that's why there was going to be a confrontation.

They were due home from dinner soon. Some new south-western-style restaurant Mom had heard about. Dad preferred eating at home because he traveled so much, but Mom and Elizabeth usually got their way, and they were just leaving when I'd gotten home. I lied and said I'd eaten at Nicki's just to avoid all the questions that always came attached to family outings. There was no retreating to your room in a restaurant.

So I'd made a decision. I was going to ask Dad if he had a minute to talk after they got home, but I was still debating how to break the news. I was assuming that the heads-up, my willingness to discuss the situation with him, was going to provide some protection. But all C's, and probably a D? I was hoping the Muse of Words would soon join the Muse of Maturity. Otherwise, it was going to get ugly.

I was also wrestling with another issue. I wasn't one for guilt—well, at least not for accepting guilt—but I hadn't been able to shake certain images of the old man from the previous day. Nicki had been right. The profile picture was incredible; the contrasts, the viewpoint. His face spoke of perspective, of confidence, of experience with life, yet I was remembering the rage in his eyes and the fierce reaction when we'd surprised him. It made me think that the story, his story, was complicated. And I was curious to know more.

I swung my legs off the bed and walked to my closet where carefully stacked rows of boxes housed the collection of pictures I'd taken. You never would have guessed such a fastidious enclave existed within my room; neatly printed labels affixed to files, everything organized by date and cross-referenced by subject matter. There was a perverse pride knowing that the files clashed with my image, which of course stoked my adolescent fire.

Hideaway Lake rated its own box, and the manila files in it were stuffed. Black and whites, color, animals, rocks, flowers, and trees; they were all chronicled. The adjectives to describe my work were as varied as the shots themselves: eloquent, idyllic, striking, conventional, poetic, intimate, imposing, bright, stark. Some of the images were dramatic, most were amateurish, a few superb. I sifted through the files, not knowing exactly what I was looking for, yet trusting that I'd recognize it.

MY FATHER'S STUDY WAS A TEN BY sixteen concocted cubbyhole tucked behind the family room where bills got paid, books read, and investments tallied. Originally designed as a long storage closet, the builder was able to extend the outside wall a few yards, install ten rows of bookshelves, and add $25,000 to the price of the house. At least that's what Mom claimed it cost whenever anyone was willing to listen. Dad never argued the point, though I always suspected he could.

My confidence inched up when I tapped the pocket-door frame to get his attention. He was behind the desk reading a magazine. Paying bills, the act of sending your money to someone else, spoke for itself, and reviewing investment results was always a dicey proposition. Reading a magazine meant relaxed. Reading a magazine was good.

"Hey, Dad." I did my best to smile. "Got a minute?"

Dad laid the magazine on the desk and removed his reading glasses. He was tall, but a few inches shorter than me, and worked at staying in shape. A full head of gray hair made him look older than his forty-seven years. "Of course I've got time, Quinn. Come on in and have a seat."

A swallow of red wine remained in the glass on his desk, and there wasn't a bill or brokerage statement in sight.

My eyes roamed the bookcase as I sat on the edge of the blue leather chair next to it. How would I describe my father's interests as evidenced by his sanctuary? Eclectic. Biographies, thrillers, classics, and reference books lined the shelves or were stacked flat on top of each other. Knickknacks and mementos and framed photographs showcased memories, and were scattered among the volumes. Some were strategically placed; others had just grabbed an open spot. It was an intimate setting. It was comfortable.

"I'm not really sure how to start," I said. Of course I'd known how to start. Start with weak and vulnerable. "It's about school."

"Okay." Dad's expression shifted into neutral.

"Yeah, well ... my grades aren't going to be so good this quarter. I guess I got a little too far behind to catch up, and I'm realizing I need to work harder on a day-to-day basis." Everything I'd just said was true, but that wasn't my motivation. I looked into his blue eyes, now narrowed a bit, and gauged my performance so far.

"Aren't there still a couple of weeks left?"

I nodded. "I'll try as hard as I can, but I doubt if it will change anything." I saw Dad's jaw stiffen, and quickly added, "I wanted to tell you now, you know, not surprise you. I could have waited until the report card came home, but that didn't feel right."

Dad considered the postscript, and sighed. "How bad?"

"Definitely an A in Photography."

"How bad, Quinn?"

Okay, so I needed some work on the sidestep technique. "All C's. Maybe a D in Pre-Calc."

There was disciplined silence from my father. It made me uncomfortable but it sure beat the heck out of yelling and recriminations. That's why I was in the study and not the kitchen.

Dad sighed again and reached for the wine. He swirled the

liquid a couple times before downing it. "I suppose we can get into the particulars later ... "

"Particulars?"

"Particulars," he said flatly. "Like half-ass homework, studying for tests with loud music, a room you need a machete to get through. Particulars like car restrictions and unplugging the computer." He trained his eyes on mine, waiting for a rebuttal, but I knew better. "So we'll talk about the *particulars* in a minute. Right now I'd like to know why you're here."

"I know I messed up, and I wanted to tell you that I'm going to try harder."

"Really? And what about your argument that grades don't matter? What about 'who needs to get into a top college?' Hell, I would have bet my last dollar you'd thumb your nose at the whole thing." His voice was controlled, but the strain was evident.

"I've never done this bad. Maybe not my best, but I've never had grades like this, and I'm kind of embarrassed by the whole thing." Arguing my previous position on grades had suddenly taken a backseat to hanging on to a computer and car keys, and swallowing a little pride seemed a small price to pay. And yeah, there was a shred of humiliation. Going from honors student to possible academic probation in one year was a bit steep, even for me.

"I'm guessing your mother doesn't know yet."

Dad could have forgotten the guess and taken it to the bank.

Another pause. True confession get-togethers always seemed to open the door to other topics, and Dad tilted his head and fiddled with a pen while he considered which low-hanging fruit to pick.

"So, tell me again about that bruise," he finally said. "And don't make me read between the lines. I want the truth, Quinn. No more bullshit."

I'd expected this question and was prepared to repeat the story. "I told you the truth, Dad. Winnie and I went up to

Eldorado Canyon after school to take pictures. He slipped on a rock and caught me with an elbow. That's it. Call him if you don't believe me," I said, injecting just the right amount of indignation into my voice.

Dad weighed the probabilities, and then moved on. "Are there other issues?"

"What do you mean?"

"I mean drugs. I mean problems at school. I mean girlfriend troubles."

We'd finally arrived at a place where I got to win points truthfully. I didn't do drugs, mostly because I looked at the people who did and didn't want to be anything like them; I wasn't in trouble at school if you didn't count lousy grades; and I didn't have a girlfriend. Jessica Winters was the closest I'd come on that front. We'd caught a few movies, even locked lips at homecoming the previous fall, but that was about it. I would have been interested in an upgrade to the relationship. She wasn't.

"I promise, Dad. There's nothing else going on. You can do a drug test anytime you want, you can call school, and you know I don't go on many dates." It was easier to meet his eyes again, and I felt my heart rate slowing. I knew I wasn't going to skate, but my confidence was growing. My parents could live with one quarter of bad grades if they didn't have to deal with the other issues, and I could hear them saying "It could be worse" later that night.

"You're sure there's nothing else?"

"I'm sure."

Dad took a deep breath and blew it through his mouth. "Okay," he said, "your mother and I will talk. I want a chance to think this through before we respond." He arched an eyebrow. "There will be consequences. I just don't know what they are yet."

I was at that age when you don't like your parents—they're controlling, unreasonable, and hypocritical—but I did respect my father. He never overreacted and stayed calm in times of turmoil. I always thought it was an essential trait for flying jets and being married to my mother.

I nodded, acknowledging Dad's promise of punishment, and kept a humbled expression on my face. Sure, I'd known there would be consequences and, even though they had yet to be announced, felt like a little starch had been taken out of them. And I was a bit surprised that I felt better. I stood to leave and seriously thought about trying harder at school.

"Quinn."

"Yeah."

My father's expression was resolute, his tone blunt. "No more surprises."

eight

The bell announcing first period rang, interrupting students still catching up on each others' weekends. I had study hall in the cafeteria and was already sitting at a far table facing the wall, creatively camouflaging my face with arms and fingers and hands. The bruise was smaller but had turned an angry purple. Several people asked about it and a few taunted me with questions like "Did you even fight back?" Mercifully, Winnie interrupted one remark and apologized for his errant elbow, which put a temporary hold on the ridicule.

The rest of my weekend was solicitous and boring. I cleaned my room, reworked some math problems and figured out why I'd blown the previous week's test, and almost got current with the assigned reading for American Lit. Perhaps more telling, I turned down the volume of my music, stayed off the computer, and away from Elizabeth, all in hopes of demonstrating a new-found passion for pleasing, or at least appeasing, my parents.

Something must have worked because on a scale of "got away with it" to "grounded for life," I came out somewhere in the middle. Mom and Dad sat me down after dinner that Sunday night and rehashed everything. There were lots of I-told-you-so's disguised by other words from Mom, and a few rah-rah attempts

by Dad before new ground rules were set. There would be no television, no music, and no computer (except to do homework) on
school nights, but I would regain those privileges on weekends
if I followed the rules. And I would be subject to harsher penal-
ties if any new infractions occurred or if I didn't make the honor
roll next quarter. All in all, not too severe, and I still had wheels.

So it was time to bear down. I had a reason to be smart again.

I'd gotten through another ten pages of *To Kill a Mockingbird*
when I felt a tap on my shoulder. I looked around and saw Mr.
McCormack standing behind me, arms folded across his chest
like a genie waiting to grant a wish, except he was obviously not
in a philanthropic mood. Then I remembered.

"You're supposed to be in my classroom this period, Quinn."
His voice was hushed, the tone harsh.

"I forgot all about it, Mr. McCormack. I'm really sorry." I'm
sure my expression conveyed my surprise; I really had forgotten.

"Get your books and come with me." He turned and walked
toward the study hall monitor, not bothering to see whether I
followed.

The kids in the cafeteria peeked from behind their books,
first at me and then at Mr. McCormack, before a whispering
chorus of questions spread. They wanted to know what had happened (getting yanked out of study hall was right up there with
crying in class), but they couldn't appear to be all *that* interested. That wouldn't have been cool. Me? I just hoped the red
flush sweeping across my face blended in with the bruise.

MR. MCCORMACK DIDN'T USE THE school district's basic
issue for side chairs. Instead of a metal frame fitted with lami-
nated wood for a back and seat, I sat on an old upholstered
wingback. Maybe it was supposed to be homey or less structured

or something, but I remember the thing needed major repairs. The legs were uneven and rocked back and forth, and I could feel springs pinching my butt. The chair was covered in faded brown leather with patches of red electrical tape stuck all around. The tape covered tears in the upholstery, but it was hard imagining that such a remedy was worth it. I figured whoever held the garage sale had definitely gotten the better end of the deal.

Mr. McCormack sat behind his desk, giving the file in his hands a slow, sour-faced look. Watching him made me nervous and, when I squirmed, the chair rocked and the springs creaked, so I looked around his classroom instead. His desk and chair and the ugly brown chair all sat on an area rug that was tucked in a corner. A row of file cabinets and two bookshelves semi-enclosed the area for privacy. It reminded me of the forts I used to build after Christmas with shipping boxes and sheets and blankets. Papers were stacked everywhere—the floor, the desk, on top of the filing cabinets. Magazines and newspapers took the most space and the yellowed newsprint suggested recycling rather than reading material. I wondered if my never-returned homework resided somewhere close, but it was hard to determine what the piles represented or if there was a pecking order.

"So," Mr. McCormack said, finally looking up from the file, "tell me about your Pearl Harbor paper." He peered over the top of his glasses, checking my reaction.

It took me a second to get my bearings. *Discuss whether FDR allowed a Japanese attack on Pearl Harbor in order to thrust America into World War II.*

"FDR knew what he was doing. I think it was a setup," I declared, relieved that he was merely testing my memory. I recited a couple of supporting facts and met his gaze indifferently.

"Yes, I read that in your paper, Quinn," he said, tapping the folder. "Interesting paper you wrote. I have to admit it's a pretty persuasive argument—all the sources, the stories, the accounts."

"Thanks." I started to loosen up just a bit. I'd done a good job? Was I experiencing positive reinforcement? I imagined my parents' reaction when they heard that I'd aced the major paper for the quarter, and then began to mentally calculate whether I'd get a B after all. Was it good enough to bring me up to an A?

"Did you write this paper, Quinn?" Mr. McCormack lifted my report from the file and held it for me to see.

"That's my paper," I said, hoping for a gesture, maybe even a half-hidden smile, anything that sent a message about A's and report cards. But there were no gestures or smiles, and I didn't see a grade on the paper.

"I asked if you *wrote* the paper."

Did I write the paper? The illusion of satisfied parents instantly cratered into a delusion and I tried to hide a swallow that didn't quite make it all the way down. I had no choice.

"Yeah, I wrote it," I said, holding back an urge to squirm between covered coils, whether they pinched or not.

"Okay." My history teacher sighed, obviously disappointed by the response. He reached to one of the stacks and lifted a magazine from the middle. "Ever see this?" He tossed it across the desk.

I looked at the cover and recognized the name of the publication. "No, I've never seen it." I was hanging my hat on a technicality; I'd downloaded the article off the Internet but had never seen it in hardcopy. It was a lame excuse and my only hope.

"You certainly didn't list it in your bibliography, I know that," said Mr. McCormack as he flipped to the last page of my report. "Not footnoted either."

Blinking and swallowing replaced breathing. How deep should I dig this hole?

"We've only got a few minutes left before second period, Quinn, so I'll stop the charade now," Mr. McCormack said, seemingly annoyed at putting me out of my misery so soon. "Except for a few lackluster attempts to disguise the effort, you copied an article from that magazine by James F. Carroll. In case you've forgotten, it's called 'Pearl Harbor: Truth Behind Lies.' Actually, lackluster is being too kind. You went whole paragraphs without changing a single word!"

"I read a lot of different articles from the Internet." I hesitated just long enough to consider whether I should argue that James F. Carroll's words had miraculously stayed with me, sentence structures and all, or plead for mercy. No contest, the game was over. "I guess I just thought he made a really good argument. You know, I wanted to make sure I presented all the evidence like he did, you know, thoroughly."

"I specifically warned against plagiarism when I gave the assignment. I wanted your words, your thoughts, not a recitation of someone else's position." Mr. McCormack's eyebrows knitted behind his glasses while he paused, reading my face and choosing his next words. "This is an honors class, Quinn, an independent study format that's supposed to challenge you and develop critical thinking. I don't care whether you can memorize facts and dates. It's why I have you write papers instead of take tests."

"I'm sorry, Mr. McCormack. I should have put the argument into my words, but I did read a lot of material. I guess I tried a shortcut and didn't take enough time." The truth was, I hadn't done any other reading. I found what I thought was an obscure article, and copied and pasted it into my word processing program. And there was no way I would ever admit it. "Can I have a few days to resubmit? I think I can have it to you by Friday."

"Friday doesn't work for me."

"I really need a little time to put things together, you know, rough drafts and stuff. Can I turn it in Thursday afternoon?" I had no idea how I'd be able to research, much less write and rewrite the paper in three days, but my negotiating position didn't offer many options.

"No good," he said.

I took a deep breath—I would have bent over if I wasn't sitting—while my mind raced through timelines for completing the work and crafting possible explanations to my mother for the marathon study sessions. "When do you want it?" I finally asked.

"I don't."

"Excuse me?"

Mr. McCormack pushed his glasses high on his nose. There was a clearer intensity, a more purposeful demeanor, like everything until then had been merely jockeying for position. His jaw stiffened, and he separated his hands and laid them flat on the desk. "The assignment was due last week. You turned yours in. You received a zero." He paused just long enough for my facial expression to appropriately reflect the connection my brain had just made. "And because the paper is fifty percent of your quarter grade, you've earned an F in this class for the quarter."

"An F? I can't get an F! Okay, I copied some words and I didn't really give you a good effort on the paper, but an F? For the quarter?" I heard the surprise, the anger, the pleading in my words, like a part of me was watching from a safe distance and listening in on the conversation. And that detached part of me was thinking I was in deep shit.

"My grading criteria were explained in detail, both in class and in the syllabus I handed out at the beginning of the quarter. And I repeat, I specifically cautioned everyone against plagiarism." Mr. McCormack narrowed his eyes, almost like a challenge. "I know how bright you are, Quinn, and I know what an F on your report card means. I also know it's important for you to take responsibility."

Any detachment from the conversation was over. My breathing became even more labored and my thoughts were jumbled, like lottery balls being blown about in a glass case. I couldn't control either.

"Responsibility? Yeah, right! And *you're* going to be responsible for me not getting into a good college. Look, I'll do the paper. I'll participate in class. I'll give you my best effort, I promise, but I can't get an F!"

The bell ending first period interrupted a dozen more promises I would have been willing to make.

"I doubt whether you realize it right now, but I care about all of my students, including you, Quinn. I take my job as a teacher seriously. I give a damn." Mr. McCormack's expression turned softer, almost gentle; his eyes mixed compassion with patience, and hinted at knowing the future. But he was confident in the decision and his resolve was unmistakable. "I'll be calling your parents this afternoon. There will be a written account of the incident in your school file."

It was as if I'd blown a fuse and everything was short-circuited. I knew my eyes were wide open, but I didn't see anything. I felt my body shaking and couldn't stop. I saw my history teacher still talking, yet I'd stopped hearing his words.

I NEVER MADE IT TO MY SECOND PERIOD class. We were supposed to do a lab in Chemistry, and that hadn't seemed like such a good idea. I don't remember whether I'd decided I couldn't concentrate, or if I was afraid that the other kids would link my shaking body and bruised face, and knock my status down another notch. I still wonder whether I should have gone. Mixing chemicals in my state of mind might have been interesting.

I went to the administration office instead and told the secretary I didn't feel well, that I wanted to go home. I must have really looked like shit because she didn't question me, didn't probe even a little bit before scribbling and time-stamping a sick pass. I'm pretty sure I didn't acknowledge her "I hope you feel better" as I headed out the door.

I didn't go home. I ended up at a table in Lucky's, a coffee bar in the University Hill area of Boulder, for the next two hours, and I *wasn't* feeling better. I was anxious, confused, and really pissed.

Lucky's was a relaxed version of Starbucks that started back in the seventies when a couple of college buddies decided that flea market furniture, freshly baked bread, and different coffee flavors somehow went together. That was all it took—that and a handful of intellectual types who carved a counterculture image by arguing philosophy and reading poetry. Students flocked and profits soared. They ended up expanding the menu and adding four other locations next to college campuses throughout the state, but the original Lucky's hadn't moved and it hadn't changed much. I liked it there. No one hassled or paid attention to you.

Did I mention I felt anxious? Three white chocolate mochas and a couple of oversized muffins had administered enough caffeine and sugar to keep me bouncing with the Energizer bunny for a week, but other than two relief sessions in the restroom, I hadn't left my chair. I figured, why bother? I had nowhere to go. More to the point, I knew this would be my last "outing" for several weeks, and that I might as well savor the moment. It was pathetic.

My pity party alternated between licking fresh wounds with a rather sharp tongue and dreaming up paybacks for Mr. McCormack. I also debated whether to quit school. Moving away from my parents was the only way I knew to avoid a total meltdown, and I'd cobbled together a budget on a paper napkin. What a waste of time. Even math students with D's could figure out that flipping burgers at five bucks an hour and paying for an apartment, a car, and all the other stuff jumped to negative integers in a hurry. It was a depressing reality check.

All in all, that Monday ranked as one of the three worst days of my life—just ahead of wearing my basketball jersey backward in the first game of my freshman year, but still behind the time Mom barged into my room while I was beating off. I shook my head, certain nothing would ever top that episode, when a voice interrupted my thoughts.

"Mind if I sit down?"

I looked up to see a man standing over me, an older man with short white hair. It was the painter from Hideaway Lake.

nine

I wasn't sure whether to run, or just duck and hide behind the table with my arms over my head, hoping the other patrons would care enough to call the police. Surely someone would pull him off me. But my feet were cemented to the floor and my elbows weighed a hundred pounds.

"Just take a minute. I want to apologize."

The man placed his drink on my table, pulled out a chair and sat before I could breathe, much less answer. He locked his fingers around the cardboard cup and stared at it. His hesitation seemed intentional, controlled and reflective, and his once-fierce eyes were subdued.

"I can't tell you how sorry I am, son. You and your friend surprised me, but I really don't know what came over me. Just lost control and I don't know why. I am truly sorry," he said, finally looking up to see my response. That's when he noticed the bruise.

"I'm sorry about the painting," I managed. I studied the old man, surprised by his apology, more surprised by my calm voice. His face had a sturdy, weathered look. The tobacco lines etched around his lips flowed into deeper wrinkles that told of unprotected years, and suggested experience, an earthy wisdom. His high cheekbones and square jaw were striking, validating Nicki's photographic assessment.

"The camera hit you in the face when you were running?" His question was more a statement. A grim look settled uncomfortably on his face.

"I thought about a version that included me saving a beautiful girl, but no one would have believed it, so the story is that my friend accidentally caught me with an elbow." A nervous smile was my only attempt at a peace offering.

"Maybe you should tell people the truth." He pursed his lips and shook his head. "I am so sorry," he said. Each word resonated, slowly and separately, distancing the apology from others I'd heard.

My fears were quieted, and I'd arrived at the awkward moment when the expectation of forgiveness hovered like an impatient child. Sure, the guy had gone ballistic, but I couldn't ignore my complicity. I wanted to tell him why we'd hidden behind the rock, to explain about taking his picture and how everything just kind of happened. But relieving my guilt would only muddy the water, and could come later. I met his eyes when I said, "It's okay."

The painter took a deep breath. "Thanks," he said before pushing his chair away from the table.

That was it? It was over?

"I didn't see a car or truck," I blurted.

"Sorry?" His hand stopped before reaching his cup.

"I mean—well, how did you get to Hideaway Lake? We didn't see a car or truck or anything. Did you hike in?" It was only one of many questions I wanted to ask.

"It's called Hideaway Lake?"

I shrugged my shoulders. "That's what I call it. I don't think it has a real name."

"Pretty good name," he said. "There's a dry riverbed just on the other side of the rocks to the west. I can get my truck within a half-mile or so. Funny, I was wondering how you boys got there."

"There's a picnic site about a mile to the south. The stream that flows into the lake runs by it."

"You can park there?"

"No, you have to hike a couple miles, maybe a little less during the summer. I thought it was the only way to get close." I matched smiles with the man. "I'm Quinn."

"Joe." He gave my hand a firm squeeze.

THE EXPLANATIONS AND APOLOGIES were clumsy and quickly demoted to the past, but they launched us into a discussion that lasted over an hour. His name was Joseph (just call me Joe) Toscano, he was seventy-four, and he'd moved to Boulder twelve years earlier, a few months after his wife had died. They hadn't had children and he didn't want to stay in California, and for reasons skimmed over, the mountains, the university, and Boulder's disposition had claimed him. He'd lived in the same apartment on 19th Street, just off Pearl, since moving to Boulder, and thought the place was just starting to get comfortable.

Joe painted because it focused his creative energy, said it came naturally, but that he hadn't taken it seriously until he was in his fifties. He was disciplined, spent at least four hours a day at the canvas, sometimes much longer. Joe didn't paint people and he seemed almost proud he'd never sold a painting, as if profiting from his work would have somehow violated a contract with nature.

Joe had a forthcoming manner, a what-you-see-is-what-you-get type of guy, whose economic use of words took a little getting used to. He wasn't withholding; the words were just simple and precise, and quite a change from babbling teachers and parents.

I had to focus not to miss anything. And there was an edge about him. It had been rounded and sanded almost smooth, but it was there, much like the trace of an accent I couldn't pin down. Both had me aware and wondering.

I liked the questions he asked because they invited me to share and weren't intrusive. Whether my answers were a simple yes or no, or something more complicated, they were accepted, not expected. Funny, but it seemed I learned more about Joe from his questions than from the answers he'd given to mine. Sure, he talked, told me about himself and all, but he didn't reveal anything. He was more intent on drawing me out.

Joe was interested in my photography: how I got started, whether it was a hobby or something more, what I was good at, where I struggled. He even asked questions about how certain pieces of equipment affected the light. He told me that the word photography meant "drawing with light" and he was curious how I captured and manipulated it, if I preferred a certain time of day, and how Colorado's ever-changing weather affected my work. Joe got it. I could tell by the way he compared his tools to mine that he got it.

"SO, BESIDES PAINTING, WHAT else do you do?" I asked. I'd been doing most of the talking for a while and figured it was okay to just go ahead and ask questions. I was betting that he went to a health club several days a week, and hoped he wouldn't mention the word television. Daytime soaps would have killed the moment.

"I try to ride my bike or jog every morning."

I nodded, satisfied with my read.

"I enjoy afternoons most, so that's when I paint. Classes are usually in the morning."

"Classes? What classes?"

"Whatever classes I happen to be taking." Joe smiled. He'd given this speech before. "I'm taking Anatomy & Physiology and Biology this semester."

"Really? You're taking those classes? Are you studying to be... like, a doctor or something?"

"Doubt I have time to get through medical school," he said, like he was mentally comparing time lines to mortality tables. "I study what interests me. Right now I'm interested in Anatomy & Physiology and Biology."

I couldn't hide my puzzled expression so I kept asking questions. "So you've taken classes before? Are you going for a degree?" I'd heard about old people going to college, but always thought they were a little whacko and had something to prove. The man who sat across from me didn't fit that picture.

"I've been taking classes since I moved to Boulder, usually two every semester. I tried taking more once, but that didn't leave me enough time to paint. So I go to class in the morning, paint in the afternoon, and study at night." Joe watched my reaction, obviously enjoying the respect he read on my face. "Not really interested in a degree."

"Wait a second. Twelve years of college? Even with only two classes each semester, that's, like, forty-eight classes. Not interested in a degree?"

"I'm retired. What would I do with a degree?" he said.

"Isn't that why you go to college?"

"I go to college to learn. I'd have to fulfill certain requirements for a degree, and I'm not interested in some of those classes. Not worth the trouble."

For the first time in an hour I felt uncomfortable, like I was sticking my nose where it didn't belong, and that it was about to get popped. Joe, on the other hand, was relaxed and apparently still enjoying my company.

"Am I asking too many questions?"

"Nope. Tell you if you were."

I shrugged my shoulders and threw a sheepish grin back at him. "Okay, well, what *did* you do? I mean what did you retire from?"

Joe reached for the coffee, his second since we'd been talking, and sipped. "I've retired twice. I spent twenty-six years in the Marine Corps and then started a plumbing business when I got out. Sold the plumbing business after my wife died."

There were so many strings for me to pull, but Joe just smiled and kept talking.

"Joined the Corps right out of high school, but it wasn't exactly a free choice. I was a bit of a hell-raiser and kept getting into trouble. Pretty clear I was headed down the wrong road, so a judge gave me a choice: go to jail or join the military. They used to do that back then, try and straighten kids out instead of just locking them up. That was in 1947." Joe looked past me for a moment, like he was watching a memory whisk by, and then said, "Retired as a first sergeant, 5th Marines. Started as a rifleman, fought in Korea. Spent quite a few years as an infantry instructor. Did a tour in Vietnam, too."

"Why'd you get out?"

Joe's eyes drifted lower and his head slightly nodded while he searched for precise words. "I could still take the physical demands but I had questions, lots of questions. About life, about my life. A man with questions shouldn't carry a gun."

I detected that nerves, protected by thirty-year-old scar tissue, were still sensitive. I was way over my head, I knew that. Joe hadn't told me to stop asking questions but I decided to change subjects anyway.

"So why'd you become a plumber?"

Joe's eyes twinkled. "Money," he said.

I laughed. So matter-of-fact, so uncomplicated.

"I was forty-four when I got out of the Corps and was getting a decent monthly pension, but I needed something to do.

Started off doing odd jobs, fixing things, handyman-type stuff. Pop was a plumber back in Chicago, so I knew what I was doing."

The word "Chicago" cleared up the accent. "My mom complains that plumbers make more money than people with college degrees."

Joe wiggled his eyebrows.

I liked the way he made a point.

Joe checked his watch and downed the rest of his coffee. "I need to go," he said. "Maybe we can do this again."

I was startled, then enticed by the abruptness. That was when I realized I was interrupting his schedule. "Yeah, I'd like that." My voice trailed off when I remembered why I was at Lucky's in the first place. Another get-together wouldn't be happening soon.

Joe sensed my hesitancy and tightened his eyes on me. "I do have one last question before I go." He crossed one leg over the other. Apparently his painting session could wait. "Why aren't you in school?"

So he'd finally asked. Maybe he had assumed there was some new three-day weekend for the school district, or maybe he'd just waited until we'd talked a little. Maybe he hadn't wanted to pry. It didn't matter. He asked, and now it was my turn to answer an uncomfortable question.

It was hard for me to trust adults, to trust anyone. I was so programmed to lie, to be evasive, but transparent words would have robbed the intimacy from our conversation. I decided to just spit it out, all of it, without the excuses and without the fluff. Unreasonable parents, boring classes, plagiarized papers, bad grades—everything.

Joe listened and other than an occasional nod, didn't move. His elbows rested on the table and his hands cradled an unflinching face. I felt a trace of familiarity when his dark eyes focused on me, like he'd known me forever.

"So I guess anything on my social calendar should be in

pencil." I tried to end on a funny note, but the joke fell flat. I sighed, and Joe pursed his lips and breathed deeply.

"Okay to ask a few questions?"

"Yeah." My apathetic tone returned.

Joe was an adult, and adults had a way of asking questions that guaranteed the desired response. Their questions were black and white, they were yes or no, and rarely left room for explanations. I knew it would only take a few minutes for Joe to wrap my legs and raise his hands like a calf-roping cowboy.

"Need a place to stay?"

"Huh?" I'm not sure, but I think I shook my head.

"If things get too rough, do you have somewhere to go? Do you need a place to stay?" Joe waited a couple seconds, then said, "I'm not suggesting you run away. That's not my decision, but you're welcome to the foldout couch in my living room."

"Thanks," I mumbled, "but I'm still hoping to stick it out at home."

"It's a standing offer. I'll give you my phone number. Leaving home is one thing. Roaming the streets takes it to another level."

Joe's expression settled somewhere between determination and sympathy, and I imagined that more than a few Marines had witnessed the same face right before their first firefight.

"Need help studying?" he asked.

I hadn't even figured out how to show my face at school, and he was offering to be my tutor? It was a nice gesture, but miles ahead of me. "I'll be okay," I said, pretending to think about it. Busting my ass just to pull C's for the quarter? That wasn't going to happen.

Joe understood, or maybe he just accepted my reluctance, and clamped a lid on any new offerings. He stared through me and blinked, like his eyes were rifling through an imaginary stack of index cards, each offering a solution to my problems. A few seemed promising. He wanted to tell me what to do, how to straighten things out, but something held him back.

"It's good you came here today, that you got away. Folks in my generation call it clearing the cobwebs."

Clearing the cobwebs? God, I was locked in a nightmare version of *Charlotte's Web*, funky designs and all.

"About all I know for sure is that my life's about to become one big shithole." I was bothered by a sudden sense of fatigue as I waited for the lecture about responsibility, how I was only hurting myself, and why God-given talents shouldn't be wasted. But Joe was finished. He'd offered help and then told me, in his own way, to figure it out.

"Here," he said, fumbling to get the wallet from the hip pocket of his jeans. "This has my name, phone number, and e-mail address." He slid out a business card and handed it to me. "It's okay to call anytime. If you want to have a cup of coffee or just talk, it's okay."

"Thanks."

I took the card and tapped the edge against the table, not sure what to say or not say. I'd wanted our talk to continue, to learn more about the painter from Hideaway Lake, and maybe even hear a solution from one of those index cards, but I knew it was time for it to end. And then I remembered.

"Do you have time to go to my car?" I asked. "It's just around the corner."

"Sure." Joe pushed the chair back and followed me outside.

"The picture I took of you—well, I can make out what you were painting. It was the rock formation on the west side of the lake." I unlocked the Explorer with the remote and grabbed my backpack from the back seat. There was a quizzical look on Joe's face when I took a manila folder from between the books and handed it to him.

"What's this?"

"I've taken quite a few shots of that thing. My photography teacher says it borders on obsession." I smiled and nodded for him to open the file. "Those are all the color shots I've taken. I have black and whites, but you said something about not being able to remember the colors. Maybe these could help."

Joe's smile widened while he flipped through the prints. "You're good, Quinn," he said, holding one picture an extra few seconds, "but I think I already knew that."

"Maybe you could still paint that picture, you know, if you wanted to."

To this day I don't know why I'd stuffed those pictures in my backpack. Perhaps it was pure chance, a coincidence, or maybe there was more to it. But it was on that afternoon I learned to trust that pesky inner voice that comes from nowhere, the one that pokes and prods until I start heading in the right direction.

"I normally don't paint from photos." Joe lingered with one print, then looked at me. "This is what I was painting. I see the colors."

"Go ahead and keep these. I've got the negatives." An unexpected pride stirred as I imagined my photographs reviving his passion.

"If I used these, I'd have to keep them for at least a couple weeks. Sure you don't need them?"

A hypothetical question—it was a done deal.

"I know how to get them," I said, dangling Joe's card from my shirt pocket and watching acceptance flash across his face. "You know, I hate to say this, but you may finish the painting before my parents grant parole. Kinda bugs me that I probably won't see the work-in-progress."

"Maybe it won't be as bad as you think."

"Maybe."

An anticipated quiet, like right before a doctor delivers a diagnosis, surrounded us before Joe stretched his hand toward me. "I mean it, Quinn. Call if you need anything."

I'd never really understood why people shook hands until then. Joe's grip was firm but not tight. It conveyed understanding, it promised protection.

ten

I'd lit another cigarette and was watching the smoke trail into the afternoon sky, dissolving into nothing, before my feet set the swing in motion. Seemed a little odd, cigarettes and playground equipment. The swing set had been in our backyard since I was in the fourth grade. I'd loved kicking higher and higher, parachute jumps, twisting the ropes and then spinning into a daze. Mom would yell at me not to go so high, afraid I'd hurt myself, while Dad reassured her I was just being a boy. Smoking was new, but it would have provided similar reactions if they'd known. Mom would have screamed and Dad would have told her I'd grow out of it. And it made me dizzy.

In the three months since I'd met Joe, the swing had become my preferred seat when I was home alone. The swaying motion was relaxing, I liked being outside, and it connected me to a time when my life wasn't so demanding, so out of control. Hanging out in my room? It had become sterile. Not clean like a hospital, but barren. The computer, the television, and the stereo had been confiscated, packed away on the top shelf of my parents' closet, so there was nothing to do but lie on my bed. And that had gotten old.

Of course I did my best to keep the mess in my bedroom at

extreme levels, but even that satisfaction was waning. Mom used to get a pained look, one that wanted to scream, "I refuse to be surrounded by such filth," one that tried to guilt me into cleaning before just doing the work herself, fuming and complaining about teenagers the whole time. I pushed that button a lot—until she replaced the pained look with a passing grunt.

I figured she'd cave in, that my attitude would outlast her resolve, and that unchanged bed sheets and a disgusting bathroom would return the status quo. That didn't happen. Our war of wills only grew stronger and my bedroom more dreadful, which was another reason I'd become partial to the swing.

Every now and then I looked at Joe's card, wondering whether to test his offer. Escaping the prison I called home, vanishing without a trace, inflicting worry, pain and suffering on my parents; it was easy to get caught up in fantasies that pitted me against the world. But that's where it stopped—with fantasies. I didn't have access to a computer for e-mail and I couldn't bring myself to phone, so I hadn't talked to Joe since our meeting at Lucky's. Maybe I was afraid he'd say "No, I didn't really mean it." Maybe I was afraid he'd say "Come on, I got a place for you to stay." Mostly, I didn't want him to know how unbearable my life had become.

As promised by Mr. McCormack, I received an F in Contemporary American History—for the last *two* quarters. After the infamous plagiarism episode, I purposely came late to class, refused to participate in discussions, and just signed my name to the final exam. Nothing else, just my name. Mr. McCormack didn't say a word when I turned it in, didn't even bat an eye, like his time was too precious to waste on a loser like me. I never really thought Mom and Mr. McCormack had much in common, but it turned out that they were both pretty good at this game.

My other teachers had been a little more sympathetic, or at least they'd tried to be. I kept C's in everything for the third quarter, even Pre-Calc. I didn't know whether the grades were already established or if they were throwing me a bone, trying to soften my fuck-you attitude. It didn't matter. I kept the attitude and lost the sympathy. My final report card had come the previous day and I'd gotten F's in everything except American Literature for the fourth quarter. I still don't know how I managed the B in American Lit. The teacher must have liked my take on *The Catcher in the Rye*.

So I wrapped up my junior year with four F's and a B. Well, *maybe* my junior year had ended. If Mom and Dad's ongoing negotiations with Principal Gendler for summer school broke down, I'd be repeating the eleventh grade. And I didn't get an A in Photography. My parents made me drop the class.

When I think back to that Monday after I came home to stone-faced parents who'd just finished talking with Mr. McCormack—well, I guess I would have done things differently. I would have been prepared, I would have anticipated, I would have been hardened. Maybe that would have helped start everything down a different track.

I wasn't a complete innocent. I knew they'd be seeing red, that lectures and punishments would join forces to attack the Quinnlan Marshall academic menace. Of course there would be yelling and screaming, but I'd also been willing to talk, ready for my parents to listen to some of the challenges I faced as a teenager. I'd just been with an adult who hadn't beaten me with words, whose do-not-cross lines were spread far enough to avoid meaningless arguments. Joe hadn't judged my actions or told me what to do; he'd just listened, and that memory was fresh.

My parents must have heard the garage door open and close when I arrived home that afternoon because they were waiting for me at the door, standing on either side like bailiffs in a courtroom ready to pounce on an uncooperative defendant. The first thing from my mother's mouth wasn't "Where have you been?" It was "Give me your cameras. Now!"

When I paused to gauge the situation, she ripped the camera

bag from my shoulder and hurled it across the kitchen floor, crashing it into the wall. Dad balked a little, but he didn't try stopping her. They'd had more than a few arguments about how his being away from home left her as the bad-guy enforcer, and that her authority was undermined when he returned. Not this time. I guess he'd heard "If you would have listened to me" one too many times.

They marched me into the living room and ordered me to sit. That's where I heard their sermon about rules, where I endured the accusations, where my parents tag-teamed guilt with shame. It's where I was told not to bother checking my cameras because they didn't matter, that my parents were making me drop my photography class. It's where I snapped.

I still can't remember everything that happened next. Maybe I don't want to. I do know the moment was locked in a surreal state. I heard multiple voices, whispering and talking and shouting, to me and to each other. Exaggerated objects zoomed in and out. Distorted faces vied for attention; some charming, some threatening, each insisting I listen to them. I know I screamed. I know I lunged at my mother and that I was restrained by my father. And then I made a choice.

I could have just let go and continued down that uncertain path; it promised sympathy and it would have been so easy, so effortless. A nervous breakdown might have wiped the slate clean, or perhaps left it eternally stained, I didn't know which. It certainly would have shattered Mom's carefully crafted image, and that proposition was tempting. But the psychiatrists and drugs, the hospitals, the behind-the-back snickers, and the knowing glances never happened. I don't know why, but I didn't let them. Reality grabbed hold instead.

It took a few days and a bunch of slammed doors before I calmed down and began a new strategy, one that played into my passive-aggressive behavior. It was simple. Anything that had a subjective interpretation—tried my best, didn't understand the question, forgot there was a test—screamed opportunity, and I attacked with a relentless energy that grew stronger and more powerful with each victory. It was pure, and in my mind, an equitable retaliation. Drop my photography class? I blew off a few chemistry labs. Confiscate my computer? I flunked another test. House arrest unless I was with a parent? My hair didn't get washed. No TV? No conversation longer than three words. When my parents became too easy and too conspicuous of targets, I expanded the playing field to any authority figure that looked at me the wrong way.

Brooding, selfish, rebellious? Yep.

I pushed the envelope on the physical confrontation front, too—the "I'm not cutting my hair and you can't make me" and "Clean my room yourself" type stuff. What were they going to do, spank me? No, Mom wasn't getting in my face anymore unless Dad was around, and I knew when to back off with him. His eyes narrowed and he wouldn't speak. Not a word. That's how far I'd take it, not always, but most of the time.

There were other ploys. I started smoking cigarettes (unfiltered Camels, of course) at school the very next day. Bought a pack from some kid I didn't know for five bucks and hoped a teacher would catch me flicking butts in the parking lot, just so there would be a confrontation. I never did get caught smoking but I kept at it anyway. God, that stuff was nasty—made me nauseous when I inhaled—so I'd play with the smoke, pretending to take long drags, and trying not to flinch when the fire brushed my throat. It all seems so silly now, but I was on a mission, staging a performance, and Camels were my newest prop.

I didn't know who was going to blink first. I desperately wanted to outlast them, but I have to admit I knew better. It wouldn't be all that long until I turned eighteen and kicking me out of the house would become a legal, albeit extreme, option. My parents hadn't played that wild card yet, but the "my way or the highway" threat was out there, lurking, ready to be slapped on the table with definitive vigor, waiting until I got too close to victory. It was an unfair advantage. Still, I'd tell myself that I could survive on my own, that I could be pushed only so far. And every few days I counted the money stashed in my dresser, confirming it was undisturbed and still a secret, but that reassurance was more illusory than real. The rubber-banded wad had lots of fives and ones, and not nearly enough twenties.

WINNIE PLOPPED ON MY BED LIKE he owned it, and locked his fingers behind his head. He wasn't a picky type of guy, and I got the feeling he'd have been comfortable crashing anywhere—couch, sleeping bag, the floor—but he wasn't there to sleep. He was just visiting, had stopped by unannounced and Mom ushered him straight to my room, probably figuring she'd embarrass me. I doubt Winnie even noticed my room was a mess.

We had talked a little at school, between classes and in the lunchroom, but I'd made sure there hadn't been much substance. He knew I ran into Joe at Lucky's, and that he turned out to be a decent guy. He knew I was grounded for life, probably even heard I'd flunked out of school, and had come by just to cheer me up. I was waiting to hear "Dude, maybe we'll be in some classes together next year."

"So, your Mom and Dad lighten up yet?" he finally asked after propping the pillow against the headboard and kicking off his sneakers.

"No," I said, "I didn't do so hot in school. It's going to get worse."

Winnie frowned and shook his head. "Dude!"

"So what's up with you? Going somewhere for the summer?" I asked, anxious to change the subject. Reliving a blow by blow, owning up to my grades? I wasn't up to it, especially when I didn't even know the summer school decision yet.

"We got two weeks in July with my Dad in California. He's thinkin' Disneyland-type stuff, but I've been pushin' Laura and Janice. Got 'em thinkin' that more than a couple days of doin' rides is a waste, that we need to be doin' the beach thing." Winnie sank deeper into the pillow and grinned. "I hear the girls, well, that they don't wear too much on those beaches. You know, bikinis and shit? I got some reflective sunglasses. Dude, they won't even know I'm lookin' at 'em!"

Even self-absorbed outcasts like me found it hard not to smile around Winnie. "Sounds like a plan," I said. Wished I had a plan. Even girl-gawking would have worked.

"And I'm baggin' groceries over at King's. Gonna get five-fifty an hour and a twenty-five-cent raise after a month. Figure I can save almost two grand by the time football practice starts up again."

"Two thousand dollars?" I envisioned paying for two, maybe three months' rent with that kind of money. But reality checked in with groceries and a car and all those numbers on the back of the napkin. Still, padding the stash in my dresser needed to be considered, and I started wondering whether Mom and Dad would have considered a halfway-house type of arrangement.

"You workin' this summer?" asked Winnie.

"Haven't thought about it much. I probably got some summer school, so I don't know. Scheduling work, homework—I don't know," I said, shrugging my shoulders but considering different scenarios.

"Dude! Summer school?"

"Don't rub it in, okay?"

"Yeah, sorry." Winnie swung his legs over the side of the bed and sat up, ready for a happier topic. "Hey, I never got to see the pictures from that day, of that buck and the lake and stuff. Still got 'em?"

It was the third time Winnie had asked to see the pictures. The first two were at school, and I'd dismissed them by saying they were at home. But now we were at my house, the pictures were in a box in my closet, and Winnie knew it. It's not like I didn't want to share them. I just didn't want to be reminded that I wasn't taking pictures anymore, that other people had taken control of my happiness.

"They around?" he asked again.

"Yeah." I disappeared into the closet and retrieved the file from that Friday afternoon, the last time I snapped a picture. "Here," I said, handing Winnie the file.

Winnie was generous with his praise. Words like tight, sweet, whoa, and cool were tossed around as he worked through the prints. "What about after the buck took off?" he asked when he'd finished the stack.

"Didn't turn out."

"And that guy. What'd you say his name was? Joe?"

I opened a drawer to my desk and grabbed the picture of Joe. I didn't bother removing the business card clipped to the back before passing it to Winnie. "It's a good picture," I pronounced.

Winnie held the print at different angles. "He doesn't look as scary as I remember. Well, not scary, but so mean." He fingered the business card. "So this is him? Joe Toscano?"

"Yeah." I hadn't shared much about Joe with Winnie other than how we ran into each other at Lucky's and that we'd both apologized. I still wasn't sure how much to reveal, but I kept talking. "He gave me the card and said to call him anytime. I gave him some pictures I had of the lake. I think he was going to try another painting."

"Cool." Winnie nodded and did that scrunchy mouth thing. "You ever call him?"

"My parents took the computer," I said, tossing my head around the room, encouraging a look, "so I can't e-mail. And I haven't called. I don't want to get into all the explanations about being grounded."

I looked at the picture in Winnie's hand. I remembered my conversation with Joe, how good I'd felt, how I was ready to get through the impending parental blowup. And I wondered if he'd used my photos to paint the rock formation. I wanted to see how it turned out.

"Too bad. Might be kinda cool seein' the painting."

Winnie needed to quit playing football and open one of those psychic shops, the kind where they ask a bunch of questions until they hone in on your specific issue, and then spout off bullshit predictions like they knew it all along. Except Winnie wasn't cheating with all the questions. He probably just saw it on my face.

"Maybe." I'd kicked around calling Joe more than a few times, but it was like running in place on a patch of ice; lots of slipping and sliding, little progress. Talking on the phone would have been sketchy and watered down. It just wouldn't have been the same.

"Come on, dude, call him. Tell him ya want a rematch!" Winnie laughed, then quickly added, "Ya know I'm teasing, right?" He put a temporary hold on the grin, and made sure I thought it was funny.

"No rematch," I said, shaking my head with a laugh. "He'd clean my clock!"

It was okay to laugh. Actually, it felt pretty damned good.

eleven

Mom and Dad had been huddling in the den since the latest phone call from the muckity-mucks at Monarch High. It sounded like the final summer school proposal, the take it or leave it offer, and my parents were deciding. Despite closed doors and guarded whispers, I gathered I was going to be allowed to repeat the second semester of Chemistry and Spanish during an eight-week program at Lexington High in Denver, and whatever grades I earned would replace the F's. That was the good news.

The bad news was I had already earned the minimum credits in Math and History to graduate so, unless I repeated junior year and retook Pre-Calc and Contemporary American History, those F's were going to stand. Repeating junior year or having two F's on my high school transcript? I wondered why I hadn't been invited to the discussion about which was the lesser of two evils.

I was betting they'd go with summer school. It got me out of the house five hours a day for two months and would have kept uncomfortable questions to a minimum. *Quinn isn't graduating this year? He's still a junior?*

There was still the question of whether I would continue playing the defiance game. Failing summer school and repeating junior year anyway was a tempting option, yet I was wavering. Milking another round of punitive damages, giving pain to get pleasure, extracting revenge—well, it hadn't been all that much fun lately. Mom and Dad had become so conditioned, so detached. It was like firing a BB gun at a brick wall; there's minimal damage to the wall and the ricochets kept coming back with stinging accuracy. Sitting in a classroom during summer vacation when I could have been taking pictures, sleeping late, and living large? What happened?

I knew I didn't have to roll over and play dead just yet. Summer school, if that was the choice, wouldn't start for another four days, and besides, I could have agreed to get good grades and then just not followed through. But I was at a point where I wanted things settled, where black and white were preferred color choices. So maybe there would be room to negotiate, maybe Mom and Dad would offer a good-faith gesture in their deal, like allowing a day off or giving my computer back. There could be tradeoffs, some this-for-that. At least I hoped so.

My thoughts of regained freedom were interrupted by the noise we called a doorbell. It didn't go ding-dong; it played *White Christmas*, and not just a few bars, either. It played the whole damned song. There was supposed to be a selection of melodies to choose from, songs for different seasons, oldies but goodies type stuff, but something had gone wrong with the control panel, and we'd been stuck on *White Christmas* since the day after Thanksgiving. Things weren't supposed to stay broken in our house for long, and I knew that fixing the doorbell sat atop Dad's to-do list. I'd seen Mom put it there.

"I got it!" Elizabeth's hand skimmed the railing as she raced down the stairs, ready to join whichever friend wanted to ride bikes or roam the neighborhood. It was particularly annoying when a never-ending stream of twelve-year-olds paraded through the house on weekends or during the summer. They never called. They rang the doorbell.

I expected to hear the door slam, confirming that my sister wouldn't be around when my parents brought me into the study, but I heard Elizabeth's footsteps instead. She walked through the foyer until she saw me, then said, "There's a man at the door. He wants to talk to you."

I OPENED THE DOOR, NOT QUITE sure what to expect. Winnie? No, Elizabeth would have just let him in. A neighbor who'd spied me on the swing and wanted to scold me about the evils of tobacco? Yeah, that was probably it. Someone who couldn't stand idly by, someone else who wanted a shot at me. Attacks and confrontations—I expected battles at every turn. I didn't expect to see Joe Toscano standing on the front porch.

"Thought about calling first." Joe glued his eyes to mine, waiting and reading. "My gut told me to come over."

I was caught off guard and my jaw, though I knew it was open, seemed locked. How'd he find me? Why'd he find me? For the first time since I couldn't remember, it mattered how I looked. I was self-conscious about dirty hair and smelly clothes, about my sister peeking around the corner, about my parents in the study.

"Got a minute to talk?" he asked.

I nodded and stepped down to the porch, closing the door behind me. "I wanted to call you," were the only words I managed.

"I figured." Joe's eyes roamed a bit. "Just wanted to make sure everything was okay, and to give you the pictures back." He handed me the manila file from under his arm and smiled. "Finished the painting. Might be better than the first."

"Really, you used my shots?" Joe's smile broke the ice; telling me my pictures had mattered melted it. "You didn't lose the sense of being there? The colors were okay?"

"I *was* there, remember? Between my memory and your pictures, well, I don't toot my own horn much, but everything came together. It's one of my best pieces."

I nodded, and then my pride and satisfaction became a smile.

"Was hoping you might drop by to take a look."

My breathing turned into a sigh. Oh yeah—reality.

"Things didn't go so well when I got home that day." I bit my lower lip, debating how much to tell. "And I'm not exaggerating when I say it's gotten steadily worse."

"I figured." Joe sat and stretched his legs down the porch steps, not waiting for an invitation. He was dressed in a golf shirt, blue jeans, and cowboy boots. The jeans and boots were familiar, but the golf shirt, a red and white striped version with a penguin on the pocket—well, it *was* over eighty degrees. I guess a golf shirt worked. "So that teacher gave you the F?" he asked.

"Which one?" I mumbled as I sat a few feet from Joe and wrapped my arms around bunched-up knees. "It probably didn't make the national news, but there's been a war going on in the sleepy little town of Louisville, and you're sitting at ground zero. My biggest weapon, the one with mass destruction capabilities, is grades." I turned my head toward Joe and said, "There are a bunch of F's."

"It did get worse."

"Oh yeah."

"Anyone survive?" Joe placed his hands behind him and leaned back. He didn't seem startled by my grades—didn't even flinch. Then he gave me a look, one that made sure I understood the question.

I left Joe's eyes and stared at the walkway leading to the street. Our house stood out in a neighborhood of manicured lawns—a six-inch-high row of round cedar logs, wedged together against the walkway leading to our front door, guarded freshly trimmed shrubs that lined either side. So orderly, so perfect. The precision matched a landscape of multicolored flowers, evergreens, and just-so hedges strategically placed and joylessly maintained.

"I think we're about to start the peace negotiations. My parents are deciding whether I should go to summer school or repeat junior year."

"What do you want?"

I looked back at Joe. Such a simple question that no one else had asked. I swallowed, my voice was weak, and my words came quickly. "I'll do the summer school, I'll get the grades, but I need my life back." It had taken just two seconds to decide whether to dig in my heels or cry uncle, whether to cop more attitude or admit I'd had enough. How long had the answer been there, ready to spill out, waiting to be heard?

Joe stroked his chin with a thumb. When he spoke, the words were slow and soft. "Sometimes folks go down roads that take them further and further from what they really want. Pretty easy getting wrapped up in details, focusing on bumps and curves, not paying attention to where the road takes them. Turning around can be tough."

I understood what Joe was telling me. I knew it was important for my parents and me to get back on track, but it just seemed so unfair. I wasn't the one who'd turbo-charged this. I wasn't an adult who was *supposed* to be mature. I hadn't thrown cameras against the wall. Why should I have to take the lead? Before my mind ranted further, I decided a reply was better than silence, at least as far as Joe was concerned.

"Yeah," I muttered.

"You don't get to start down a new road right off the bat, Quinn. There's some backtracking." He raised an eyebrow with another smile, then reached his arm toward me and placed his hand between my shoulders, just below my neck. Joe waited a few seconds before he said, "Been up to Hideaway Lake recently?"

I managed a half-laugh. "Not since I crunched your painting."

"Take me with you next time you go." Joe patted my back and stood.

"Sure, I'd like that," I said, wondering when that would happen, and why he was leaving so soon. "Hey, how'd you know where I live?"

Joe began to answer when the latch to the front door clicked.

I turned and saw Dad standing next to the partially opened door, his left hand resting on the knob. Mom was behind him, peeking around his right shoulder, not yet ready to claim a front row seat. They took turns looking at me, then Joe.

Joe stepped toward them and extended his right hand to my father. "Joe Toscano," he said like it was a cocktail party. "I'm returning some pictures to Quinn." He offered a warm smile, and waited for Dad to take his hand.

"Dennis Marshall." Dad shook Joe's hand. "This is my wife, Sharon."

Joe reached further and grabbed Mom's hand. "Nice to meet both of you," he said matter-of-factly.

Mom slid past Dad and onto the front porch next to Joe to play her gracious hostess part. "So, Quinn shared his photography—that's interesting." Her tone was sweet, but I knew better. She lasered in on Joe, just like when she would ask if my homework was done. "So how did you two meet?"

"We met at Lucky's Coffee House in Boulder a few months ago." Joe met my mother's eyes and didn't let go. "You must be proud of Quinn. His photographs are quite remarkable." Joe turned and reached for the manila file in my hand. "I was able to finish a painting from these." He opened the file and handed a couple prints to Mom and Dad.

Mom didn't miss a beat. "Yes, we're quite proud of Quinn," she said without looking at the pictures.

Dad nodded as he looked at the shots and then reached for the ones Mom held.

Joe took it in, all of it. It was like he'd found a few more pieces to my puzzle and knew exactly where they fit. He blinked several times, rifling through those index cards with answers. The picture was becoming clearer.

"Mr. and Mrs. Marshall, could we talk privately for a moment?" Joe fixed his stare on Dad with a purpose.

My mother and father replied at the same time.

Mom said, "It's not a .. ."

Dad said, a little louder than Mom, "Why don't you come in so we can be more comfortable."

I WAS BACK AT THE KITCHEN TABLE, imagining outcomes and managing emotions, and once again waiting my turn. Joe was talking to my parents? The Joe from Hideaway Lake who had chased me around his easel? What would they think about me having a seventy-four-year-old friend? Damn, I was already in enough hot water!

I'd talked to this guy and told him everything; all my feelings, the anger, the frustration, that I'd used my grades as a weapon. Well, I guess I should have given Mom and Dad more credit; they'd probably already known that, but still, I had confided in him, and he was talking to my parents—alone.

At least Elizabeth was enjoying the proceedings. She sat twenty feet away pretending to watch television, and she hadn't said a word. She didn't need to. She just sat on the couch and smiled. Elizabeth knew I was jumpy. She knew there was a story behind Joe, and was patiently waiting for the right moment. Sort of like a hungry wolf spotting a caribou stuck in the snow.

Then it hit me. It wasn't like it could get worse. There weren't any more possessions to confiscate, no privileges left to revoke, and hey—besides plumbing and painting, maybe Joe was a master negotiator and had taken my case pro bono. He could have been in there getting cameras and a computer and car keys.

Good things coming my way? Probably not. I'd been in a full-fledged funk for over a year, longer if you counted the attitude no one recognized, and I knew how it worked. I'd just start to feel good, get my bearings, have something to look forward to—then splat. Someone, or something, flattened me. Took my legs out and didn't look back. Who was that guy in Greek mythology that dragged this huge boulder up the hill, and every time he got close to the top it fell to the bottom? And he struggled to the top and fell back down for eternity. Sisyphus? Yeah, I knew Sisyphus only too well.

I heard the door to the study slide open. It was over? So soon? I stood, waiting to answer to someone, ready for the verdict. I could make out Dad's and Joe's voices; sounded like friendly chitchat. I didn't hear Mom.

Joe, Dad, and then Mom emerged and walked toward the front door. Dad looked over his shoulder and said, "Quinn, come on over and say goodbye to Joe."

Goodbye? What did *goodbye* mean?

I walked through the family room, purposely lingered in front of the television (every opportunity to irritate Elizabeth counted), then joined the three of them at the front door.

"Joe explained how you two met," Dad said. He sized me up, waiting for a response or an excuse, maybe even an apology.

I looked at Joe, unsure what he'd said to them. His nod was slight, almost imperceptible, but it told me exactly what I needed to know. I inhaled and stared at my feet before speaking.

"I was pretty embarrassed about sneaking up on someone to take a picture, Dad. I think Winnie and I scared Joe—well, startled him. One of my cameras hit me in the face when I was running. It wasn't his fault."

"Joe said he saw you at Lucky's and that you worked things out." Dad cocked an eyebrow at Mom, satisfied with my answer.

"It was after I talked with Mr. McCormack. I couldn't believe I was getting an F, and, well, I didn't want to stay in school, and I didn't want to come home. It wasn't that I was trying to skip or anything. I just needed time to think about things." The words came easy. I'd practiced them driving home from Boulder that afternoon.

Dad's willful side always surfaced when he was in control of the Marshall household. He talked faster and a little louder, his manner crisp and to the point. That piece of Dad would appear after he'd considered the facts and when there was some kind of resolution at hand. That confidence was apparent now and, knowing Dad was navigating, I began to relax. Mom must have recognized it too, because she didn't interrupt.

"Anyway," Dad said, "why don't you two take a few minutes, and then, Quinn, come on into the study. Mom and I want to go over what Mr. Gendler had to say. We need to let them know a decision."

Mom gave a polite excuse and said something to Joe that I didn't really hear. She shook his hand and headed toward the kitchen. Her walk was slow, subdued.

Dad turned and pumped Joe's hand. It was a thank you and relief handshake, the kind you don't know you're overdoing.

"Joe," he said, "thanks for telling us about your meeting with Quinn, and for the insight. Putting a little perspective on the situation—well, teenagers aren't easy." Dad pressed his lips into an I-should-have-known-that smile. "Anyway, thanks. I appreciate ... Sharon and I appreciate you being direct."

"Like I said, Dennis, I'm no expert. No kids, no grandkids, but I've had a few eighteen-year-olds under my wing."

Joe grinned and Dad laughed, and Mom was in the kitchen—perfect.

"So," said Joe when we were alone on the front porch.

"Do I want to know?"

"Not that much to it, really. Wanted them to know the circumstances between us, and that I think you're a fine young man."

Joe paused, picking pieces of their conversation. "Your dad liked that I was a Marine. We talked about discipline, about maturing young men, what they go through."

"Why did you think they'd even listen to you?" My voice was edgy. It pissed me off when people talked about me. Still, it had been Joe in my corner, and not some counselor from school confusing me with three hundred other students.

Joe listened and read my face. "Probably should have cleared it with you beforehand. Sorry, Quinn. Just seemed to be the right time."

In that instant I knew three things about Joe: he trusted his instincts, stepping on toes wasn't a deal-breaker when it came to doing the right thing, and he would apologize once—only once.

"Well, whatever you said, my dad bought it. He was almost in a good mood."

"Be honest with your dad, Quinn. He deals it straight up."

"And my mother?"

Joe blinked a couple times, then squinted. "She's pretty tightly wound. Thinks the more she squeezes, the more she controls. She'd have been a good Marine." He put a finger to his lips and had a vacant look, as if a memory had sliced through his thoughts. "I don't know her that well," he said, "but sometimes rigid people change. They find out what's important."

"In my lifetime?" I was relaxed again. Joe had pegged my parents. He wasn't on their side.

"You never know."

"Well, don't keep me hanging. What are the terms of my parole? I'm getting paroled, aren't I?"

Joe shrugged. "Beats me," he said.

"What? I'm a good kid, my dad's a straight shooter and my mom's the Gestapo—I already knew that! Come on! Tell me you talked about computers and car keys!"

"Nope."

Shaking my head to jar loose the clumps of dirt that must

have been lodged in my ears seemed like a smart thing to do. I couldn't be hearing correctly. Dad was talking and smiling, Mom had her tail tucked, and I was having a conversation with Joe on my front porch—and nothing was resolved?

"Like I said, Quinn, you got some backtracking. I can't do it for you."

Joe stretched his arms toward the sky and arched his shoulders like he was warming up for a yoga class. It was a little too nonchalant for my taste.

"So you opened the communication channels—that's all?"

"Seemed like a good first step," Joe said. "Talk to your folks, work out your deal. It's between you and them." He knew I wanted more details and that I needed words, specific words, to tailor my position, but he didn't bite off. "Just remember one thing."

"Yeah, what's that?"

Steadfast eyes, those ebony circles with unyielding intensity, momentarily appeared. "Keep your end of the bargain." Joe watched me process the words, then added, "*Everyone* should have complete confidence in your word."

It was the honesty thing: truth, justice, and the American way. Oh, I knew all about honesty. I knew about skirting the issue, selective memory, and literal translations, and all the other techniques adults used. If I had been talking to Mom, I would have already fired back. Instead, I held my eyes steady and gave Joe the benefit of the doubt.

"One more thing." A smile played on Joe's lips. "Assuming you don't detonate any more mass destruction weapons, we're on for tomorrow. Meet me at Lucky's at nine."

twelve

I was right. I wouldn't be repeating my junior year.

Dad was pragmatic and concluded that even if I'd erased all the F's, the admission officers, those men and women who sign the "congratulations" or "too bad, chump" letters, would have still known. Why waste another whole year when top schools were now out of the question anyway?

Mom struggled. She dabbed her eyes, sniffled, and quivered her lip before finally relenting to Dad's logic. Her stories of math ribbons and spelling bees and teaching me to read when I was three—well, they were history (no pun intended). Her oldest, so bright, so much promise. It must have been hard for her to accept reality when she was joined at the hip with ambition.

Me? It was a no-brainer, so I was onboard. Eight weeks of classes for five hours a day or thirty-six weeks of eight hours a day. Not too tough a choice.

So we had a unanimous decision. One that soothed nerves, offered a cleaner living arrangement, and reclaimed privileges. I guess the battle had gotten old for both sides. And there was an interesting twist to our negotiations. Dad purged the grade requirement in exchange for me giving up distractions during homework sessions. That was it. There were no other conditions.

He knew the previous game plan, whatever that was, hadn't worked, and he was ready to try something else.

And for the first time in over two months, I was driving. I was behind the wheel and headed for Boulder, ready to drink coffee, eat pastries, and talk to Joe. I had to smile when I glanced at myself in the rearview mirror, at the way I looked and how I felt. I didn't see a sullen teenager with greasy hair hanging in his face. I saw clean and combed hair, a freshly scrubbed face, and way-cool shades covering my baby blues. I was energized and ready for a fresh start.

I'd had a few of these before; the stopping and the starting, rolling my boulder up and down the hill, but that day seemed different.

JOE FLAGGED ME DOWN LIKE HE WAS guiding a 747 to the gate. I saw a newspaper stretched across his table; the disorderly pages and half-full mug of coffee suggested he'd been there a while. He had replaced the golf shirt with a faded blue work shirt, but kept the jeans and cowboy boots.

"Morning, Quinn." Joe deposited tip-of-the-nose reading glasses into his shirt pocket, and stood to shake my hand. "Just catching up on my investments," he said, folding the newspaper and stacking it on a chair.

"Make any money?"

"Just enough to buy you one of those fancy drinks you like. What's it called?"

"White chocolate mocha. Did you make enough for a blueberry muffin too?"

"Barely." Joe walked to the counter and placed the order, and when he returned with my breakfast, said, "Suppose you're covering any of the major food groups with this?"

"Probably not." I peeled the wrapping from the muffin and took a bite. "Just coffee for you? They've got whole-grain breads. You know, healthy fiber stuff."

"I had breakfast three hours ago. Right after my walk."

"I thought you jogged or rode a bike."

"Felt like walking this morning." Joe watched me devour the muffin, looked at the crumbs on my plate and shook his head. "It's like magic. I blink and the muffin is gone. Want another?"

"Maybe later." I sipped the mocha and eased back into the chair. Joe's eyes stayed with mine, but I knew he'd taken stock of my hair and face and attitude. They would have been hard to miss, yet there was no comment.

"So, everything worked out okay, or are you still haggling with your folks?" Joe rested his forearms on the table and interlocked the fingers of his hands. He was interested, but it was hard to know how many details he wanted.

"Dad took over as quarterback after you left," I said. "He talked about moving forward, that we both saw how ugly it could get, and that we needed to understand the other guy's position." Joe nodded, so I continued. "I'm going to retake Chemistry and Spanish in summer school. Mom and Dad gave back all my stuff, you know, the computer and stereo, and I promised not to be distracted when I study."

"Good." Joe knew there was more, and he waited.

"Mom's still a bit touchy. I mean, she was really intense during all this, like her life depended on not giving an inch, so I don't think she's too happy that Dad took charge."

Joe puckered his lips like he was debating whether to comment, then shrugged his shoulders and said, "We all have tools to get through life, Quinn, and for whatever reason, your mom keeps a hammer real close. Driving nails, slamming them flush. When you get good at using a hammer it becomes the first choice, a reflex." Joe saw the puzzled look on my face and wriggled his eyebrows.

"You left a few nails dangling that she thought needed pounding."

"She's pretty good with a screwdriver, too."

Joe laughed out loud while he visualized. "You can't solve everything with tweezers, and you don't just swing away with a hammer. Different problems require different tools. Give her a reason to use different tools."

I sighed and sipped more mocha. I liked the tool metaphor. It broke everything down into simpler terms. It had me thinking.

"Get your cameras back?"

"Yeah, it's tight." I had examined my equipment and everything seemed fine, but I didn't bring my cameras to Boulder that day. I hadn't known what Joe had in mind, and I didn't want taking pictures to interrupt my time with him. I also wanted to be alone when I got reacquainted with photography. I was looking forward to private moments, seeing which image grabbed me first, and listening for the voice that whispered "now."

"You asked a question yesterday. Talking about your cameras made me think of it." Joe sipped from his cup. "Nicole Strandlund," he said.

"Huh?"

"You asked how I found you. Nicole Strandlund."

I was busy connecting the dots when Joe finished.

"Figured you might be grounded, but I thought I'd hear from you after a few weeks. Wondered if you lost my card, that maybe you didn't know how to get ahold of me. So I called Monarch and got the name of the photography teacher."

"You called Nicki? She told you where I lived?"

"Not right away," Joe said, and chuckled. "We had a little discussion about the bruise on your face before much else happened."

I raised an eyebrow. "She wanted to call the police," I said.

"She told me that. Pointed a finger in my face when she did."

"You saw her?"

"Yeah. Went by her studio." Joe's look suggested that anything less than a face-to-face hadn't even been considered. "Didn't think she'd give me an address or phone number over the phone."

Good point. I could see Nicki's finger waving and wouldn't have been surprised if she'd poked Joe in the chest with it. "I told her it was just as much my fault, you know, that day at Hideaway Lake. I hope she wasn't too hard on you," I said.

"We had ice cream."

"What?"

"I bought her an ice cream cone. There's a shop around the block from her studio."

"I know about the shop," I blurted. "You went for ice cream? The two of you?"

"We got along fine once I explained that you and I met again. I showed her the file you gave me." Joe was amused by my reaction, like licking ice cream and talking about Quinn Marshall just went together—didn't everyone know that? "She said your mom called and told her that you were struggling in school, that you didn't have time to take Photography. Nicki asked about you. Said she wanted to call but didn't know if it was appropriate."

My surprise had something to do with guilt. I knew Mom had called her, and that Nicki had gotten at least some of the story. Still, I hadn't faced her. I was embarrassed and didn't want to admit my parents were taking away something that mattered. (Several years later I realized I also wanted to avoid the one person who could have kept me from waging my war.) So I hadn't told her what happened, didn't even have her sign the form for dropping photography class. I'd left it at the administration office, and went out of my way to avoid her.

"Courtesy call might be nice." Joe paused, then winked and said, "I really go for women who play in darkrooms and eat chocolate chip mint."

"Whatever." It was the word, a crutch teenagers used when they needed a witty response but drew a blank. I wasn't a big fan. It reminded me of bubblegum-chewing airheads with too much makeup, or grunge types riding skateboards, and I'd thought of myself as smarter than that.

Joe decided not to press the point and changed the subject. "Have an interest in seeing that painting?" His palms were flat on the table, ready to push up.

"Absolutely!"

"I want you to see it," he said. "Why don't you follow me over to my place?"

"Sure," I said, but before I stood, a man approached our table. He was middle-aged with well-oiled brown hair that was unevenly parted on one side. His glasses were thick—the proverbial bottoms of Coke bottles—and I couldn't tell if they were broken or just lying crooked across his wide nose. Only the front and back tails of his short-sleeved dress shirt were tucked into wrinkled Dockers. Disrepair. He was a walking state of disrepair.

"Joe?" said the man. "Well, hello Joe. Are you feeling better?"

Joe nodded and stood. "Much better, Dr. Leakas. Thanks for asking."

"Good. Ah, that's good." The man bounced his head up and down in short strokes. "I got your message, and of course I knew the final exam didn't matter. I remember our talk. But I was concerned. I got the message and I was concerned. Everything is okay, though?"

"Just under the weather a few days," Joe said. There was a gentle, almost embarrassed smile on his lips, like when people sing *Happy Birthday*. "Dr. Leakas, this is a friend of mine, Quinn Marshall. Quinn, this is Dr. Leakas. He's a professor of Anatomy & Physiology at the university."

"Hello, Quinn." Dr. Leakas took my hand, shook it once, and then let go. "Are you a student, too?"

"No," I said, pushing the chair back and standing. "Well, I am a student, but at Monarch High School. Over in Louisville."

"Ah, I see. Well, maybe you'll be one of my students in the future, then." He gave me a perfunctory smile, then drifted back to Joe. "I could still give you the exam. I normally don't make such concessions to students, but we could set something up. I don't have to turn in final grades until Friday. There's still time."

"Everything is fine, and thanks, but I won't be taking the exam." Joe rested his hand on Dr. Leakas' back, and walked him toward the counter, positioning him in line. It was hard to tell whether Joe was being courteous or taking steps, literally and figuratively, to end their conversation. "Don't worry about the final grade. I haven't looked at one in twelve years."

"I know, I know. We've had this discussion. I just, I just ... "

"It's okay, Dr. Leakas, really." Joe arched his eyebrows and dropped his chin a notch, a that's-just-the-way-it-is look. "I enjoyed your class. Learned a lot." Joe offered his hand to seal the decision.

"Yes, well ... " Dr. Leakas' face moped with acceptance. "Yes, well, Joe, it was a pleasure. A top student, a very fine student indeed." He shook Joe's hand like they were contestants just before the toss-up question on *Family Feud*.

"Quite a selection of drinks." Joe inched the professor forward and pointed at the overhead menu. "Take care of yourself, Dr. Leakas." He waved goodbye with one hand and pointed me to the door with the other.

Dr. Leakas' eyes darted across the overhead board. He seemed tempted and confused, and his lips twitched while he read and reread the choices. "Ah yes, goodbye Joe," he said without looking in our direction.

"What was that all about?" I asked once we were outside. "You didn't take the final exam?" I walked beside Joe, trying to keep up with dictating steps that headed the opposite direction from where I was parked.

"I'll tell you later."

thirteen

I kept looking for the "I love me" wall, the one that validated success, attested to skill, or certified talent. It's the wall that reminds you, and tells everyone else, that you're somebody. Everyone's got one. Some are obvious, with plaques and certificates and diplomas and citations. Others take a more subtle approach to bragging; family pictures and handicrafts are accomplishments, too.

I had figured an ex-Marine would have plenty of masculine trophies—swords and guns, pictures of buddies drinking beer, souvenirs taken off dead enemies—but we were almost done with the tour and I still hadn't seen the wall. It had to be there. Maybe it would be a little different, like Nicki's "no award is better than another" attitude, but Joe had to have one. I admit now to a certain degree of relief at not being overwhelmed with gung-ho Marine shit when I'd first entered the apartment, but then I began getting curious. I wanted the wall to tell me more.

"That's it," Joe said as we left his bedroom.

"Nice place," I said without enough enthusiasm.

Joe's ground-level apartment was one of four units in a red brick two-story that, other than the absence of uncut grass and thriving weeds, was not much different than a couple dozen other neighboring multifamily units that catered to university students. Affordability, not amenities, was the operative word.

I guessed Joe's place was built back in the sixties. The appliances, plumbing, and fixtures weren't dirty, just old—really old. You had to light the kitchen stove to turn it on, the cupboards had been painted but were still aggressively ugly, and the bathroom—well, the bathroom was pink. Pink tile, pink sink, pink bathtub. It made me glad I was born in the eighties.

"Everything works fine. Fix it when it doesn't." Joe smiled at our difference in taste, or maybe it was just priorities. He was content with worn comfort; I would have been Home Depot's best customer.

"Hey, it's great."

Actually, other than the kitchen and bathroom, I wasn't blatantly lying. The place had three bedrooms, a living room, and an eating area off the kitchen. Joe had converted two of the bedrooms. One, an art studio that, despite an open window, blasted your nostrils with the smell of turpentine as you entered. The current work-in-progress (it looked like the bridge across Varsity Lake) rested on an easel in the middle of the room with a once-white sheet spread at the base for a drop cloth. A few feet away an eight-foot folding table was crammed with supplies. Not only did paintings cover the walls, canvases leaned against them five deep.

The other bedroom, a study, had a metal desk in one corner, the kind schools provide their teachers, with a computer monitor and keyboard on top. I couldn't see the CPU that everything connected to, but I was sure it was old and really slow—technology's version of pink. At least a dozen bookcases, some tall and thin, some short and wide, and some stacked on top of each other, filled the remaining space. None of them matched and they were full of books. Nothing else, just books.

Joe's bedroom was the smallest. It was stark and strict. The dresser was basic: blond oak, chest high, five drawers, and there weren't any pictures or knickknacks on top. The double-bed butted against the wall without a headboard, and was tightly tucked. Two pillows were fluffed and perfectly aligned with a folded back sheet; a crisp gray blanket covered the sheet. There wasn't an alarm clock or a lamp on a nightstand because there was no nightstand. And Joe's bedroom was the only room in the apartment where paintings didn't fight each other for space. The walls were bare.

"This is the only place you've lived in Boulder? For the last twelve years?"

"Yep." Joe's nod was proud. "The kids who rented it before me really trashed the place. I met with the owner, told her I wanted to live here, that I would fix it up, keep it in good shape if she bought the materials. Been good for both sides. She keeps a reliable tenant. I pay affordable rent."

"So you're a live-in caretaker?" I said, trying to imagine the place twelve years ago.

"Just keep up my place, but I get to know everyone in the building. Had quite a few interesting neighbors over the years," he said. "Usually takes a few weeks to reach an understanding when new ones move in." Joe headed toward the kitchen and opened the refrigerator. "Want something?" he asked, grabbing a jug of water.

"I'm fine."

My mind was reeling, trying to imagine the stories: Joe breaking up too-loud parties, Joe smelling marijuana and calling the cops. Don't get me wrong, I already thought he was a great guy and I knew our friendship was growing in an odd-couple sort of way—but going off to college, being on your own and away from your parents, and having him for a neighbor?

"Quite a few stay in touch, Christmas cards and e-mails." Joe took his glass of water and headed into the living room.

"So what are you? The grandfather everyone always wanted?" I laughed, but Joe lowered his eyes and offered a polite smile.

"I like being around young people," was all he said before sitting on the couch.

"I don't do the Christmas card thing, but I'll send you e-mails." I took a chair across from Joe and hoped my little joke relieved the tension. Then I saw it. On the wall behind the couch. The painting of the rock formation at Hideaway Lake.

"I expect you to be honest, Quinn."

"Huh?" I hadn't really heard the words.

"What do you think of the painting?"

I didn't remember getting up, but I was standing, and I knew my mouth was open because I was using it to breathe. I had captured more images of that rock than anyone, so I knew the exact angle of the painting, but it was like I was seeing it for the first time. It wasn't a replica, like a photograph, but an interpretation. The trees were grouped differently, the lake wasn't really as close, and the hill to the left was steeper. But the rock formation—there was no mistaking it.

"Well?"

I closed my mouth and swallowed. "It's incredible!" I moved closer to the painting, trying to determine why I was so taken. It was the colors. They were judiciously exaggerated. Bold and raw. The colors commanded attention.

Joe couldn't hide a look of inner satisfaction. "I changed a few things," he said.

"Yeah, I see that. But it works! Look at the shadow on the water ... here." I stepped forward and pointed to a spot on the painting. "That's why the colors on the rock are different. Well, at least not what I've seen before. I'm torn between knowing you invented the color but not absolutely sure you did. That's it! That's what has me hooked."

"What?"

"These colors, your colors; they *could* be real. I look at your painting and I *want* them to be real." My only passion had been photography—capturing the angle, the light, the split second—but at that moment I was mesmerized by a piece of art. I can still recall the sensation of recognizing every detail, every distinction. It felt like I understood the reasons and the results of each stroke, and that I was a part of his painting.

"I painted it, so thank you," Joe said. "But I didn't make up the colors. I got them from your pictures."

"No way! Hey, I took the pictures. I'd remember these colors."

"Not all from the same picture. Got them from all of your pictures." Joe stood and turned toward the painting. "I kept asking myself 'Why couldn't it be this color' so I started playing a what-if game. What if it was raining and the sun was shining, what if it was twilight and a full moon, what would those colors look like together? I didn't want to be outlandish, just a little out of the box."

"Nicki's got to see this."

"I wouldn't want to bother her."

"Tell her you'll spring for a double-scoop of chocolate chip mint. But believe me, she'd want to see this!"

I'D LOOKED AT ALL OF JOE'S PAINTINGS and we had talked about most them—when he had painted them, what he was trying for, his own assessment. Though I hadn't looked at the works in chronological order, I felt that I could, if I went back and forth a bit, see a progression in Joe's work. His first few paintings were all watercolors—lots of beaches and crashing waves. They were good, but for lack of a better description, they were stiff, the kind you'd buy at starving artist sales for $49. Joe said he'd painted them before moving to Boulder.

He went a different direction after moving to Colorado. He'd switched from watercolors to oils, the canvases were small, and the subjects were specific and close-up. Joe went for nuance and captured details. One in particular, a greenish-blue-breasted hummingbird, was striking, and to this day is one of my favorites. Joe laughed when he recalled how he had to position the feeder several times a day to catch the right light. He said it constantly interrupted his work and that it had irritated the hell out of the hummingbird.

Then Joe got comfortable. Not lazy with an "I'll get to it when I get to it" attitude, but more relaxed with his journey. I saw variations, probably techniques he learned in class, and I saw more interpretation and symbolism. Joe told me that he'd tried different brushes, experimented with palette knives for texturing, and that he became fascinated with creating color by mixing paint.

Joe was hesitant to label his current work—thought it dictated too much to the viewer—but admitted to being influenced in the Fauve style of Matisse, or as Joe interpreted, "the wild beast." He liked brilliant colors, vivid and contrasting expressions of yellow and red and blue, and he spent as much time mixing the oils as he did actually painting. Joe claimed the discipline and patience required to extract the perfect hue allowed his eventual brush strokes to be bold and decisive, uninhibited, like he was releasing a force of energy and emotion onto the canvas.

I remember how Joe responded to my barrage of compliments. He said, "I got good when I was willing to be bad. When I finally allowed each piece to have a voice, when I dared to ignore what others thought and just let loose, I became an artist." He told me how he'd listen, actually close his eyes and meditate, waiting for direction, and then allow his hands to follow the image. Joe believed that all artists—whether they're painters or writers or photographers or actors or dancers or musicians—welcome guidance from the creative spirit, and crave those "where did that come from" moments. He called it an artist's greatest pleasure.

"YOU COULD HAVE STOPPED ME AN hour ago," he said. We'd finished reviewing Joe's work and reclaimed our seats in the living room. "People ask about my paintings all the time, but I can tell when I go into too much detail. They get that glassy-eyed look, like I'm reciting the periodic table." Joe gave a trusting smile. "Hope I didn't bore you."

"Would have told you if you did."

"Good," he said. "That's the way it's supposed to be."

"Okay to ask a few questions?" The role reversal thing was getting fun.

Joe laughed. "Only if I get to keep my computer and car keys."

"Okay—well, this apartment is wall-to-wall pictures. I mean, they're everywhere." I noticed Joe fold his arms across his chest. Not a good sign, but I was in too deep to retreat. "How come there aren't any paintings in your bedroom?" I wanted to add something about a Marine barracks bed and dresser, but didn't.

Joe's eyes tightened. He pursed his lips and nodded acknowledgment of my question. After a couple of measured breaths he said, "I'm happy spending my days studying and painting. I experience the joy of learning and I express myself, display my passion with paints and canvas." Joe breathed deep again, and this time he blinked. "I only sleep two or three hours a night, Quinn. Not because my body only needs two or three hours. Because that's the most I can sleep."

"Oh." I was embarrassed by my dimwitted response, and an uncomfortable pause spread throughout the room. It was my turn to blink. Not index cards. Just nerves.

"Sort of used to it now. If I don't fight, if I just get up and get going, I'll usually get a thirty-minute nap in the afternoon. Funny, I really look forward to that nap."

I instinctively looked at my watch. It wasn't quite noon, and I didn't know what part of the afternoon sleep claimed. "You okay now?" I asked.

"I'm fine, Quinn, and nap time's at two." Joe waited for relief to register, then continued. "You asked why I don't have paintings in my bedroom. It's because I don't want to taint them. Sounds silly, but I don't want to expose them to that other side of me, like the demons will rub off and somehow ruin my twenty *good* hours every day. So I sleep in that room. It's not a pleasant experience."

I'd read about veterans who had flashbacks, how they relived the atrocities of war over and over again, how they were afraid to sleep, terrified they would remember details, the pain. I envisioned beads of sweat pooling on Joe's brow as he battled a recurring enemy. I heard screaming, felt the suffering. And even though I knew there had to be an instant when his black dots enlarged and focused on a new day, an exact point when reality took over, I struggled to understand how this could go on every night. Joe was a regular guy. So normal.

"Maybe if you put paintings in there, you know, make it more comfortable and surround yourself with good things—maybe you'd sleep better." I was fumbling because I wanted to fix it. I desperately wanted to fix it.

"Tried that," he said flatly. "Not here, but in California. Decorated my bedroom, filled it with paintings and pictures, all kinds of relaxing images. Didn't sleep at all. Nothing. Not even the two or three hours. And I began to hate painting. The very thought of putting paint on a canvas was exhausting. It depressed me."

"Sorry." I hung my head at my naïveté.

"So I took it out, all of it." Joe's patient gaze told me the ending before his words. "Fell right to sleep that night. Only three hours, but they felt pretty damn good. Started painting when I woke up." He clasped his fingers around the back of his neck and casually stretched his legs trying to get comfortable, as if he wanted to physically detach from the memory. "There's something buried inside me that wants to be isolated, to be left alone, and it exacts a price if I interfere. I don't understand the arrangement, but I keep to it."

"This has been going on since California?"

"Started in '74."

I was dumbfounded. No way—almost thirty years?

"I'm probably going somewhere I shouldn't, but I'm going to ask anyway. So is this a Vietnam war thing?"

Joe pasted a brave smile and said, "Yeah, Quinn. It's about the war."

fourteen

Eating lunch at Joe's apartment was like going to a garage sale; there was always a variety of inventory that could have easily been thrown away. Frozen casseroles, leftover pasta, and I-dare-you lunchmeat shared refrigerator space with endless jars and cans, each covered with patches of aluminum foil that disguised conditions and colors. Wasted leftovers? Hardly. The defrost and reheat buttons on Joe's stand-alone microwave went through daily workouts.

We had salad, bread and lasagna that day. The salad came from one of those ready-to-toss bags, and Joe coated it with Italian dressing. The bread, half of a long French roll, was crunchy. Pieces of crust scattered when Joe broke off a hunk and handed it to me, but the middle was soft and tasted good as it squished in my mouth. Even though Joe said he'd made our lasagna the previous Sunday and that it hadn't been tampered with since, the center layer was still lukewarm after four sessions in the microwave. Joe dug in while I popped my plate back in the microwave and punched "full power" at three minutes. Too hot would cool, too cold didn't work.

I had said, "Whatever you're having" when Joe asked what I wanted to drink. We both drank milk, but that was before I'd seen the inside of the refrigerator. I like to think of myself as an adventurer, a sort of when-in-Rome type of guy, but I have to admit I sneaked a peek at the milk carton to make sure the expiration date was a future event.

So we were at a yellow vinyl-topped table pushed against one wall, and lunch was a mishmash of leftovers. It could have been that I was just hungry, but it tasted good.

"I got banana cream pie," Joe said after wiping his mouth with a paper napkin. His plate was clean, his glass empty, and I was still fiddling, dabbing at everything. He walked to the refrigerator and returned with a Marie Callender's box. He lifted the lid and showed me the prize—a swirling white topping sat atop three quarters of a pie; some of the yellow filling had drizzled into the open space, but most of the dessert was intact. "Gave up smoking ten years ago. I eat healthy and exercise every day, but this ... " Joe sighed and shook his head. "My self-discipline goes right out the window."

"A good tradeoff. I'd trade in my Camels for a slice of pie, too."

"Camels, huh?" Joe cut a slice of pie and dumped it on my plate, right next to the lasagna and salad.

That's it? Not even a shocked look?

"Yeah, I figured if I was going to smoke, I may as well experience the real thing, you know, be a man, get hair on my chest." I scraped the lasagna and salad away from the pie, hoping I could still prevent a disgusting collision.

"Pretty much how I started, except I smoked Lucky Strikes. Kept 'em rolled in my T-shirt sleeve when I was your age. Hell, *everyone* in the Marines smoked." Joe dropped a slice on his plate and scraped the tin for loose parts. "Glad I quit. Can taste the pie now."

I watched Joe carve a piece of yellow goo and white topping with his fork, and stuff it in his mouth. A smile erupted—the poster boy for the simple pleasures in life.

"Why'd you quit?" I asked. "I mean, ten years ago—you were sixty-four. What did it matter?"

"Mattered plenty." Joe nodded at my plate, wanting me to join him in banana cream nirvana. "Meant I stopped doing something harmful to my body, meant I felt better, meant I *could* quit." Joe attacked his plate again, not bothering to gauge my reaction.

I decided not to respond. What was I going to say? Cigarettes tasted good? Blowing smoke rings was just too cool?

"I get a fresh pie once a week," Joe said. "Make a special trip to their place in Westminster." He eyed my serving, probably wondering why I hadn't wolfed it down yet. "I change the flavors around, but it's hard to beat Marie Callender's cream pies."

What were we doing, talking about pies? About smoking? I poked a fork at the mess on my plate, then figured what the hell, and scooped a mouthful. Lasagna, salad, and banana cream pie—all ended up in the same place, I guessed.

"So, no lecture about the evils of smoking?"

"Good heavens, do you need one, Quinn?" Joe's look was of surprise, not sarcasm.

"No." I avoided Joe's eyes by burying my face in the plate and shoveling more food.

"So." Joe wiped his mouth and tossed the napkin on the empty plate.

I raised my head like I was listening, but kept eating.

"I'm going to be out of town for a few days. Got some business to take care of and I won't be back until after your summer school starts."

I groaned with a mouthful of food. I had three days before classes and tests and homework, and I had hoped to spend some time with Joe. Hang out, talk, maybe take pictures while he painted. And now he wasn't going to be around. Figured.

"What time are your summer school classes?"

"Start at seven-thirty. I'm supposed to be done at one."

"Might work," Joe said, holding a finger across his lips. He was looking at me, but with a vacant stare, like he was mentally calculating possibilities. "Quinn, what do you think about being study buddies for a few days each week?"

I was glad for the wad of food that needed swallowing. Study buddies? Okay, how did I answer that one? I finally managed, "You mean like quizzing each other, that kind of stuff?"

"Maybe. If you need it." Joe slid his plate to the side and rested his elbows on the table. He blinked a few times and said, "Having a reason to start, making a commitment to study with someone makes it easier." The vacant stare disappeared and Joe focused on me again. "I'm enjoying getting to know you, but I don't want to interfere with summer school or your social life. You could come over around two-thirty. Give you time for lunch and to wind down, and I'd have my nap. Studying together might work."

I was struck by a distinctive image as I watched Joe speak, a vulnerable side that I'd seen only once before, when he was standing over me at Hideaway Lake. It was like taking frontal pictures and then changing angles; same subject, but you notice different features. I knew my new friend was moving me in the right direction, sort of like mixing business with pleasure, and that he had my best interests at heart. That hadn't changed. But there was more to it now. I detected a sense of loneliness in Joe. I saw it in a face that was unaccountably tired, and I felt it in an apartment where cooking resulted in leftovers. I'd been so wrapped up in me—how Joe understood me, how he accepted and didn't judge me, how his eccentricities excited me—I'd never bothered to think that maybe our friendship was important to him.

Me, me, me. Yeah, I was good at that.

"Not saying we have to study every time we get together. There are other things. Might even be a few places in Eldorado Canyon you haven't seen." Joe's voice faltered a bit, but his eyes held steady.

"Are you taking a summer class?" I finally asked.

"No, got to catch up on some reading. I won't be watching you study, if that's what you're thinking."

"I don't know what to think. Don't know what my folks will say," I mumbled. Actually, I did know what to think. I thought it was a great idea, if I could get Mom and Dad to buy in, but my tone didn't express enthusiasm. My flare-up in attitude wasn't about studying together; it was about being insensitive to Joe's situation and it was about the first time I'd noticed "selfish" tattooed across my forehead.

"Don't know about your parents, but one thing's for sure, you need to be straight with them. They want to know what's going on, and they want results, so connect the two. Explain why you think it will work, then live with their decision."

"I can do that."

Joe smiled again. Maybe it had been tough to float the study buddy idea. Or maybe he was relieved that I was interested in spending more time with him.

FAMILY DINNERS REMINDED ME OF getting a physical from the doctor; you expect a certain amount of pressing and pushing that's mostly nuisance and not too uncomfortable, but you also know to be on guard, ready for something more invasive. My parents poked and prodded during mealtimes. Mostly it was stuff I could handle, but I was always alert. I knew plastic gloves could be snapped on at any moment. Actually, I think I preferred physicals back then. They only came once a year. I had to eat dinner with my family almost every night.

The eating area off our kitchen mimicked the rest of the house: fashionable, tasteful, defined. The oval walnut table seated six, and was perpetually decorated with freshly cut flowers displayed according to the guidelines of a book stored in the pantry. Mom rotated placemats with color coordinated cloth napkins, always arranged a full complement of silverware, and our everyday dishes were anything but. Adding to the ambiance were two star-shaped candles that, according to the label, produced an engaging and lively essence of blueberry. I wasn't all that enthusiastic about smelling blueberries and flowers while I ate, but at least that night's version of family time didn't include Elizabeth. She had gotten an early start on a sleepover at a friend's house.

Mom used to say our dinners were special, that they let each family member share what was going on in his life. I had a simpler take—booor-ing. Looking back, I will admit it was a good plan, but engaging, interesting, sharing of what was really going on? It never happened.

So that night's conversation was sedate and controlled, with polite questions and efficient answers. *Joe's fine, everything is set for classes on Monday, I was careful driving, Elizabeth's report card came today and she got all A's.*

I was participating—sort of.

Even though my face pointed mostly at my plate, I could tell Mom and Dad were conversing through knowing looks. They'd raise an eyebrow or tilt their head, alerting each other, assessing my reactions and words. My family was good at nonverbal communication; outsiders would have needed a codebook or at least a little practice to understand us. Slamming doors, indiscernible mumbles, retreats to the study, and shopping excesses all sent messages. I had been so conditioned to say as little as possible that initiating conversation with my parents, actually bringing up something I wanted to talk about, was a challenge I rarely undertook. But it was time for me to speak, to say what I'd practiced twenty times. I had to moisten my lips first.

"I really had fun today," I said, meeting Mom's eyes to my left, and then Dad's to the right. "Thanks for letting me see Joe."

Mom smiled, looked at Dad and then me, and said, "You're welcome, honey. He's an interesting man, maybe a little different than I would have guessed for a friend, but nice." She dabbed her mouth with a blue and white checkered napkin, clueing my father it was his turn.

"So, what did you and Joe talk about? Did he tell you any good war stories?" Dad had served in the Air Force for ten years, but Vietnam was over when he started flying C-130 cargo planes. Still, he loved hearing stories and reliving the accounts of the war, maybe wondering what he would have done.

"Joe didn't really talk about anything specific," I said, conveniently forgetting to add that I wouldn't have divulged anything important to them anyway. What Joe and I talked about was between us. Still, I had to get their approval for the study plan. Bits and pieces. I decided to share bits and pieces. "He did say he doesn't sleep well, but I guess he's learned to live with it." That was my stopping point. I wasn't going to share anything else.

"War is a terrible thing. A lot of good men struggle with their memories." Dad nodded like he understood.

Maybe he did. I realize now that he might have been torn between relief and embarrassment that he hadn't had to fight, and maybe that was why he gravitated toward war stories.

"What else did you talk about?" he asked.

"We talked a little bit about school, I mean my summer school."

"Really?" Mom was interested again.

"Uh-huh." Okay, I had this part down. I just needed to take it nice and slow. "He said how it was important for me to stick to a study schedule, and that just getting started every day would make it easier." I reached for my glass and gulped the remaining milk, acting as if I couldn't care less about study habits and getting started, while silently applauding my reverse psychology skills.

Mom smiled and said, "Joe's right, honey. A little discipline goes a long way, especially when you're more than capable of doing the work." She watched me for a moment, then added, "What do you think?"

Was she hooked or just playing with the bait? Then I remembered: *Be straight with them. They want to know what's going on, and they want results. Connect the two.*

"Joe thinks we could study together. He said he doesn't want to interfere with summer school, but that setting a time to study, you know, making, like, an appointment would help. He said he's got reading to do and that he'd be around if I needed help."

"I see." Mom's lips tightened and she forced her next words silent. Not exactly what she had expected.

"I think it would help, too," I stated, "but I also know you don't have a lot of confidence in me right now." Was I playing the "I wish you'd trust me" card? You bet.

"That's not it—"

"So," I interrupted gently, "I thought you could look at what's been assigned, and I'll show you my work and all the grades so you know exactly what's going on. The grades will tell you whether it's a good plan." I couldn't believe I was saying this. Jesus! Checking up on me? Like I was a little kid? And I was suggesting it?

Mom frowned, not because she was angry or upset, but because she was confused. She'd invested so much time and energy, made such a commitment to our three-month war, and now I was just giving in? You'd think she'd be running a victory lap.

"Dennis?" she finally said, her voice drifting toward exasperation.

Dad had been fingering a spoon, watching and listening, gathering information. I knew I'd made points with him by talking about responsibility and discipline, and keeping them in the loop, but I was still anxious to hear his words—the verdict.

Dad said, "I think we should talk to Joe. Let's make sure we're all on the same page before any decisions are made."

fifteen

"Dude! Let's hit it!" Winnie snapped his seatbelt, then removed sunglasses from the brim of his turned around baseball cap, and pressed them into place on his nose.

The rest of Winnie's outfit highlighted an imposing physique: baggy tan shorts that hung past his knees but didn't hide calves and ankles that seemed bigger around than my waist, a black muscle shirt that displayed tree-trunk arms, and sandals that made his feet look like giant waffle irons. I knew Winnie grabbed whatever clothes were handy without thinking about his football player image, but the fashion statement still declared "Don't mess with me."

"You eat yet? I didn't bother with breakfast. I just wanted to get going," I said, sliding into the driver's seat. My blue jeans and oversized shirt were intentional cover for skinny arms and legs.

Winnie turned his head toward me and pulled the shades down his nose so I could see his eyes. "Like you really have to ask if I want to eat? Where we goin', anyway?"

"Let's check out City Park and then head over to Larimer Square. Today's a people day. Just taking pictures of people," I said, covering a yawn with my free hand. The truth was, I was still half-asleep. Not only was midmorning a couple hours before my normal waking time, I'd tossed and turned and didn't sleep well the previous night. The anticipation of taking pictures again—well, it felt like the night before Christmas when I actually cared about opening presents.

But my struggle with sleep had been about something else, too. I was still sorting out how I messed up with Joe by not thinking about his feelings, and it had mushroomed into more personal areas. Assessing my social life was an uncomfortable exercise, even for an experienced loner like me. Admitting I didn't have all that many friends, that maybe I could extend myself more? I finally managed to sleep when I decided that Winnie was a pretty decent guy even if he did wear a letter jacket, and that he might want to tag along that day.

"Let's just get some donuts and drive," I said. "That'll hold us for a couple hours, and then we can have lunch."

"Gotta be Krispy Kreme, and better make it a dozen."

"I'm not believing this. You're telling me that if I plop some Winchell's donuts in your lap, you won't eat them. Come on, Winnie, even I know that guys who use shovels instead of forks don't have taste buds."

"Dude." Winnie slid the sunglasses down again. "Either go first class or don't go at all," he said with a serious tone before laughing. "Hey, thanks for calling this morning. I was just hangin', watchin' some cartoons with Janice. Takin' pictures again—I'm there." Winnie laid his palm open for me to slap.

"I didn't tell you, but Joe came by my house a couple days ago."

"No way! He came to your house?"

"He brought back the pictures." I got my bearings with the traffic, then trained my eyes on Winnie. "He talked to my parents."

"Dude!" Winnie's expression, the wide-open mouth and shaking his head thing, was worth the look.

"No shit. He got everybody talking. I don't know all the details, but I think my dad liked the Marine stuff." I was focused on the driving again but still talking. I really wanted to tell someone about Joe, about eating reheated lasagna and banana cream pie, about pink bathrooms, about the rock formation he painted from my pictures. "The next thing I knew my parents were working out summer school details and handing back car keys."

"Tight," Winnie said, pressing his lips together. "I mean, who woulda thought that guy would turn out to be so cool? Think about it. You, like, totally demolished the dude's painting."

"He did another painting. He used my pictures." I swallowed back a smile. "I went to his apartment in Boulder yesterday and I saw it. It's exactly what he was painting that day at the lake. It's amazing."

"You went to his apartment?"

"Yeah, we met at Lucky's for coffee and then we headed over there. Joe showed me around, made some lunch." I was trying to be laid back, as if hanging out with people like Joe was the norm, but then I remembered, hey, it's Winnie. Forget the pretense. "He's not like other adults. What I mean—well, he's easy to talk to."

Winnie settled in the seat a bit, then said, "My grandpa was kinda like that, except he died when I was like six or seven, but I still remember him. He played with me and gave me Life Savers. Always had a roll of 'em. Grandma talks about him like he's still around." Winnie paused, bit his lip, remembering. "My dad's folks, they live in California. We see 'em every once in a while, but it's like visiting company or being interviewed for a job or somethin'. They expect certain answers, ya know, and they're always fussin' about the way we look and the clothes we wear." Winnie let loose one of his laughs. "Takes a lot of energy being 'round *them.*"

"I never knew my mom's parents," I said. "They were both killed in a car accident before my folks were even married. Pop and Gram, my dad's parents, they're okay. I mean they're fun. They meet us places when we go on vacation, so it's not so bad when we see them."

I was trying to imagine Joe as a grandparent, as my grandfather, but it wasn't a good fit. True, Joe was easygoing, but I figured that most people in his generation were more at ease with life and didn't get whacked out over insignificant bullshit. But it was different with Joe. There was an understanding, an acceptance that was deeper and more personal. And then it clicked. Winnie, the two-hundred-and-forty-pound lineman who pushed people to the dirt, had just zeroed in on the issue. Joe was natural, he was being himself. He didn't waste any effort—or energy, as Winnie had just said—living up to expectations or crafting an image. His lines were clearly drawn and you knew where you stood. It was so simple, so efficient.

"Dude."

"What?" I was still putting the pieces together, amazed at how easily they fit.

"Turn around. You just passed Krispy Kreme and I'm starving."

MAYBE I NEEDED TO BE ON A RANCH, mending real rather than figurative fences. I'd just fixed Mom and Dad and tightened up Winnie, yet there was more work ahead. I still had eight weeks of summer school staring me square in the face, an army of Monarch teachers were ready to pounce on me next semester, and there was Nicki.

I guess I could have made her the first stop. I'd been liberated on Friday and it was Sunday morning, but I told myself I needed more time; time to think about what to say, time to gather courage. The truth was simpler. I was getting caught up in what-ifs. What if she was mad I hadn't talked to her, what if she said only students could use the darkroom, what if she slammed the door in my face—what if, what if, what if—what a waste. I'd wanted to talk to Nicki for over two months, to explain what happened, to let her know why I had avoided her. It was time.

Pine Street was deserted. Well, almost. A couple cars were parked down the block but nobody was walking around. Made sense, I guess—it *was* Sunday. I was betting Nicki was in her studio. She lived in an apartment on the second floor and wasn't the Sunday brunch type. She read the newspaper and drank coffee on Sunday mornings.

After a final deep breath, I rapped my knuckles on the heavy glass door. The storefront blinds were closed, so she wouldn't know who was outside until she peeked from a lifted slat or opened the door. We would see each other, with expressions to hide or share, at the same time. My heart pumped a bit faster when I heard footsteps.

I guess I shouldn't have been nervous. Nicki unlocked and opened the door, stopped, placed both hands over her heart in disbelief, and pretended to fall backward. I would have preferred a scowl; then I wouldn't have felt so bad about avoiding her.

"As I live and breathe, it's Quinnlan Marshall." She was wearing a lime green shirt with an art festival logo on the front, and cut-off blue jeans with frayed bottoms. Her hair was pulled back in a braided ponytail and seemed grayer than I remembered. "Well? Are you coming in?"

"Hi, Nicki. Yeah, I can come in." I hoped my nervous smile distracted her attention from eyes that refused to engage. I looked at the floor, the walls, even at Nicki in a big picture sort of way, but not her eyes. Not yet.

Nicki locked the door behind me and led the way to the sitting area across the room. She had one of those puffy couches—hers was covered with chocolate brown corduroy—and a couple white wicker chairs against a wall. I guess you could call it a reception area. Stacks of the Sunday paper littered the floor next to the couch and a nearly full ceramic mug sat on the adjacent coffee table.

"Want something to drink?" she asked.

I nodded. "Yeah. A Coke's fine."

"Have a seat, and I'll be right back."

I watched the thick braid swing across her back as she disappeared and, for the first time, I was hesitant about making myself comfortable in her studio. I'd stretched across these chairs, even napped on her couch, but I felt like an uninvited guest that morning. I knew she would ask and that we would talk, but I was still nervous. It was hard to pick up where we'd left off when so much had been left out.

"I thought Sunday mornings were sacred with you. Sleep until your back hurt or you had to pee or something." Nicki handed me a cold can of soda and sat on curled-up legs in one of the wickers. "Well, are you just going to stand there?"

"Thanks for the Coke," I said, then sat on the couch. That was a big mistake. I sank into the cushions and immediately felt like I'd been swallowed by corduroy. I struggled back to the front edge and rested my arms on my knees. "I was grounded, so I didn't come by," I said, staring at the coffee table.

"I see."

I waited, hoping she'd ask a question or make a comment that required an answer. Some sort of response. But there was nothing, no easy way to start. She just watched me, waiting to hear what I had to say.

"I wanted to talk to you about school, I mean, dropping your class and everything. I had some problems in History, and my mom lost it. She made me drop Photography."

Nicki reached for her mug and sipped. "I talked to your mom. She said you were struggling with all your classes. She said Photography was taking too much of your time, and that she didn't want you to be distracted."

All I could do was shake my head.

"I take it that means her plan didn't work."

"She threw my cameras against the wall, Nicki." I closed my

eyes and swallowed as the memory stirred. It was an image I couldn't shake, the one that made me still want to fight back. And then the story started without an invitation. It wasn't exactly what I'd told Joe; he was so abrupt and to the point, I guess I'd filtered his version so I wouldn't seem like a crybaby. But Nicki? I was talking fast, like there was a finish line to cross, and it poured out. And I'm not sure whether any of it made sense.

Nicki listened and occasionally nodded her head. She didn't scrub my words or search for hidden meanings, and her eyes never left mine. They were gentle; they gave me permission to talk, and told me I was being heard.

I sucked in a breath when I was done venting. Even then I knew it was one-sided, and if pushed a bit, would have admitted there was another version, one that spoke of past deeds and responsibilities, and let Mom reclaim her status as a human being. But letting loose, just getting it out—well, I'm sure Nicki allowed for my uncharitable interpretation. Mom's replay would have probably left out a few details, too.

But now we were to the tough part, the point where the bug on the wall would have said, "Why didn't you just pick up the phone? Why did it take over two months to tell her this?" I wish it would have been that easy.

It was time to say I'd messed up, not with Mom and school, but with how I'd handled the situation with Nicki. Blowing off a friend because I was pissed at my mother? I reached for the soda because I was anxious and still didn't want to look Nicki in the eye.

"So is it too late to say I'm sorry?"

Nicki paused. She toyed with the idea of saying "Sorry for what," but she knew it would be easier on me if I didn't have to list the offenses. Instead, she puckered her lips and squinted her eyes, like she was debating which refrigerator to buy, the almond or the white. "Okay," she finally said, "you're forgiven, but you have to take out the trash before you leave today."

Since I had expected to be dragged through the mud at least a little bit, there was a momentary hesitation before I let loose a sigh of relief.

"Deal," I said, and clinked my soda can against her mug.

"So, have you taken any pictures lately?"

"I went with Winnie to City Park and Larimer Square yesterday. People pics."

"Well, don't insult me by making me ask you to get your film so you can develop it, or you'll have to clean my kitchen, too."

sixteen

"So you've taken some chemistry courses, right?" I asked. Of course I already knew the answer; Joe had taken General Chemistry I and II, and had helped me through tricky parts of my summer school homework before.

Joe looked up from his reading, some historical book about a president, and peered over the top of his reading glasses. He was sitting in the recliner in the living room with a clear line of vision to the kitchen table where I was spread out. Comfort was a primary consideration when Joe settled in to read, so the familiar blue jeans and cowboy boots had been replaced by an outfit more appropriate for ninety-degree days. Joe was wearing a gray T-shirt, red gym shorts, and ratty white socks.

"What are you working on?" he asked.

"Gases. We're supposed to compare relative rates of diffusion."

I dropped my pencil into the spine of the open textbook and blew out a bit of frustration. I'd finished writing up the day's lab, was working the homework problems—and I was totally fed up with periodic tables, velocities, and temperature. The workload never ended; quizzes every day, labs every other day, and a test every Friday. God, I never wanted to see a graphing calculator or hear about inverse proportions again.

And I never wanted to conjugate another Spanish verb. My other summer school class wasn't a cakewalk either. Sometimes I thought I was losing it, like the time when I started writing a lab in Spanish. Christ, cramming all that stuff together made my head hurt!

Payback. I figured I'd completed five weeks of payback.

Don't get me wrong, school was fine. I listened in class and completed the assigned homework every afternoon. But more importantly, I was spending almost every afternoon with Joe. Mostly I studied while he read, but we also managed to comb Boulder's campus, explore used bookstores, and hike several trails in Four Mile Canyon just outside of town, all the while talking and sharing. It was the first time in my life that I wasn't afraid to just be me, and I was soaking it up, all of it.

Joe stared hard at one of the holes in his left sock. "Graham's Law," he finally said.

"Shit." I rubbed my forehead with my hands, partially hiding the scowl plastered across my face. I looked back at Joe and said, "I knew that. I've been fixated on temperatures and pressures for the last fifteen minutes and didn't even think about molecular mass. Square root, right?" Time had become a prized commodity in my life, and fifteen minutes was a careless waste.

Joe nodded and twisted his lips into a grin. He liked it when I struggled. Not that he enjoyed seeing me in pain or anything, but he wanted me to fight back and not give in to challenges.

"Take a break," he said, closing his book. "Come on, I have a fresh key lime pie in the fridge. I'll get you a slice."

"Fresh? I'll bet half of it's already gone."

"Smart-ass. I got hungry, painting last night, so I had a snack. You want some or not?" Joe lowered the leg rest and stood. His gym shorts drooped like they were a size too big, and he hitched them higher on his hips as he padded across the living room to the kitchen. "A little pie and a glass of milk. Give you some energy."

IT WAS THAT TIME OF DAY, AFTER Joe woke from his nap and read a bit, for his preferred afternoon snack—a slab of Marie Callender's pie. I remember Joe saying a pie would normally last him a week, but I think we averaged closer to three. Seemed like there was a new flavor every other day, and I wasn't even eating that much. Joe's sweet tooth must have kicked into overdrive, because he inhaled the stuff like he hadn't had a meal in days, but then he picked at everything else. I was the opposite. I chowed down on sandwiches and leftovers, and managed small helpings of pie just to be polite.

"So, what's captured your photographic fancy lately?" Joe wiped his mouth with a paper napkin and watched my reaction as he tossed it on the empty plate.

I pushed my pie with a fork as an excuse to avoid Joe's eyes, but didn't break off a piece. Truth was, except for our hikes, I wasn't taking many pictures. "I haven't really gotten out that much. There's always more homework or a quiz or another test. I don't know. I guess there's so little down time now that I just want to sit and veg."

If Joe had pushed a little harder, I would have admitted to being afraid, of becoming addicted again, of using photography as an excuse for not keeping up with school. I had A's going, and I would have told him that I didn't want to risk being distracted.

"You got a helluva schedule. Five hours of classes, plus three or four hours of studying every day. Take it your folks are pleased."

Pleased? I was up by 6:30 to make Spanish, there was a fifteen-minute break before chemistry class, and I studied at Joe's apartment three hours every afternoon, plus a couple more hours before I went to bed. So, other than a room that looked like an imploded Laundromat and a couple of pointless but satisfying fights with Elizabeth, I'd been a model citizen. *Pleased* was an understatement of gigantic proportions.

"They're pretty happy about the A's," I said.

"The A's are okay."

"Okay? I'm busting my balls to get A's!"

"I know you're working hard, Quinn. Setting a study schedule and sticking to it, focusing in class. You've been disciplined and you should be proud." Joe took his dish to the sink and rinsed off the crumbs. "Okay to talk straight?" he said.

"Go for it." Like it wouldn't have been okay. I don't know why or even how it got started, but Joe and I didn't bullshit each other. Sure, we'd kid and both of us took turns messing around, but shooting straight when we talked had been in place since the beginning. That Joe was asking if it was okay had gotten my attention.

"Grades aren't important. The end result isn't a grade."

"Yeah, right. My F's didn't mean a thing. That's why I'm killing myself in summer school."

"The end result is learning, and you didn't learn the material. That's why you're taking summer school classes." Joe narrowed his eyes a bit and fixed them to mine with an easy familiarity, waiting for his words to sink in. "Don't misinterpret what I'm saying. I'm proud of what you're doing, really I am. But you could make a careless mistake on the final exam or misunderstand an assignment. Hell, maybe a teacher gets a wild hair and you end up with a B or C. Know what? The grade doesn't matter. Your level of knowledge, what you mastered in that class, won't have changed."

I could tell by Joe's words, the rehearsed emphasis and the measured tone, that he'd wrestled with this awhile, so I backed off being defensive and just laughed. "Don't tell my parents grades don't matter. I'll be banned from your apartment forever."

Joe laughed, too, then rejoined me at the kitchen table. He nodded and said, "There needs to be some way to measure achievement, I'm not arguing that. My point is we've somehow messed up the system. Good grades used to be a byproduct of learning. Nowadays, folks don't care about anything except the bottom line, the grade."

"But grades measure what you learn." I couldn't believe I'd said that. Good God! The kid who'd told his parents he didn't give a shit about grades, the one who'd argued Bill Gates and Warren Buffett, the one who knew Advanced Algebra inside out but got a B-. Yeah, that kid. The one who knew better, but was proud of the A's scrawled across all the homework and quizzes and tests for the last five weeks.

Joe reached for my fork, picked the sliver of lime off the top of my pie, and took a bite. His latest confiscation made me wonder about the healthy lifestyle I had assumed was part of his daily routine. I didn't know whether he'd trashed his focus on nutrition or just fallen off the wagon, but either way, gorging on pie certainly hadn't made him fat. In fact, Joe seemed thinner. His face was drawn and a bit off-color, more yellow than tan, and there was a sharper edge to his cheekbones and jaw. His muscles were still prominent—the T-shirt and gym shorts left no doubt the guy was in good shape—but they were wiry and not as thick as I remembered.

"Grades are an imperfect estimate at best, a disguised weapon at worst," Joe said.

"You told me that you try to score high on all the exams," I said, "that you don't just blow them off. If grades are so imperfect, if they can be used as weapons, why do *you* bother? Hey, take the class, learn, forget the bullshit stuff."

"I take the tests to verify that I *did* learn the material. The grades?" Joe grunted again, one of those sarcastic through the nose types, and shrugged his shoulders. "I haven't looked at a report card in the twelve years I've been here."

I didn't believe it. He had to have looked. One peek? One time?

"Remember the Anatomy & Physiology professor we talked with at Lucky's, Dr. Leakas? When he said he *understood*, that we'd had a discussion? I meet with every teacher the first week of class and tell them the same thing: I'm in class to learn. The grade doesn't matter. Tell them I don't do extra credit and that I don't make up tests. If I miss a test it's because I have a damn good reason, and I'm not going to turn my life upside down over a retake." Joe paused and strummed his fingertips across the table. "I study hard, I take tests, and I see how I did on the tests. It's a tool I use to measure how well I understand the material."

I couldn't disagree with the logic but I was still miffed. There were plenty of reasons I wanted A's, not the least of which was Joe's approval, and that seemed to be evaporating like the gases in my chemistry lab that day. "So is there a point?"

"Yeah, there is." Joe laid the fork on my plate and paused while our eyes met across the vinyl-top table where spirited discussions and inconsequential chatter had taken turns deepening our friendship. "I'm concerned that you're not taking pictures, Quinn. You bring cameras when we hike, but I don't see the excitement, I don't feel the intensity. What happened to the young man willing to risk life and limb, not to mention a bruised cheek, to catch the perfect shot? Where's the curiosity that aches to know why a lone wildflower grows between rocks, or what circumstances brought a homeless man to a cardboard box stuffed with newspaper?" Joe wriggled his eyebrows and waited for me to catch up with the images he'd just created. "I've seen your pictures. I know what's inside you. Are you too busy chasing A's to notice?"

It had only taken a minute. I'd gone from racing through chemistry problems, pumped with adrenaline and reveling in success, to a physical void where I was more numb than tired. My thoughts and emotions swirled like a sheet of newspaper in a gusting wind, settling only briefly before another flurry resumed its disorderly journey. Joe wasn't beating me up; in fact, there was a growing tenderness in his voice. But I was still deflated. I was just getting back into the flow, piling up victories, and then the rules changed.

"It's good you're back on track with school, Quinn, but you don't have to choke off photography."

"Yeah, and maybe I'm supposed to be a doctor or a lawyer or some other pillar of the community who makes a shitload of money and belongs to a country club. Maybe photography is just one of those things kids become obsessed with, like video games or skateboards, until they grow up and move on to a real life."

I knew Joe wasn't saying I'd totally fucked up—he'd said I was disciplined and that he was proud—but telling me I'd lost my passion for photography? Reminding me that I had conformed? He'd hit a sensitive nerve and I was struggling to keep a civil tone.

"You'd be a helluva doctor, and I don't even want to think about the poor schmucks facing you in a courtroom." Joe laughed and grabbed the fork for another bite of pie. Joe knew the point had been made, that the lesson was over, and for reasons I'm only now beginning to understand, he trusted that I would frame his words in a way that worked for me.

"I can't imagine being a doctor or lawyer," I mumbled while taking back the fork and shoveling a piece of pie into my mouth.

THE CHEMISTRY PROBLEMS WERE finished and filed in the notebook, I'd reviewed my notes for the next day's Spanish quiz, and I was sitting alone in Joe's office, feet propped on his desk and tapping a pencil against my knee. I'd been sitting like this for twenty minutes, contemplating the discussion at the kitchen table, filtering words, trying to understand. I knew the difference between imposing beliefs and honest reflection, so I wasn't pissed at Joe. But maybe that complicated the situation. Maybe it would have been easier if I were pissed.

It wasn't just about photography. Sure, Joe was right. I'd been consumed: Getting A's in summer school, driving a point home with my parents, proving all those teachers wrong. It was another crusade, just like the war with Mom, except this time everyone was clapping and cheering my performance. And I suppose, all things being equal, I would have been rooting for the guy getting A's, too. But that wasn't what was bugging me. It was my all-or-nothing approach to everything, the violent swings back and forth. I ran hot or cold; there was no in-between, no lukewarm. It was a pattern that was hard to miss, yet one I'd chosen to ignore.

I stood and made my way to the art room where a faint rendition of *Maria*, one of the songs from *West Side Story*, was being hummed. I should tell you that Joe's singing *The Sound of Music* at Hideaway Lake wasn't a fluke; he sang, hummed, and sometimes whistled songs from musicals while he painted. Not anything new, or at least semi-modern like *Phantom* or *Miss Saigon*, but the ancient stuff. It was embarrassing that I could actually sing along to more than a few selections from *My Fair Lady*.

Joe had altered his daily routine since we began studying together; he painted mostly in the evenings after I'd gone home. But he was singing, so I knew he was painting, and I eased through the doorway hoping to catch a glimpse of him at work. I loved watching Joe dab the palette and mix colors, witnessing the eagerness with which he attacked the canvas. He was intentional, every stroke was deliberate and decisive, each touch of the brush strengthened a vision that Joe dared to capture. Without question, Joe's paintings were terrific, but watching the process was what I enjoyed most.

"Hey."

Joe turned with palette in hand and smiled, not even a little self-conscious about me having overheard off-key notes or butchered lyrics. "Tell me Graham's Law was right. I'd feel bad if I sent you on a wild-goose chase."

"Right on the money and I'm done with everything. I actually get a night off."

Joe cleaned the brush he was holding and placed it in an empty coffee can. I didn't know if it was just time to take a break or if he was shifting priorities because of me. Joe wasn't a temperamental artist, the type who'd throw a fit if he was interrupted, but I remembered our first talk when he'd said that he painted every day. It bothered me to disrupt his schedule.

"And I've been thinking," I continued, hoping it was an okay time to talk. "You're the one who set up this study buddy deal, you're the one who got me focused on school and keeping to schedules and all that. And you're the one who got my parents to sign on." I paused, letting my words trail off.

"Yep." Joe twisted a couple of caps into place and started stowing his supplies.

"I got F's and now I'm getting A's."

"Uh-huh."

"But you're not happy with that?"

"It's not about *me* being happy, Quinn." Joe wiped his hands on a towel and walked toward me. "You're the one who needs to be happy. Just you." Joe touched my arm as he passed. "Come on," he said, "let's go for a walk."

JOE TOLD ME ONCE THAT HE BELIEVED wherever he was, that was where he was supposed to be. Our walks adhered to the premise. We'd wander without agendas or destinations, never knowing that we'd arrived or when it was time to turn back. There weren't rules or rituals or requisites when Joe and I walked. We chatted and joked, and sometimes we solved the world's problems.

I'd followed Joe out of his apartment and down to the sidewalk outside his building. One of Boulder's ten-minute rain showers had just blown through. The air smelled of refreshed grass and wet asphalt, and a silent breeze was moving an overhang of gray-puffed clouds to the south. It felt a bit chilly, and I was ready to grab a sweatshirt back in the apartment, but Joe was already ten yards ahead of me.

"Aren't you cold?" I said a little louder than normal while catching up. He was still wearing the T-shirt and gym shorts, but had lost the raunchy socks in favor of flip-flops. It was an unusual combination considering the weather, but Joe enjoyed the brisk air, and I could tell by his pace that it was invigorating him.

"Sun will break through and it'll warm up. Always does." Joe started up Pearl Street toward the main campus, looking over his shoulder, making sure I didn't want to go a different direction.

"You said I'm supposed to be happy," I said, figuring I should just pick up and go with the previous discussion. "Well, I was happy. I mean before I got grounded and stuff, before the grades. Before that, I was happy." I was walking stride for stride with Joe, trying to sidestep puddles and talk at the same time. "Okay, I'm disciplined now. I'm dead-ass tired, too. So why am I jumping through hoops and keeping study schedules when I was fine before?"

Joe paused at a stop sign and checked for traffic before crossing. "Good question."

"Well?"

"So, you were happy? Before the history paper fiasco, you were happy?" Joe started walking, but cocked a cynical eyebrow.

Okay, I'd walked into that one. Teenagers aren't happy—everyone knows that—but on a relative basis? Hell no, I wasn't happy. I hated school, resented my parents, and thought that life sucked most of the time.

"I had my share of problems," I said.

"And what was the best part of your life?"

It took all of two seconds to finally get it, to see what Joe was trying to ignite. I had turned off my enthusiasm to the one thing I truly enjoyed, and it just clicked that doing well in school didn't have to be an all-or-nothing proposition. Two seconds, but I waited longer to answer.

"Taking pictures was the best part of my life," I finally said.

"And now?" Joe splatted through a puddle he didn't see, which added a squishing sound to his flip-flops.

"Now I don't take as many pictures." My tone was short and curt. I'd only developed a couple of rolls of film at Nicki's since our Sunday morning reunion, and that had been almost three weeks earlier. I was okay with her, we were back to being friends; it's just that I hadn't needed to use her darkroom. Between classes and studying and being with Joe … it wasn't like I could just gather my equipment and head off for extended picture-taking sessions.

"But everything else, not the photography, but everything else is better?"

"Yeah, it is," I said, shrugging my shoulders. "I mean, I like showing people I'm smart, and my parents aren't in my face all the time. It's hard work, but it feels good in a strange way, like there's a purpose or something. Yeah, everything else seems better."

The sun, as Joe predicted, had reclaimed its position, causing colorful reflections to bounce off the pavement as it warmed the damp air. When a rainbow peeked through a patch of lingering clouds, we headed toward it.

"Like I said, I'm really proud of your effort. You made a commitment to your parents and you've kept it. A's are great and, from what I can tell, they fairly represent your knowledge of the material. But getting hooked on atta-boys, being seduced by grades? That's letting other people dictate your happiness." Joe stopped in the middle of the sidewalk and draped his right arm over my shoulder. He waited to speak until I looked into his eyes. "The way taking pictures makes you feel? That's real."

Joe was so much shorter, that wrapping his arm around my shoulders felt clumsy, and I was aware of the people passing by us, like they were listening, waiting to overhear a choice word or two. But curious looks and secret glances didn't dilute Joe's presence or his gentle concern. I knew he was walking me through these steps, yet allowing me the freedom to accept or reject. Funny, but not cramming it down my throat, letting me kick around what fit and what didn't—well, it took me to the buy-in point.

"Forgetting my parents and teachers for a second," I said, "I like the A's and I like the challenge of learning, but learning the stuff that's important to me, not all the crap they make us memorize or read for no good reason."

Joe released my shoulder and smiled.

"And I love taking pictures. What I do with my cameras? It makes me feel good."

"So a little tweak, some fine-tuning. Sounds to me like that's all we're talking about," said Joe. "And from my own experience, I can tell you that's a lot easier than major overhauls."

We'd just jumped from first to third gear. What had Joe overhauled? Sure, I knew him, and he told me what he thought and how he felt. I'd experienced the discipline of a former Marine, the imagination of a painter, and the quirks of a perpetual student, but where were the skeletons buried? What would have made a warrior become an artist? I was debating my next question when Joe grabbed my arm.

"Hey, look! It's touching the ground! The rainbow is touching the ground! What do you think, Quinn? Should we get a shovel and start digging?"

"Huh?" I felt Joe's hand in the small of my back, pushing me to the spot.

"The rainbow. It's touching the ground. You know, the leprechaun's pot of gold?"

Joe was standing in the multicolored hue, looking to the source of the reflection and wondering, I'm sure, how he could transform the vision to canvas. Basking in the unexpected perfection, a smile crept across Joe's lips and he closed his eyes.

He said, "Too bad you can't count on rainbows to pinpoint all of life's treasures, but there are other signs. It just takes a little effort to recognize them."

seventeen

It was finally over. The ruin-my-summer, wreak-havoc-with-sleep, and fry-my-brain reckoning was completed. No more jarring alarm clocks, numbing homework, or pointless tests. They were done, or maybe I should say *terminado*, since I'd fulfilled the school district's foreign language requirement when I wrapped up the Spanish final exam. I'd paid my debt to society and I was free—at least until senior year started in three weeks.

I'd considered celebrating, maybe getting someone to buy me a six-pack and spending a private afternoon drinking beer and eating potato chips at Hideaway Lake. I wasn't much of a drinker, but listening to rustling leaves, assigning bizarre images to clouds floating by, belching—well, you get the idea. Doing stupid shit just because.

Instead, I was lying on my bed listening to music with my eyes closed, feeling relaxed and experiencing the joy of doing absolutely nothing. Maybe it was too much hassle to find a buyer, or maybe I was just tired. I really don't remember. But I'm pretty sure it had crossed my mind that doing stupid shit just because might lead to another stretch of hard time, and that was a price I wasn't willing to pay.

What I really wanted was to go to Joe's apartment. Eating

leftovers, checking out the latest Marie Callender's purchase, listening to his take on current events—that's what had gotten me through those tortuous eight weeks, and it had become a comfortable routine. But Joe was out of town. He'd left six days earlier on a business trip to Texas and wasn't due back until Sunday. I hadn't known Joe still had ongoing business issues since he'd sold the plumbing company, or that he even knew anyone in Texas, but we'd promised to toast cardboard cups of white chocolate mocha at Lucky's when he returned.

It was a challenge not having our study buddy system in place while I prepared for finals. Joe did offer me the apartment, said it would be the same environment even if he wasn't there, but I'd said no. It wouldn't have been the same without him. So I struggled to keep the computer and stereo turned off while I memorized formulas, worked and reworked problems, and finished a five-page paper, in Spanish, about Eva Peron.

That week wasn't a total bust—I had *some* fun. Winnie had gotten back from California and we hung out all weekend. We spent a couple hours exploring Hideaway Lake and laughing about our first encounter with Joe; we rented a couple of new video games; and I brought him by Nicki's and showed him how to develop film. And we went to the movies and ran into some of his football buddies one night. I tensed up at first—not exactly my crowd, if you know what I mean—but they treated me okay, especially after Winnie told them about all the F's and summer school. That was an interesting evening—yucking it up with a bunch of jocks over bad grades and then going home and sweating the Spanish paper.

A double knock on my door interrupted any further reflection. It was Mom, and she was already in my room. She was dressed in one of her summer outfits that all looked pretty much the same: a sleeveless cotton shirt tucked into coordinated walking shorts that showed off tanned arms and legs, and white sandals. Mom had one pair of sneakers that still needed breaking in, and four pairs of white sandals. That day's shirt, light blue with yellow lines, was collared and appropriately buttoned.

"Everything go okay?" she asked.

"I did fine, Mom." I didn't roll my eyes at the predictable question, but I didn't sit up from my position on the bed either.

Mom smiled, not the hollow type she always had ready, but a friendlier version. Maybe it was more sincere. "Your dad gets back from a trip in a couple of hours. How about an end-of-summer-school dinner celebration? You pick the restaurant."

I wasn't at war with my parents any longer, but going *out* to dinner? It was tough enough at home; why add public scrutiny to the mix? But saying no, at least the way it would have come out, would have been an escalation, and Joe and I had talked several times about avoiding that trap. So I stared at Mom, not saying a word, hoping she'd get the message.

"You like lobster, Quinn, and we haven't been to Coronado's in ages. Come on. You're finished with summer school, and there's still three weeks of vacation. Let's splurge a little."

This wasn't going to go away. Mom wanted to go to dinner, Coronado's was way expensive, and the end of summer school set it up.

"Yeah, I guess we could celebrate with a dinner, Mom," I said, straight faced. "It's okay if I pick where we go?"

"Sure it is, honey. You deserve it."

"You know," I said, swinging my legs off the bed, "I really feel like pizza. Having dinner at Valentino's would really hit the spot."

IT WAS FRIDAY NIGHT AND VALENTINO'S was jammed with families waiting; for an empty table, in the salad bar line, or to place an order at the counter. Music designed to please the under-thirty crowd was blaring from elevated speakers throughout the restaurant, little kids were yelling and screaming at video games while their parents dug for more quarters, and packs of thirteen- and fourteen-year-olds were doing group-date at tables in the back corner.

We had to wait twenty minutes for a table. It was closer to some kids from school than I would have liked, and not directly below a stereo speaker, but it didn't matter. There were no waiters reciting thirty-dollar entrée specials, my parents weren't enjoying a relaxing glass of wine, and we weren't talking in hushed tones because everyone else was.

Okay, so I wasn't eating lobster. Other than that, it was perfect.

"When do you think the final grades will come?" Dad had finished studying the menu that doubled as a placemat, and was the first to pit conversation against the environment.

Mom was busy popping aspirin and didn't hear the question, and Elizabeth was pouting because she hadn't been allowed to join her friends at the far end of the restaurant.

I shrugged my shoulders and said nothing. I guess there was still some doubt since the final exams counted twenty-five percent of the final grade, but I had breezed through both of them. I would have never admitted it, but keeping up with assignments and not cramming at the last minute? Well, it had worked. The finals had been easier than most of the unit tests along the way.

Dad leaned closer and raised his voice: "Mom says A's."

"I knew all the material," I said. I wasn't as evolved as Joe. I was definitely going to look at the grades. Seeing A's instead of F's on an official report card would be satisfying, and I still needed that validation. But I wasn't obsessing. I was leaving that to Mom and Dad.

"I couldn't hear you, Quinn. You said A's, right?" Turned out Mom had been listening.

"Yes, Mom."

My parents were probably mistaking my grin for courteous compliance. That would have been wrong. I was grinning because I was back in control, because my parents didn't get it. They didn't understand that I was living my life on my terms, not theirs. Sure, there were some overlaps—their terms and mine—but I chalked that up to coincidence and didn't let it bother me. Hey, we were at Valentino's, weren't we?

"Oh, shit." Mom's words surprised us. Her tone reeked with disgust.

I followed Mom's eyes long enough to understand. My pulse quickened and my stomach turned queasy. It was Mr. McCormack, the guy who'd started the summer school mess, and he was walking toward us. I hung my head and fiercely focused on an oregano sprinkler on the table, hoping to be just another student, one whose face was familiar but whose name drew a blank, one he'd pretend not to see. No such luck.

"Hello, Mrs. Marshall." Mr. McCormack stretched his hand across our table, acknowledging his fiercest adversary, the one who had negotiated and pleaded and threatened. Mom barely squeezed his hand, offered her best you-know-I'm-just-being-polite look, and said nothing. I wasn't surprised. Mom was good at this.

McCormack then offered his hand to my dad. "I'm David McCormack, Quinn's history teacher from last semester. We've talked on the phone."

Dad stood and hesitated, like he wanted to send his own message, then shook McCormack's hand and introduced himself. "Dennis Marshall," he said. "This is our daughter, Elizabeth." Dad towered over Mr. McCormack; his lanky features contrasted a squatty physique, and added an additional layer of awkwardness to the moment.

"Hello, Elizabeth."

Elizabeth's face brightened and she propped her elbows on the table, now fully engaged in our family dinner. I was betting she wouldn't say much, probably wouldn't talk at all, but she was going to hear every word. She would process each gesture, every twitch, and any indecision.

"Hello, Quinn." Mr. McCormack had allowed enough time for me to initiate a greeting. He pushed his glasses higher, started to fold his arms across his chest, then let them hang by his side.

"Hi." It's all I could manage. It's more than I wanted to say.

"Saw you folks come in and just wanted to say hello."

Mr. McCormack's smile was so intent on being friendly that it warned of the opposite, and told me that he'd done this before. Was he waiting for an insincere invitation to join us? Was appearing comfortable in an uncomfortable situation some sort of psychological game, something adults always seemed ready to play?

"How thoughtful of you," Mom said in an ice-cold monotone.

McCormack nodded in victory and said, "And I wanted to say I've heard some very good things about Quinn. I know Mr. Truell over at Jefferson. He said Quinn aced his chemistry class this summer, said he was the best student in the class. So, congratulations, Quinn. I'm very pleased to hear that you're back on track." Mr. McCormack angled his body toward me and his expression changed. He wasn't battling Mom. He was meeting my eyes with a peculiar warmth, almost respect.

My heart was still pounding against my chest, but I pasted on a brave façade, one that wanted to scream, "If you would have just given me a second chance, I could have aced your class, too." I didn't. I didn't want to hear about the syllabus or plagiarism warnings or a final exam with just my name scribbled at the top. That would have dragged me back to a place where I wasn't in control, where cocky grins were too easily replaced by unpredictable emotions, and where accomplishments gave way to attitude. I couldn't go there. Not again.

"Thanks, Mr. McCormack," I said. "I worked really hard this summer." Once the words were out, when I'd beaten back the voice urging me to fight, I managed a couple of deep breaths and felt myself relaxing. I imagined Joe sitting at our table. He would have folded his hands or maybe cocked an eyebrow, just to let me know I had said the right thing. That I'd said enough.

SO MY PLAN TO DROP MOM IN THE middle of a two-hour dinner from hell backfired. It never occurred to me that Coronado's pricey menu would have been a deterrent to chance run-ins with any of my teachers. Damn! And I could have had lobster, too.

Predictably, Mom didn't let things slide after Mr. McCormack left the table. We had to rehash all the crap, go over the issues, relive the phone calls and analyze the meetings. Mom made sure I knew how hard she'd fought, how she'd tried every imaginable option, and what strings she'd pulled. And all the while Elizabeth just sat there, sucking up juicy tidbits like a human vacuum cleaner.

The drive home topped it off. Mom was still wailing on Mr. McCormack; how dare he come up to our table, what right did he have to talk about me with my summer school teacher, but when she vowed to write a letter to the school board—well, that's when Dad exploded. I guess he had heard enough and didn't flip the safety valve in time. He told her she was not to do any such thing, that everything having to do with my school was now under control, and wasn't the purpose of the dinner to celebrate my good grades, or had she forgotten that? And he told her to get off of her goddamned soapbox and to get off it now.

How was the rest of the ride home? All I can say is that I still remember the distinctive blinking of the turn signal in Dad's car, and how many seconds the light stayed red at the corner of Bellevue and Manor.

I didn't wait for Dad to park the car in the garage when we pulled into the driveway, and hopped out while the automatic door was still opening. I didn't slam the car door and I wasn't mad; I knew I'd handled the situation with Mr. McCormack well. I just didn't want to be ringside in case Mom and Dad decided to go a few more rounds. I was fumbling with the key to the door when the phone rang. I normally didn't make much of an effort to answer the thing (taking messages for Elizabeth was beneath me), but it was a convenient excuse to distance myself from my family. I picked up the receiver on the fourth ring.

"Hello." We were supposed to say "Marshall residence" when we answered, but I thought that too formal. Just like the rest of our house.

"Hi, Quinn."

"Joe?"

A little laugh, then, "It's me."

"What's up?" I was confused and a bit concerned. Joe rarely called. We used e-mail or instant messaging, and he wasn't due back from Texas for three more days.

"Quinn, I know you like to hike, but I guess I never asked whether you've ever backpacked. Seems silly I wouldn't know that."

Joe's voice sounded different, not confident, and he was calling to find out if I backpacked? I was curious, searching for signals.

"Yeah, sure, I backpack. Did some when I was in Scouts. Haven't been in awhile. Why?"

"I'm still not coming back until Monday, but I've been thinking. There's a two-day hike in the Indian Peaks Wilderness that's pretty special, and I got an itch that needs scratching. Interested?"

"Yeah, sure!"

"Is your dad home?"

"Yeah."

"Good. Let me talk to him."

eighteen

I suppose I could have felt at least a little pity for Mom. After all, she did carry me around for nine months, giving me life, sustaining and nourishing me, and all that. And I caused hemorrhoids when I was born (it was her favorite story on Mother's Day or after her third glass of wine), but neither of those events seemed relevant. I reserved my pity for undeserving recipients of bad breaks. I didn't let guilt interfere. Mom could have tripped over a curb and broken her leg, and I would have been there, feeling sorry for her and even helping around the house.

But her leg wasn't broken, and her suffering had nothing to do with jagged streets or unseen hazards. It was about Mom being Mom. It was about rousing the troops for another battle, one more nasty fight even though the war was over, and this time Dad didn't bite off. So Mom's injury wasn't physical—there were no gashes or scars or scabs—but I guessed her pride hurt worse.

Dad had said yes to Joe's backpacking request. He asked cursory questions, glanced at a calendar, and jotted down a couple notes, but that was the extent of his due diligence. Maybe the results spoke for themselves. Maybe my grades and my attitude had proven Joe's value, and Dad wanted to keep the momentum going. I'm sure that played a part, but Dad never made rash decisions; he wouldn't say yes or no if there was still information to be analyzed or facts to be considered. And he'd always ask Mom's opinion. Not this time. No heads-up, no conference, no unified front. Dad granted permission; said those exact words into the phone while he glared at Mom, daring her to interrupt with "But" or "What about?"

Like I said, I could have felt sorry for Mom. But I didn't.

Dad was driving me to Joe's apartment and then taking us to our starting point just past Lake Granby because Joe didn't like leaving an unattended vehicle overnight. Looking back, it makes sense that Dad also wanted to see where Joe lived, but I also think he wanted to talk to him again. Do the polite thing; say hi, compare notes, give an in-person thank you. Then again, maybe he was just stepping in because we needed a ride and he knew Mom had other plans, no matter when we planned the trip.

"You're sure Winnie's okay picking you up tomorrow?" Dad asked.

It was a bright, cloudless Tuesday morning, and he was guiding my Explorer through Louisville's developing web of suburban sprawl. It would take just a few more minutes before we hit Highway 36, and then another ten to reach Joe's apartment.

"Yeah, he's got Wednesday off, and I know you're leaving on another trip. Winnie's okay with picking us up."

The truth was Winnie wanted to join Joe and me that day, said he would call in sick and that he didn't care if the store manager didn't believe him. Backpacking, a little fishing along the way— Winnie didn't beg, but he would have if I hadn't gotten in front of the idea. I explained that Joe and I wanted to do this by ourselves, that it was a special trip. Winnie understood.

"Summer vacation has finally arrived."

"Thank God," I said, not worrying about a reprimand over my choice of words. Dad was cool with some cuss words. He tossed in a few around me and didn't seem to care when I said God in nonreligious ways.

We'd merged onto the highway and Dad was gaining on the car in front of us. I knew what came next. It didn't matter that it was nine in the morning and there wasn't any traffic. Dad's checklist wouldn't change. He signaled, used the rearview mirror, then the outside mirror, glanced over his shoulder, and when everything checked out, he switched lanes. I guess airline pilots get comfortable with routines.

"So, Joe's taken this trail before?" he said, repeating the procedure when we passed the car.

"He says it's been a couple of years, but he remembers that it wasn't too tough. There are only a couple of steep grades, and even though we cross Cascade Creek a few times, Joe thinks it should be mostly dry."

Dad nodded and kept his eyes fixed to the road. When he wet his lips I knew there were more words, but then he swallowed them back. We'd already been through "Got everything packed?" and "Make good decisions," but I figured another checklist was headed my way. My parents had a habit of repeating instructions, even if music wasn't blaring.

Since I was still bothered by the car ride home from Valentino's, it only took another two miles before our silence became uncomfortable. My parents didn't fight, at least not in front of Elizabeth and me, and the harsh voices from that night had remained unpleasantly fresh. I wanted to talk so I switched the radio station to something a little less edgy, and lowered the volume.

"Dad, I want you to know I appreciate you sticking up for me, you know, letting me be friends with Joe. I wish Mom understood."

"Mom understands."

"I don't think she approves of our friendship."

Dad glanced at me, not wanting to take his eyes off the road for more than a few seconds and said, "Intellectually, Mom knows Joe's a good guy, that he's good for you. She's told me that a couple of times." Dad cleared his throat. "Emotionally? Well, it's a struggle to think someone else motivates your kid better than you do."

I guess I'd known that. Not the part about Mom liking Joe, but that she felt threatened by him. She was such a control freak. Giving it up, or at least making the handoff to someone else, had to be tough.

"Are you and Mom okay?" I asked.

Dad sighed, not in disgust, but with resignation. Maybe it was just experienced acceptance. "We're fine, Quinn. We have different styles, different approaches, that's all. Sometimes one of us goes to an extreme until the other pulls them back toward center. That happens in a marriage." Dad eyed me and smiled. "I love your mother very much, Quinn."

I hoped Dad was shooting straight. Even with all the yelling and screaming, the fights and the punishments I'd lived through with Mom ... deep down, I would have felt bad if I'd caused a breakup.

"Do I turn here, or the next one?"

"Next one," I said.

"You know, it's not easy being a teenager, Quinn." Dad turned his head toward me. "Gee, I bet you never heard that one before," he said, and then laughed.

"Never."

"And my job takes me out of town a couple of weeks every month."

I nodded. "Yeah, I know. I'm okay with that."

"That means Mom gets a lot of the responsibilities at home." Dad paused, still uncomfortable with the talk now under way, then pressed ahead. "So even though we both enforce the rules, it may seem that she's harder on you. If I'm on a trip, she has to make the call."

"It's this left." I was surprised and then confused by Dad's sudden need to protect Mom. I'd always depended on him to be the voice of reason in my family, the one who would at least listen to me. He'd told my mother to pipe down and then given the thumbs up to the backpacking trip, and now he was sticking up for her?

Dad pulled down the turn signal and stopped at a red light. He pursed his lips like he was struggling, not with the words, but with how to say them. "Quinn, I hope you know that parents want to be friends with their kids, too. We want to be open and honest and talk about things. But we also have to make decisions that might seem harsh or unfair. We have to enforce rules." Dad looked at me with a resigned look. "Parents need to be parents, and sometimes you can't be a parent and a friend at the same time."

It had taken a minute, but I finally figured out this conversation wasn't about Mom. He'd just backed the parental team and offered reasons and excuses for her, but that wasn't the primary objective.

"How do you feel about Joe, Dad? Are you okay with him?" I asked.

Dad swallowed again but held his eyes steady. It was the question he'd wanted. "I'll be honest, Quinn. I'd love to be the one who turned you around, the one taking you on a two-day back-packing trip. But sometimes that doesn't happen with parents and their kids."

"Take a right and park anywhere on the street." I pretended to look for an open spot so I didn't have to endure my father's eyes, and wondered why this moment of truth hadn't happened ten days, or even ten minutes earlier, and not in front of Joe's apartment.

"I don't know if you remember, but we used to do a lot together—Little League, basketball, campouts with Cub Scouts. You used to help me wash the car on Saturday mornings." Dad guided the Explorer between two cars, shifted into park, and cut the engine. "But being seen with your parents isn't too cool at your age, is it? Establishing your independence is a priority."

"I don't mind being seen with you guys."

Dad let loose a yeah-right chuckle, but without the attitude.

"A lot of teenagers, for whatever reason, need someone besides their parents. I know. I did, too."

I felt my father's hand on my shoulder and I turned to meet his eyes. His face was tense, almost like he was wincing, except there was no physical pain. Then I remembered that face. I was nine years old, and Dad was carrying me into the emergency room with a broken arm after I'd wiped out on a skateboard. I was afraid; of being in trouble for causing such a commotion, of being rushed to the hospital, of pain. Then I saw Dad's face, and I felt safe. I knew how much he cared.

"Joe hasn't replaced you," I said, feeling both guilt and comfort in seeing my father's expression. "He's a friend."

Dad smiled. "I'm a little jealous of Joe, but I thank God you have him. Someone you feel comfortable talking to, someone you trust."

"But—"

"You don't have to explain, Quinn. I understand. I want you to know that I understand. And I want you to know that our relationship *will* develop into friendship. You may not see it now, but as you get older and more mature, and as I get older and less inclined to tell you what to do, we'll become friends, too."

nineteen

It's hard to imagine that lugging thirty-five pounds on your back, sweating, fighting burning muscles, and smiling all go together. It must be an example of paying the price for something you want. Joe and I had hiked over four hours, through open meadows where random patches of brilliantly colored wildflowers exploded from the prairie grass, up hills dense with fir trees and scattered with aspen, and across a swollen stream that kept coming back to greet us. I knew, even then, that the physical exertion was a small price.

We'd made progress penetrating nature's defenses; the trail had narrowed, inconvenient rocks had replaced bare dirt, and I hadn't seen a candy wrapper or cigarette butt for the last forty minutes. We walked single file. I kept three feet behind Joe, mimicking his steps and avoiding the obstacles, because he knew where we were headed and because I'd wanted him to set the pace.

"There's a good spot just ahead if you're ready for a break," Joe called out.

"Break sounds good." I could have gone a little further, but we were in no particular hurry. It was only 3:30, plenty of daylight left, and we'd already covered six, maybe seven miles. Even with the steep climb still ahead, we would make our campsite at Crater Lake in a couple more hours.

Joe wedged through an opening between two outcroppings of rock, and worked his way to a level section that was shaded by pines perfectly pitched into the angle of the mountain. He slid his arms from the straps and let the backpack fall to within inches of the ground, then caught the weight just before impact.

"Might see an interesting shadow," he said.

"Maybe." I'd already shot a roll of film, mostly of a waterfall where I'd tinkered with the light and the shutter speed. And since we hadn't seen any wildlife to speak of, I'd gotten creative with a couple of wildflowers by using an open aperture to diffuse the background and force attention on their colors.

Joe pushed his Chicago Cubs cap high on his forehead and wiped away beads of sweat, then reached for the canteen stuffed in a side pocket of his pack and sipped four or five times while leaning against the trunk of an aspen. "Everything okay at home?"

"Everything's cool." I'd claimed a rock-free area and was sitting with my legs stretched straight in front of me. Losing the weight of the backpack and getting off my feet reminded my body how hard it had worked. My ankles were a bit stiff and my shoulders were sore.

"Your dad gave permission for this trip pretty quick. He sounded strained on the phone."

Joe fidgeted with his pack, adjusting straps and checking compartments, but he didn't seem ready to hoist it back on yet. Sweat continued dripping from his forehead, and he looked shaky, not like he was going to keel over, just drained. I assumed he needed more rest so I massaged my legs, hoping to send the message that I wasn't ready to shove off either.

"You remember me talking about Mr. McCormack?"

"History teacher, right?"

"Yeah," I said before letting out a deep breath. "We ran into him at dinner that night, right before you called, and my mom got all worked up. She went postal, on and on about everything that happened, and my dad told her to can it."

"I see." A few more beads of sweat dropped, causing Joe to blink. At least I thought it was the sweat.

"I kind of get where Mom was coming from. I wasn't exactly thrilled to see the guy or make small talk, either." I paused, visualizing the scene at Valentino's, remembering how I felt. It didn't seem like McCormack was trying to pick a fight, but showing up at our table after everything that had happened? "He was nice enough. Said he'd heard I aced Chemistry, but when I saw him? All I could think about was failing History."

"Do you blame him for what happened?"

How'd I know that was coming?

"I want to. I mean, he could have given me a second chance." I looked at the mud wedged into the bottom of my hiking boots and started breaking off clumps with a stick, knowing there wasn't any reason to stall. "No, I don't blame him. I'm the one who messed up on the paper and then took a zero on the final. And it's not like he changed the rules in the middle of the game or anything. It's just ... I failed History." I shook my head and sighed with a resigned look that acknowledged my complicity. "I got some pride back with Chemistry and Spanish in summer school, and Pre-Calc—well, math is easy. But seeing Mr. McCormack? It just reminded me that I failed Contemporary American History."

Joe's penetrating look didn't reveal his thoughts or suggest an opinion. He was replaying each of my words, matching them to experience, before choosing his own. He finally grunted and said, "Failure sounds so final, too black and white. Never liked that word."

"Yeah, well, I've seen the report card, and I'm here to tell you—it *is* black and white."

"We've already talked about grades, so don't lock onto the F's here. I'm talking about the word 'failure.' I have a problem with what the word implies." Joe scratched the hair above his ears, then rubbed his temples like he was conjuring an answer, before resetting his Cubs cap. "Failure says 'game over.' Failure says 'quit trying,' " he said.

"Well, yeah. So what's your point? It's a nice way of saying, 'You fucked up, pal.' What's wrong with that?"

"You can't fail unless you quit, and you're the only one who decides that. Nobody can make you quit." Joe tapped his forefinger against his lips and waited, giving me some room. "You don't get a promotion? You keep trying. You get cut from the football team? You keep trying. You don't get the right image with your camera? You keep trying. If you don't quit, if you're still trying, how can you have failed?"

"Semantics," I said with a hint of superiority. "You're talking semantics. Hey, people fail at things all the time. So what, by just saying 'I'm still trying,' they haven't really failed? Come on. That's not the way the world works. We're judged, every day we're judged, by lots and lots of people."

"Did you fail Chemistry or Spanish?" Joe's unyielding stare forced my eyes to his.

"I got A's. I know they don't *mean* anything, but I got A's."

"But your report card, the same one listing that history class, says you got F's in Chemistry and Spanish."

"I retook the courses. I got A's," I said a little too sharply.

"You didn't quit," Joe said matter-of-factly. "And why don't you care about Pre-Calculus? I'm not hearing any moaning and groaning about failing that class."

"Because I scored 740 in math on the SAT, and that tells everyone what I know about math," I said with a smile threatening to break out. I was getting it. It was still a little too theoretical, the in-a-perfect-world stuff, but I was getting it.

"Ah, so grades don't always reflect what you know." Joe wriggled his eyebrows. "But it still intrigues me that your history teacher, Mr. McCormack is it, has somehow convinced you that you failed Contemporary American History. Too bad seeing him caused such a problem."

"Don't even think about saying I haven't given up yet because I have. I'm not retaking that history class. Forget it. Nada. No fucking way."

"Then don't."

Joe was done. I heard it in his voice and saw it in his face. An unspoken but fragile truce lingered between us while he untwisted the cap and sipped from his canteen, drinking in slow motion like he was drawing out the silence.

Finally, he replaced the cap, wiped his mouth across his arm, and looked at me. "People fail, Quinn, but only because they've quit."

MARRIAGE COUNSELORS SHOULD take their clients back-packing. Think about it. There could be half-hour shrink sessions during water breaks when issues get put on the table with some back and forth discussion, but there'd be a time limit, a built-in stopping point because you'd have to get back on the trail in order to make camp before dark. There wouldn't be time for yelling or name calling. Between fumbling with packs, struggling not to fall, and focusing energy on navigating rocks and trees and breathing thin air—well, maybe trading nasty barbs about toothpaste caps and toilet seats wouldn't be a priority. Maybe understanding a different opinion gets easier when you're not totally focused on defending your own.

Joe and I weren't married, and we didn't fight. Still, putting space between some of our talks, and not picking apart every word, worked well for us. It wasn't about winning or losing an argument and it wasn't about telling the other guy what to do. It boiled down to trust, and I was just beginning to understand that trusting people means giving them the benefit of the doubt, giving their words a chance.

Not giving up? It felt like I should be swarming out of a locker room with my teammates, ready to snatch victory from the clutches of defeat, getting juiced from the crowd's frenzy, the rah-rah-rah thing. But Joe didn't play to crowds, and I hadn't received a pep talk. I knew that.

So we pushed another two hours, trudging over rocky terrain, fighting a relentless sun, mapping our steps, hoping the current set of switchbacks would be the last. We'd kept a steady pace so we could make camp and have time to gather firewood for cooking before it got too dark. It was a quarter 'til six, and Joe thought Crater Lake was just over the next ridge. Good. Joe was straining, and I was ready to call it a day.

I'd also made a decision. After dinner, after we were stowed away for the night, I'd ask some questions. Not an interrogation; no, nothing like that. I was just curious how Joe knew all this stuff, and why he was so good at passing the torch of life's experiences, the lessons. And he'd sidestepped quite a few of my questions about Korea and Vietnam over the last few months. It wasn't like Joe hadn't shared. He had, but there were times when I'd wanted specifics, wanted more. Like what was it like to shoot at somebody? I didn't need or want to hear about blood and guts, but I wanted to know how he'd rationalized killing someone. What went through his head? How had he drawn his lines? I mean he'd *volunteered* to go to Vietnam.

Sure, I'd heard some Marines' stories, examples of how discipline and mental toughness and pride carry forward into all walks of life, and about the men who made something of themselves. But then, why wasn't Joe more rigid with the gung-ho, 'Yes sir, may I have another, sir' stuff? How could he spend over twenty years in the Marines and *then* decide he didn't have to accept all of society's rules?

I knew there were missing pieces, and I was going to ask.

twenty

Joe and I had decided against established campsites near the shore and found a flat clearing perched fifty yards above Crater Lake, where a cluster of ponderosa pines guarded our privacy even though we hadn't seen anyone since midmorning. We were treated to a panoramic view of the lake carved in the middle of a mountain, and a nearby creek. The sound of water gurgling over rocks and down a winding path toward the lake was soothing, almost hypnotic, but only if you listened. A steady breeze rattled leaves and pushed the campfire smoke away from us, jumbling the scent of pine, rocky moss, and burning wood.

My breathing was deep and satisfying, my muscles relaxed, my spirit revitalized as twilight settled.

There was plenty of dry wood, and we'd already boiled a couple pots of water for drinking and cooking. Yes, cooking. No hotdogs speared with sticks, no dried snacks, and no sandwiches.

"Bet you didn't think I'd make spaghetti." Joe grinned as he watched me heap another mound of glistening red pasta on my plate, no doubt pleased there wouldn't be leftovers. "It's messy, but it'll stick to your insides. Give you some energy."

"Tastes good," I said, bending my head over the plate. I was scooping and sucking and shoveling noodles with a spoon, too hungry to care about much else. It was my third helping, and I'd already inhaled four hunks of bread.

Joe picked at his food, then sighed and set it on the ground. He hadn't eaten much; just a little spaghetti to taste his cooking, and a few nibbles of bread. I couldn't believe he hadn't wolfed it all down. We'd hiked nine miles so he had to be famished, yet he was tentative, almost put off by the food.

"I got a surprise for dessert," Joe said, reaching for his canteen. His voice was livelier than his appearance.

"No way," I mumbled through bites. "There's no way you brought a Marie Callender's pie on a backpacking trip." I moaned when I saw Joe's grin widen. "Okay, let me guess. What kind of pie ... what kind of pie would be so tempting, so hard to do without for two days? Hmmm, you wouldn't have risked a cream pie. I mean you wouldn't be sitting there so calm and collected. You would have checked it by now."

Joe laughed and sipped water.

"It has to be a fruit pie. And since I don't know what you ate last week, I'm kind of in the dark about what kind of fruit pie. I know you like apple, but you have apple pie all the time. I'm thinking blueberry ... no, peach. You've been talking about peach pie."

"Is that your final guess?"

I took a drink and swirled it in my mouth, considering the options. "I'm sticking with my answer. Yep, we're having peach pie for dessert."

Joe sat on one of those cushion chairs with a back that snaps into place. He propped his feet on a rock and settled lower, turning and twisting like a dog circling until the perfect position is claimed. "Not even close."

"Not even close? Bullshit. No Marie Callender's? Joe, the sun will rise in the east tomorrow morning, and we're having Marie Callender's pie for dessert tonight. You're full of surprises. I mean you're like a modern version of the Renaissance man, but

dessert? Don't even try. There's a Marie Callender's pie somewhere within twenty feet."

"German chocolate crème." The campfire magnified the
twinkle in Joe's eyes. He waved a hand toward his backpack
leaning against a tree not far from me. "Check it out. There's a
black vinyl case in the bottom pouch. Got an ice pack that keeps
stuff cold for twenty-four hours."

"Spaghetti and German chocolate crème pie, huh? Nothing
like roughing it." I shook my head and laughed while I retrieved
the goody box. "Are you going to eat some of this? You hardly
even touched dinner."

"Maybe later." Joe pulled the bill of his Chicago Cubs cap
lower, shielding his eyes from me. "You go ahead. The day isn't
over until you've had a piece of pie."

The pasta and bread had finally convinced my brain I wasn't
dying of starvation, and the thought of a rich dessert? Let's just
say it wasn't how I would have chosen to end the meal. But I
sensed Joe was eyeing my reaction and that there was a bit of
pride involved. I knew it wouldn't take much to play along so I
unzipped the vinyl container and lifted a plate, tightly wrapped in
aluminum foil, above my head in homage. "Thank you, God!" I said.

Joe slapped his leg and chuckled. "Still cold, right?"

"It's cold, but let me just undo this baby. I mean, what if it got
squished? Wouldn't be the same, you know." I narrowed my eyes
and raised an eyebrow, warning that further inspection was
required. I loosened the foil, exaggerating the delicacy of my
task with sweeping hands and just-so fingers, then peeked
beneath the covering. I looked back and forth between Joe and
the plate, trying to muster a profound look of disappointment.

"Goddamn comedian. Did it make it or not?"

I walked toward Joe shaking my head and holding the plate
with extended arms.

"Shit," he said. "I really thought I could pull it off. Damn
cooler bag cost me ten bucks."

"It's ... it's ... " I leaned forward and lifted the foil for Joe. "It's perfect!" I gave Joe my best imitation of Winnie, stupid grin and all, and waited for his reaction, but I'm pretty sure he knew I'd been hamming it up all along.

"Ah, don't be doing that to an old man."

"Old, my butt. You're fifty, hell, almost sixty years older than me, and I'm the one ready to inject Advil and crawl into my sleeping bag. You'll be hiking mountains when I'm in a retirement home." I reclaimed my seat, licked spaghetti sauce off my spoon, and tried to be enthusiastic with my first bite of pie. It was good, in a way-too-sweet kind of way.

Joe instinctively shifted in the chair and his face toughened. "How's it taste?" he asked, the eagerness now drained from his voice.

"Hits the spot. Come on. You have to have some."

"Just not hungry, Quinn."

Anxiety seeped through the hardened face. I hadn't remembered ever seeing Joe so uncomfortable, so ... so ... vulnerable.

Then it hit me. I was looking at Joe, but it was like I was seeing a stranger, someone who merely resembled Joe Toscano. The Joe I knew was in great shape. He biked and jogged and backpacked, and kept such a demanding schedule that I'd often wondered where he got the energy. Joe was tough, a fighter; maybe not physically imposing, but the attitude, the presence? You didn't cross him.

That wasn't who I saw.

The man curled by the fire seemed dependent, almost frail, though I suspect such a comment would have ignited a temporary surge of energy. His face was thinner and his eyes, those fierce black circles that probed and challenged and held onto you—they were smaller, more flat, like they'd been sucked back into their sockets. It struck me that the Cubs cap had been in place and pulled tight since Dad and I picked up Joe that morning, and that it was camouflaging more than protecting. I'd missed those things with the excitement of our trip, our focus and calculated pace earlier that day, but I saw them that night.

"Okay to ask some questions?"

Joe nodded.

"Are you all right?"

There was a slight twitch on Joe's lips, almost a smile, and he shook his head. "No, Quinn. I'm not all right."

I wanted to say "What's wrong?" or "What's the matter?" but my tongue was glued to the roof of my mouth, and all I could do was hold my breath and wait.

"We've got some things to talk about." Joe lifted his legs from the rock, planted them on the ground, and sat more upright. The moves were slow and deliberate, maybe because his muscles were tired and tight, or maybe because he was struggling with words. Joe leaned forward when he faced me, then took a deep breath with his eyes closed. When they opened, he said, "I have cancer, Quinn."

I was dazed, too stunned to feel grief or pain, yet I knew they were nearby, waiting, ready to strike. And I knew, without question and without recourse, my life had just become complicated.

What kind of cancer? When will the treatment start? What's the prognosis? Come on, Quinn, say something!

"Is it terminal?" I asked, biting my lip and holding my breath.

Joe's eyes were strong again, inviting me to grab on, but they told me the answer. When Joe spoke, his voice was gentle, as if a near whisper would somehow soften the stark words.

"It is terminal, Quinn. None of the docs have called a date, but we're talking two, maybe three months." Joe sensed I was about to break down, so he kept talking. "I have cancer of the pancreas. Short version? It went undetected long enough to spread into my lymph nodes and liver. There were no symptoms, no hint that anything was wrong. By the time it was diagnosed? Well, the damned thing had free rein for quite a while, and that means it's too late."

I'd heard the words and I'd understood them—Joe was dying, he had a few months to live—but the words weren't real. They couldn't be. I didn't want them to be. I kept swallowing, trying to get rid of the lump in my throat, and I couldn't breathe. When I caught a scent of German chocolate crème pie, I almost vomited.

"Don't they ... can't they do something? Chemotherapy?"

"They could."

"So they do that in Denver?"

Joe's forehead puckered before he finally responded. "Won't be any treatments, Quinn. There's no chance for anything but a minor remission, and only a ten percent chance I'd even get a few extra months. Pretty severe treatment at this stage. The only guarantee is that I'd be sick as a dog."

"But you have to try, even if there's only a small chance. You have to try."

"Think about what I just said, Quinn. *If* it works, *if* I'm the lucky one out of ten, I'll be hooked up to machines spitting chemicals into my blood for three or four hours a day. Those chemicals will make me feel like shit. I'll have no energy, I'll be puking my guts out, and I'll have no life other than chemo treatments and lying home in bed. All that so I can be sick and miserable for a couple extra months?"

I hid from Joe's eyes and stared at the campfire. It crackled every so often, launching miniature flares that dissolved into ash before disappearing. I walked to the fire and poked it with a stick, agitating the wood and sending more embers popping into the sky.

"Did you get a second opinion? Are there other doctors?"

"I have second and third opinions." Joe sighed and rolled his eyes like he was reliving a stream of crowded waiting rooms, out-dated magazines, and unpleasant examinations. "I was diag-nosed by my doctor a couple of months ago. In fact, that's why I didn't take the final exams in Anatomy & Physiology or Biology. I was undergoing medical tests and I just didn't feel up to studying. When the results came back, my doctor referred me to a specialist in Denver, and she did more tests. Same conclusion, except she was a little more exact with the progression. She's good. Dr. Shirley Houseman over at University Hospital, and I would have left it with her opinion, but she wanted to try one more avenue. Remember I told you I was in Texas on business last week? I was at the M.D. Anderson Center in Houston. Pretty much the final say-so when it comes to cancer."

"What did they say?"

"Exactly what I just told you, and what Dr. Houseman told me before. Because it spread to my liver, there is no surgical option. I can go through chemo and radiation and it might prolong my life a few months. But those extra months, if I get them, come attached to being sick and miserable the whole time." Joe paused and kept his eyes steady. "The other option is no treatment. I'd have medication to help with the pain, but without treatment the cancer will kill me in a couple of months."

"You don't want to at least try to get a couple extra months?"

"I don't want to be sick the rest of my life, Quinn. I want some quality time."

"Quality time?" I said, glaring at the fire.

Joe struggled to his feet and joined me by the campfire. He kicked the base of the burning wood a couple times, jump-starting the flame. I could tell without taking my eyes from the fire that a determined look had gathered on Joe's face.

"I'll be uncomfortable and there will be some pain. But at least I'll be mobile. I'll be able to get around. I'll have time to enjoy things. The last couple of weeks will be rough, but I get to live my life until that point." There was another void marked by silence, by anguish. "Yeah, quality time," he said.

I hung my head a bit and still refused to look at Joe. "Why did you wait until now to tell me?" I asked. "You could have told me before. You could have told me you had health problems when we first met. Why did you have to spring it on me like this?"

"I screwed up, Quinn. I'm sorry."

I was caught off guard with the apology and instinctively looked at Joe.

"Want excuses?" he said, shrugging his shoulders. "How about I don't like bellyaching, or I didn't know the final results until last Friday, or maybe I didn't want to interrupt your progress in summer school. Those would be my excuses." Joe sighed and took a breath before managing a weary smile. "But the truth is I'm not good at sharing my secrets. I've never shared them."

"We're friends," I said, "and friends trust each other." My tone was somber, not demanding or threatening. I was okay with Joe not telling me this before, but I wanted him to know that I thought our friendship had grown, that being there for each other wasn't a one-way street.

Joe swallowed hard, returned to his cushion-seat, and gingerly lowered his frame into position. When he wiped his brow he accidentally bumped the baseball cap high onto his forehead, revealing a strained face and tormented eyes.

"We are friends, Quinn. And there's something else I need to tell you."

twenty-one

I grabbed the sweatshirt from my pack and sat on the ground next to Joe. A few minutes had passed since he'd said there was something else, and even though I was trying not to think, images raced through my head. None of them were pleasant. Telling me he had cancer ... that he had a couple months to live ... so he could get to *this* point?

"What you said, about us being friends? You've got that right, Quinn, but I'm not a mushy kind of guy. It's just not me." Joe straightened his cap and leaned back against the cushion like he was settling in for a long talk. "The last two months, even with finding out I have cancer? They've been very special."

"They mean a lot to me, too."

"You're a terrific friend, Quinn. I can't tell you how much I look forward to the days when you come by the apartment. Studying, taking walks .. ."

"Eating pie," I said, and we both laughed.

"But there's more to it, and I think you, of all people, deserve to know the truth."

I didn't say a word. My eyes were riveted to Joe.

"One of the reasons our time together means so much is that it's given me a chance to make up for some horrible mistakes."

Joe hesitated, kind of like a kid who's about to take his first jump from the high dive and wants one last look. But then he shook his head, tightened his lips, and looked me squarely in the eye. "I didn't tell you the truth. My wife and I weren't married when she died. She divorced me in 1972."

All of my senses were activated. I heard the whispers of creatures making nightly rounds, I felt tiny pebbles against my butt, and my tongue still tasted dinner. The campfire was playing tricks, distorting our shadows onto trees, making us out to be hulking creatures, powerful and menacing, but it also lit our faces, revealing expressions and vulnerabilities. I saw that Joe was in pain ... and all I could do was listen.

"And I lied when I told you we didn't have children. I have a son. His name is Jack, and he lives in Denver with his family. Has a wife and two daughters."

"I don't get it. You have family in Denver. What's the big deal? Why couldn't I know that?"

Joe moistened and then twisted his lips. His eyes were watery but he wasn't crying. "I haven't seen or talked with my son in over thirty years. Never met his wife, Abby. Never seen my granddaughters, Melinda and Patricia."

"What happened with your son? Is that why your wife divorced you?"

"True confession time," Joe warned. He leaned back farther and locked his fingers behind his neck. He'd jumped off the diving board and was about to hit the water. "I was still in the Marines and I took it pretty seriously. Hell, I took everything seriously. Everything in our lives was orderly, everything was by the book. Probably why I understand your mom so well. You could say I was rigid, but that would be an understatement. And Jack ... " Joe chuckled and said, "Jack was a lot like you—intelligent, rebellious, independent. Not exactly the dutiful child in a Marine household."

No, dutiful had never been used to describe me.

"So you two had a fight?"

"Yeah, we had a fight." A tear trickled down Joe's cheek that he didn't bother to wipe. "It was during the height of the Vietnam War. He was into the hippie thing. Had long hair, used drugs, protested the war. So we had ultra-establishment and anti-establishment, and my wife in the middle. She played the part of peacemaker. Did a pretty decent job of keeping the family together."

"But?"

"Jack was drafted. He didn't show up to the induction."

I'd seen news footage of the sixties: protestors burning flags, police breaking up demonstrations with teargas and nightsticks, flower power and love-ins. It made my generation look wimpy. I tried imagining Joe with close-cropped hair and a freshly starched uniform, dealing with his son, a stranger I knew all too well.

"I thought a lot of kids did that kind of thing, refused military service, burned draft cards and stuff. I can see how it was a big deal, you being a Marine and all, but if everyone else was doing the same thing ... "

"When I came home that night and found out he was a no-show?" Joe sucked on his lower lip, then swallowed. "It got ugly. Lots of screaming and yelling. He called me an ignorant robot who killed innocent women and children. I told him he was a lazy good-for-nothing excuse for a human being. And all the time, Mary, my wife, kept pleading for us to stop, to leave each other alone." Joe started blinking, and it was obvious the reflex wouldn't hold back his tears for long.

I touched his arm, letting him know I was there, that I understood.

Joe stared fiercely at the campfire, like it was providing glimpses of a not-so-recent replay. "Told Jack I might be able to fix the induction, get it rescheduled or something, but he said not to bother, that there was no way he'd ever serve in the military. Said he didn't want to be an American, that he was going to Canada."

I wanted to take on Joe's pain, the winces and shallow breaths and gritted teeth, but they kept crashing, wave after wave; a relentless test of my will to be strong, to stay connected to him. But I was drained. I couldn't take another blow and silently pleaded for the story to end. *Please, let it be over.*

Joe turned his head and looked straight at me. His body shook and his lips quivered when he tried to speak. The words were close but they couldn't escape. Tears flooded his eyes and streamed down both cheeks. Joe pressed, swallowing over and over, forcing fragments of what he needed to say.

"I called ... Jack ... a ... a ... coward. I said I was asham ... ashamed of him and that ... that I would never ... " Joe took a deep breath and pushed hard. "Never speak to him again." Joe's tears turned to sobs as he buried his face in his hands.

I rested my hand on his shoulder and slid it back and forth. I felt his chest heaving and heard short, intermittent gasps for air. Except for my hand, I sat perfectly still. I wasn't going to say "It's okay" because it wasn't. I wanted to cry, too.

Joe finally raised his head. His face was stained with tears and his eyes were swollen. He searched my eyes for permission, and then whispered, "I told him from that moment forward, I didn't have a son."

IT WAS EASY TO BE COCKY, TO CARRY A teenage attitude during the day. There was always someone looking, someone to impress, or someone to show that I didn't care what they or anyone else thought. It combined style with performance, and I could dial in "sulking" or "arrogant" or "smug" at will.

Nighttime was a different story. That was when I was alone

with my thoughts, when I unzipped whatever mask I was wearing, and faced reality. There were times when reality comforted and encouraged me, but since reality didn't bend or pretend the truth, it had been an infrequent ally.

It was 2:15 and Joe had been asleep almost three hours. Our talk—his confession or admission or whatever you want to call it—lasted awhile longer but then it became obvious that Joe was spent, physically and emotionally. He just couldn't keep talking. He needed rest.

Joe decided against the tent and unrolled his sleeping bag on a flat area fifteen feet from the campfire. He'd burrowed deep and used the edge of his backpack as a pillow. His snoring was intermittent and loud, his breathing heavy and uneven, almost as if sleep was purging anything left out from that night's talk. Other than smacking his lips while adjusting his head, Joe didn't move.

Me? I didn't even bother trying.

I sat with my back against a boulder, resting my chin on cradled knees, rocking a bit to break the monotony and to keep my butt from going numb. The campfire had been an agreeable companion, one that allowed my mind to wander while I watched its flames dance and skip across the wood. When the fire tried to sleep too, settling into a slow, almost invisible burn, I poked it back to life. The simple truth was I didn't want to be alone in the dark with reality.

I had crying jags every twenty minutes or so. I alternated between anger and pity, and cursed God and my life, and sometimes even Joe, but those sessions didn't provide much of a release, like it did when Joe cried. I figured you had to store tears for a bunch of years before that happened.

I wasn't totally worthless after Joe called it a night. I'd tried to sort things out, thought about the future, and fiddled with different plans. But I kept coming back to a calendar I saw in my mind's eye. I thought of November and December, and I wondered which of their days would claim Joe's life.

I also couldn't shake the image of Joe being so alone for so long. He'd told me that his son packed a bag and left the house that night, and that his wife locked herself in their bedroom. When Joe reported for duty the next day, he volunteered, actually asked to be sent to Vietnam so he could offset Jack's act of shame, so he could make things right. And it didn't matter to the Marine Corps that he'd fought in Korea, that he'd been wounded and been brave and had a bunch of medals to prove it. Joe said the Marine Corps is a warrior society that understands any request for a combat assignment, and that his commander grunted an approval and expedited it. Joe didn't consult his wife. Just came home that night, told her what he'd done, and shipped out five weeks later.

It was like a story as he talked, a make-believe story. I'd only known Joe for a few months, but we were tight, and it was hard for me to imagine him being such a hard-ass. He was right. The old Joe put Mom to shame.

When Joe got to Vietnam, he was assigned to a platoon whose primary mission was to hunt and kill Vietcong and their sympathizers. He said they'd go on patrol, sometimes eight or nine days at a time, and that there would always be firefights. Joe said that he wasn't afraid, that he took crazy chances all the time, but that risking his life didn't make dealing with Jack's situation any easier. Joe said there was a lot of killing and that all the dead bodies, on both sides, seemed too young. He said it got to the point where he didn't want to know anything about the replacements assigned to his platoon because he figured they'd be dead or wounded and sent home within a month, so why bother.

Joe's turning point came when his platoon was sent on a mission to destroy a village thought to feed and support the Vietcong. They had surprised the villagers one morning but didn't find any Vietcong or weapons; just women and children and old men pleading for protection, insisting that the Vietcong had threatened to kill any man old enough to fight who didn't go with them. Joe believed what the villagers told him—said he could see the truth in their eyes—but that the lieutenant in charge didn't hesitate, and ordered his men to set fire to the village.

In the melee, some of the villagers begged the Marines to stop, screaming and crying Vietnamese words that didn't need translation; but most scattered, frantic to salvage possessions from their burning huts. Joe said one of his men fired a rifle into the air and that the lieutenant, fresh from college and on his first patrol, panicked. He hit the ground and sprayed bullets at three figures racing behind one of the huts. The lieutenant killed a woman and her two children.

Joe said the lieutenant claimed he was firing at fleeing Vietcong, that it was an unfortunate accident, and that the woman and her children ran into his line of fire while he was engaging the enemy. Everyone in the platoon knew what happened, but no one, including Joe, contradicted the lieutenant's statement because no one could conclusively say there *weren't* any Vietcong. So there wasn't an inquiry or follow-up, and no consequences; just another quickly filed and forgotten field report whose mention of fleeing Vietcong justified the mission.

Joe returned from that patrol grappling with an identity he hadn't questioned in over twenty years. He was a Marine. Someone who, despite the ugliness and brutality of war, believed in God and a straightforward order to the world. Someone who lived by a code not subject to interpretation; someone who didn't question authority. But now Joe had questions. He thought about his son and how he'd refused military service. He struggled between guilt and relief that Jack was safe in Canada. And he was haunted by words that had become so prescient.

Then there was the envelope from Mary, her first letter since he'd arrived in Vietnam. It was manila folder-sized, thick with papers, and Joe eagerly ripped it open, craving pictures and words and smells that would reconnect him to another place and to his life. But Mary's envelope didn't hold any pictures and didn't smell of her perfume. There were words, pages and pages of typewritten words, but Joe read only three: *Petition for Divorce.* Mary included a handwritten note that said, "You may not have a son, but I do—so just sign it, send it back, and stay away."

That's the day Joe started sleeping only two or three hours a night. It's the day he realized he'd lost his family forever.

twenty-two

"What time is it?"

"A bit after eight."

Joe rubbed his eyes, then pushed himself from the ground so he was sitting with the sleeping bag still wrapped around him. His body was stiff and he appeared disoriented, not with the surroundings but with the situation, while he tried to free himself from a sleeping bag turned cocoon. He looked at the sky, confirming the sun has risen to a spot matching my claim about the time, then glanced at his watch. He cleared his throat and took a final peek upward. A smile erupted on his face and through his eyes. "I'll be damned," he said.

It was hard for me to hit the snooze button on nature (babbling birds tend to ignore just-ten-more-minutes pleas), so I'd been sitting quietly, creatively stretching my legs and enjoying the sun while it climbed the wall of rock to the west. I admit being relieved when the murmurs of night became dawn, confirming that the worst night of my life was finally over.

"You slept over eight hours," I said.

"Don't remember sleeping." Joe shook his head like he was trying to jumpstart his brain. "Didn't wake up at all. Don't even remember dreaming."

"How do you feel?"

Joe extracted his legs from the sleeping bag and slowly tested them. "Uhmm ... I'm ... I'm okay." He twisted his upper body back and forth, a little farther with each turn, and then raised his arms and started making circles. "I feel rested. It's strange, so different, like I was comfortable sleeping."

"Oh, you were comfortable, all right. I checked on you a couple of times," I said with a laugh.

But my relaxed manner belied several anxious moments. The truth was that each time Joe's labored breathing stopped, I was terrified that the night's ordeal had erased decades of guilt and allowed Joe to pass, and that I would be left with the burden of what to do next. So I'd crawl toward Joe, needing to stretch and wanting to make sure, until I clearly saw his sleeping bag inching up and down.

"You sleep much?"

I thought about lying, about fudging just enough to avoid spoiling Joe's good night, but I knew he'd see through it. It had to be the truth—especially from this point forward, it had to be the truth.

"Not really. Maybe an hour or so. Dozed off a couple of times right at the end."

Joe just nodded. "Dumped quite a bit in your lap. How you doing with everything?"

"Better than last night, but still pretty shitty."

Joe bent over his backpack and reached inside a pocket. He took out two breakfast bars and tossed one to me. "I wish I could tell you it was going to get easier," he said, peeling back the foil on his bar. He took a couple bites and swallowed. "It won't get easier, Quinn. You may get used to the idea of me dying, but it won't get easier."

I ripped into my breakfast and lowered my eyes. I was still sitting cross-legged against the boulder, postponing rickety knees and stiff joints for a while longer. I knew it wasn't going to get easier. I also knew I couldn't handle it getting any tougher.

Joe sensed my uneasiness and knew not to press. "We're running a little behind if we don't want to keep your friend waiting," he said. "Grab a banana and some water, and let's get packed. We can talk while we hike."

THE PREVIOUS DAY'S HIKE WASN'T a pushover. We covered nine miles and gained almost two thousand feet in elevation while an insistent sun beat through fair-weathered clouds and thinning clumps of trees. Not a hike for beginners, yet not intensely challenging either. The next day was different.

We retraced our trail, but since we were hiking mostly downhill and our pace was quicker, we took a few side trips along the way, bushwhacking through canyons and climbing over rocks and along cliffs. Even the forest, normally a place of cool respite, tested our resolve. Fir trees with stripped trunks and canopied tops were pressed tightly together; they required us to change course every few steps, warning us to follow the normal path. Yet Joe and I achieved a certain rhythm to our pace. It was methodical and refused to be intimidated by nature's barriers.

Our efforts were rewarded. We walked behind an ice-cold waterfall that crashed past rocks fifty feet below, we saw curious and unafraid animals go about daily tasks, and we marveled at imposing vistas that would have humbled even the most self-centered. Maybe I was lightheaded because of the altitude or maybe I just became more philosophical when I was around Joe. Hell, maybe I was maturing. But it struck me that what we'd experienced was unique, and that it was reserved for those who persisted, for those willing to sacrifice. It was the first time I remember wondering what other of life's prizes I'd missed.

At Joe's insistence, I was more active with my camera. It was a bit clumsy with the backpack and all, but I still managed to shoot two more rolls. And Joe wasn't his normal grouchy self when I took pictures of him. He wasn't smiling when I pressed the shutter, but he didn't wave me off either. That had me looking forward to a session at Nicki's.

I was leading our current descent into a plunging ravine. Joe said there was a dry riverbed at the bottom that would wind back into the trail, and that it would take another two hours to reach our pickup spot from there. We were supposed to meet Winnie at four, and it was almost one o'clock. I figured there was plenty of time for a lunch break.

"Okay to stop?" I said over my shoulder as we approached a couple of invitingly large rocks surrounded by plenty of shade.

"Good idea."

I quickly slid my arms through the backpack straps so I could help Joe.

He started to protest as I approached, but I could see the strain in his face. He gave in with a half-smile and said, "Thanks."

Lunch wasn't much: an apple, a bagel that had managed to stay soft in a Ziploc bag, and water. No use carrying extra supplies when we didn't need them. Winnie and my Explorer were only a few hours away with standing instructions to find the nearest McDonald's after we emerged. Bread and fruit were fine until then.

Joe and I had talked a little during water breaks that morning, mostly about how he'd found out about the cancer, and why there wasn't much that could be done other than manage the pain. He said it was hard to detect pancreatic cancer because it hid behind so many other body parts, and that there weren't really any symptoms to have raised a red flag earlier. He said that was why it was so lethal; by the time you found it, it had already metastasized into other parts of the body. When it spread to the lymph nodes or the liver, as it had with Joe, even the most aggressive surgical options weren't an option. And like he'd said, chemotherapy was provisional, not promising.

Joe said he had felt a slight pain in his stomach that previous May, but had assumed he'd just pulled a muscle. He cut back on his exercise regime and took it easy for a couple weeks, figuring the discomfort would go away. It didn't, but Joe still didn't see a doctor. Only when he'd lost weight, almost twenty pounds, did he own up to the possibility there might be a problem. By then the cancer had spread. The initial diagnosis, later confirmed and reconfirmed, was stage IV pancreatic cancer.

"How do you feel?" I asked.

Joe wasn't breathing hard. In fact, I think I was probably more tired than him, but his face winced almost continuously.

"I'm okay," he said while pouring water into the Cubs cap and fitting it back on his head. Water glided down his face and joined beads of sweat. Together they trickled to an already drenched T-shirt. "The hiking is fine, actually feels pretty good, but my damned stomach hurts like hell."

"A couple more hours?" My tone asked the implied question.

Joe met my eyes. "Couple more hours," he said.

I chomped into my bagel and breathed deeply, hoping the combination of oxygen and nourishment would convince my body *it* could make a couple more hours.

"How about you, Quinn?" Joe laughed out loud. "You look wiped."

"I can sum up how I feel in four words: hot shower, soft bed."

"And I'm hoping for two nights in a row."

I'd been reluctant to break the unofficial moratorium on that subject, and I was still in shock over seeing Joe cry, so I wasn't sure I could handle Round Two. But I'd also kicked around, more than a few times, the connection between Joe's confession and his sleep problem, and I wanted to ask questions. What the hell. He could always tell me to mind my own business.

"You said you and Mary became friends again a couple years after your tour in Vietnam. Did she tell you anything about Jack?"

I watched Joe for a reaction, any hesitation. There was none.

"I didn't even try connecting with Jack when I returned stateside. I was angry. At Mary for divorcing me, at the Marine Corps for making me such a rigid, hard-ass monster, at myself for allowing it all to happen. Yeah, when I explained what happened in Vietnam and how I felt, Mary let down her defenses. We became friends again after a couple years." Joe sighed and sipped from his canteen. "But she laid out ground rules. We weren't ever to discuss Jack."

"Never? He never came up?"

"Made her too uncomfortable, and I gave my word. But I did convince her to forward a letter I wrote. It was quite a few years after our blowup, when I was ready, when I was capable of apologizing." Joe stared vacantly at the trees behind me and blinked as though he was remembering the words. "I apologized for what I'd said and done, for the way I'd treated him and his mother, for the unrealistic expectations. I meant it, too, all of it. And then I really let go. I told him about the divorce, why I thought Mary did the right thing, and how I'd not only lost my son, but also the love of my life. I told him about the incident with the Vietnamese woman and her two children, how it made me feel, and that I'd left the Corps. I talked about the plumbing business. I even told him that I'd started painting, that I didn't care what my Marine buddies thought. Good God, that letter must have been fifteen pages."

"And?" I imagined one of my parents telling me their deepest secrets, allowing an inside view, and it didn't click. Parents just don't do that.

"He sent the letter back to Mary—unopened." Joe grimaced at the thought and swallowed back watery eyes. He labored through several deep breaths before continuing. "After that, Mary took pity. She shared a little bit about Jack's life. I think she believed the changes she saw in me, so she'd tell me things. Not where he lived, but other stuff. I knew that he'd finished college and when he got married. She told me he was a lawyer and when his children were born."

"He's a lawyer?" I don't know why, but I'd had this image of an outdoorsman, someone who kept to himself and lived off the land to stay away from the authorities. That's why I figured he chose Colorado when he returned to the United States.

"Surprised the hell out of me, too," Joe said. "He flunked out of the community college in California, but I guess he buckled down in Canada. Anyway, when President Carter granted amnesty to draft dodgers in 1977, Jack came back to the States, and was accepted at Creighton University's law school two years later."

"How'd you find out he was in Denver?"

Joe's shrug was embarrassed, and he dug a hole in the dirt with the heel of his boot. "I found everything about Jack in Mary's papers. I went through them when she died." Joe bit into an apple and chewed it slowly, not wanting to eat but forcing the calories and nutrients anyway. When he swallowed, it was intentional, like he was beginning the second set of a weightlifting session. "Went by her house one afternoon. Found her dead in the garden out back. A heart attack. Just sat next to her and cried."

I debated whether to call a halt to reliving memories as Joe tensed his jaw and clenched his eyes shut. Too late.

Joe's eyes were clear when they opened, and his voice was strong. "I knew the authorities needed to be called, and there weren't any relatives nearby. So I called the cops and filled out paperwork, then phoned her sister in Milwaukee. She couldn't get to L.A. until the next day." Joe shrugged. "After the coroner left, I looked inside Mary's house."

"Kinda creepy."

"I guess," Joe allowed. He touched an index finger to his lip and slid it back and forth while he momentarily watched high white clouds drift overhead. "You know she packed everything and left me while I was still in Vietnam. Didn't have a chance to claim much, so yeah, I wanted to see our pictures. I wanted to take memories that I thought rightfully belonged with me, but God, what a night. I spent five hours thumbing through pictures and scrapbooks, looking at school programs, rereading birthday cards." Joe focused back on me and smiled. "I cried a bit that night, too."

"So you kept the pictures and stuff?"

Joe shook his head and bit the apple again. "Decided they weren't really mine," he said while chewing. "Mary's sister and Jack needed to see them, needed to decide where they belonged. But I kept two pictures. One is of Mary and me on our wedding day, feeding each other cake. I can look at that picture and know she was the best thing that ever happened to me. She was beautiful."

I couldn't help but smile. Joe's recollections, his description of his wife, were so pure and innocent, like a romantic movie that's way too mushy but you like it anyway. I suppose he could have been blocking out the harsh words, the tough times, but that didn't fit his character. I got the feeling that the not-so-pure-and-innocent moments had been factored in, too.

"And the other picture?" I asked.

Joe tossed his mostly uneaten apple into the trees for some lucky creature to finish, and wiped a hand on his jeans. "It's a picture of Jack on my shoulders. He was five or six. Went to a Dodgers game. They were playing the Cubs." Joe stared through me, then he squinted and smiled. "He had a glove on one hand and a pennant in the other. I had him by the ankles."

"And you found out about Jack, that he was in Denver, from what you found at Mary's house?" I felt like I was interrogating my friend, and I was waiting for him to say "enough." But sometimes, even when I knew to be patient, to be sensitive and just listen—sometimes I just charged ahead anyway and hoped I didn't damage too much along the way.

Joe nodded, seemingly comfortable answering questions. "It was all there. Address, phone numbers, pictures of his wedding and of the kids, my grandchildren. He changed his name to Jack Torrance. He's a partner in the law firm of Sullivan & Wright. A tax attorney, of all things. Lives in Cherry Creek, and yes, that's why I moved to Boulder. I had no ties to California when Mary died, and I was ready to retire again. Wanted to go to college, so I figured Boulder was a good fit. Hoped I could reconcile with Jack, make up for lost time."

"Tell me you pounded on his front door. Tell me you talked to him." I arched my eyebrows and held my hands out, palms up. With everything I'd been told, with all I knew about Joe being direct and saying what was on his mind—that had happened, right?

Joe gave me one of my own "yeah-right" looks and said, "I wasn't quite *that* aggressive. Didn't want to make a scene or cause problems for his family. Still, a face-to-face seemed the best choice, so I showed up at his office one morning about six months after I'd settled in. Gave my name when I asked to see him. Didn't know quite what to expect."

"And?"

"His secretary came out, at least I assume it was his secretary, and ushered me into a conference room. Guess they didn't want anyone else to hear. Anyway, she said that Mr. Torrance did not ever want to talk to me and that if I didn't leave the premises immediately, they would call the police. I felt bad for her. She had a job to do, but I could tell she didn't feel right about it."

"After all that time—what was it, like, twenty years—and he wouldn't talk to you?"

Joe shrugged again.

"And you just left? You didn't call his bluff? I'm not buying it. Move a thousand miles so you can live close to your son and his family, and then never see him?"

Joe looked at me with sad resignation. "I'd said some pretty awful things to Jack. Calling him a coward, telling him I would never again claim him as my son. Guess he has reasons to carry a grudge."

"But—"

"So I left a note. Said I'd found his address in his mother's things, that I had respected Mary's sister's request not to be present at the funeral so he could attend. Told him I still had the apology he sent back, and that it said things I thought he should know. Wrote down my address and phone number. Said it didn't matter when or where, that I just wanted to talk to him."

I saw Joe's eyes droop, and he looked weary. There was no reason to ask whether Jack had responded.

twenty-three

I guess I should have been nicer to Winnie. The guy took a couple of hours on his day off and drove fifty miles to pick us up, and all he got out of the deal, at least from me, was a half-hearted thanks. Joe was more gracious. He invited Winnie into his apartment for a soda and a piece of pie (of course there was *more* German chocolate crème), but I nixed that idea. Said I was really tired and needed to get home.

Our drive from Joe's apartment to Louisville was torture. Winnie wanted to know why I was so tired, why he couldn't see Joe's paintings, and why we didn't even stop at McDonald's. I just stared straight ahead while he rambled, trying to ignore an enthusiasm that I just couldn't handle. When Winnie finally got it, when he finally shut up, I slumped down in the seat, closed my eyes, and tried to ignore that I was being an asshole. I apologized when he pulled into my driveway; said I'd call and tell him what had happened, and that I just couldn't talk right then.

Mom was a different story. I put up with fifteen minutes of questions that I answered with more than "yes" and "no." I told her I'd taken quite a few pictures, and even mentioned that Joe and I had some pretty serious talks. She watched me carefully, like I was some strange creature inhabiting her son's body.

Maybe she was shocked that she and I had managed to have a normal conversation.

I didn't bother taking my dirty clothes to the laundry room or raiding the refrigerator. I just turned on the shower in my bathroom, stripped, and climbed in. I was in there awhile, maybe twenty or thirty minutes, and didn't accomplish anything like washing my hair or scrubbing away dirt. Well, that's not entirely true; a steady stream of water managed to rinse off most of the grime.

I sat facing the faucets, letting the water pelt my chest or my face or my shoulders, depending on how I leaned. Mostly it relaxed me, like warm hands rubbing the tension from my body, but my solace was brief and the comfort was temporary. Every few minutes another round of despair began.

I cried and couldn't seem to stop. I tried choking back the tears, thinking I needed to get a grip, and that I could somehow conquer tattered emotions and erase the pain. That didn't happen. Too many images refused to cooperate.

I thought about being alone again, about losing the only person I'd ever completely connected with. I imagined how I would react to the gruesome proof that cancer was claiming Joe's life, to seeing skin marred by bruises and shriveled from weight loss. And I remembered a face, Joe's face, that couldn't repress a thirty-year pain that begged to be heard, to be forgiven.

It wasn't like I was sobbing or bawling like a little kid ... well, maybe I was.

I kept trying to talk to God, wanting to believe all this could be cleared up, hoping that he'd somehow made a mistake. I dusted off prayers from Sunday school and folded my fingers together in submission, I crossed myself, bowed my head, and closed my eyes. But the rituals didn't fit; they were distracting, artificial, and I just didn't think God believed me when I used them. Something told me he wasn't big on hedging bets.

So I decided to just have it out with him: to say what was on my mind, talk instead of recite. It was hard. Asking questions, justifying feelings, explaining motives—my words weren't perfect and they were disjointed, and I'm pretty sure I didn't make a logical argument. But I told myself it was okay to struggle, that genuine emotions mattered.

I didn't hear a booming voice or see a burning bush. Instead, the steam continued gathering and the only noise I heard was water thumping me and the ceramic tub while the drain tried to keep up. But maybe there had been answers. Lots of ideas drifted in and out of my conversation with God that afternoon. Maybe I even felt better. It seemed the bitter anger and sorrow that always precede a good cry were replaced by a sense of renewal.

I'D THOUGHT ABOUT NOT GOING to Boulder the next day, about taking some time off and escaping into a temporary refuge of video games or a mind-numbing session of television, but then I realized diversions wouldn't work. I would have still been wrestling with questions, still trying to map out some sort of plan. Besides, wasting time, doing nothing to avoid doing something? I was like a kid the day after Halloween—a little queasy with taking another bite.

So instead of moping around my house, I was at Joe's apartment. It had been less than twenty-four hours since our backpacking trip, but he didn't seem to mind that I came by unannounced. It was almost like he was expecting me.

"So I'm dying to know," I said, placing a mug of coffee on the kitchen table. I winced after I said the words, then shook my head. "Sorry, I need to be more careful. I didn't mean—"

"Hey," Joe said sharply, "I got one rule going forward. Don't treat me differently. You start acting like a first date ... well, just don't do it, okay?"

Joe wore a red shirt and blue gym shorts that looked like he should have been playing basketball on an inner-city playground. The outfit made him look smaller.

"Yeah, okay." I still felt awkward.

"So, what do you want to know?"

"If you slept. I mean, did you sleep more than two or three hours last night?"

Joe wriggled his eyebrows and smiled. He was freshly shaven and smelled of musk cologne. His eyes were lively, almost energetic. "Nine hours, baby! Not counting the stomach pain, I feel great."

"Yes!" I had my fingers crossed that it had been more than a one-night stand. I held out my hand and waited for Joe to join the high-five. His slap stung my hand.

"How about you, Quinn?"

"I'm okay," I said with a shrug, and reached for the coffee mug. I'd slept a little more than the previous night but had still tossed and turned. I hadn't even bothered trying to sleep in. Just got up and drove to Boulder.

"Talk to anyone?"

Joe had encouraged me to open up with Mom and Dad; said they would help me get through everything, and that he wouldn't be hiding his condition. Joe said I should use my own judgment about discussing his family issues, that it was still a private matter for him, but that I shouldn't hold anything in if it would help me deal with the situation.

"I talked with my mom last night, after I was home for awhile and had a chance to think about things. I told her about the cancer, but not about your family. She surprised the shit out of me. She actually listened, didn't try to tell me what to do, just let me talk. And just so you have a heads-up, she's going to call. She wants to know what she can do to help."

Joe nodded. "That'd be fine."

I could have been more complimentary about my mother's reaction. Besides giving her traffic controller's job a rest, Mom seemed to understand how I was feeling. She'd even talked a little about her parents, opened up more than anytime I could remember. And she'd hugged me when I got up to leave for my room. Mom hugged a lot (it was particularly annoying when she barely knew someone), but this was different. Both parties participated. It felt good.

"Okay to ask a few questions?"

"Go ahead," Joe said.

"Have you thought about why you're sleeping? I mean, it's kinda weird."

Joe traced his finger around the top of his coffee mug and pursed his lips. He took a few seconds, then said, "I've got some ideas. Don't know if I have definitive answers, but I've thought about it. Guess I always assumed not sleeping was a punishment, a kind of penitence for what I'd said and done, a distorted justice. Suppose I felt I deserved it." Joe tried but didn't quite manage his familiar smile. "Maybe I was taking the easy way out."

My eyes were glued to Joe. I knew not to talk.

"I thought the letter to Jack was enough. Good heavens, it took a week to write the damned thing. I admitted mistakes and accepted responsibility. I wrote about the pain and the loneliness. Said I was truly sorry. And coming face to face with everything was a big deal, a kind of catharsis. I moved forward, changed my life." When Joe shifted in his chair and crossed his legs, there was a hint of pain that he tried to ignore. "But Jack didn't read the letter. Nobody knew what I'd written."

"You told me about the letter and what you wrote."

"Bingo! That's the one change after all these years, wouldn't you say?" Joe laid his hand on my arm. His touch was light. "I never felt compelled to talk about what happened after writing that letter. Figured it was nobody else's business. Figured the apology was between Jack and me."

And now we were getting to the part that confused me, the other reason I'd asked how Joe slept. He thought I'd made a difference, except I didn't know why. Hearing Joe say that no one had heard or read his apology, that telling me his secrets had somehow released him? It was unsettling, an uncomfortable role.

"But I can't forgive you," I said. "I mean I would—you're sorry and all that—but you didn't do anything to me. I can say I forgive you, but you didn't do anything to me."

"You don't have to forgive me."

"Then why does telling me everything make a difference?"

Joe patted my arm. "Because I'm not hiding behind the letter anymore."

twenty-four

My life had been turned upside down, inside out, and then . . . I was actually sitting in the stands cheering on Monarch High's football team.

Go Coyotes! Unbelievable.

The last Monarch football game I'd attended was three years earlier. I was a freshman, still locked in the mold of being a good citizen and wanting to take part in student activities. *And* I had a serious crush on a cheerleader named Janelle Jenkins, a junior with the bluest eyes and whitest teeth I'd ever seen, whose every kick, cartwheel, and flip aroused more than a desire to cheer the football team. I had naïvely believed that if I yelled and screamed and hollered, if I let her lead me in school spirit . . . well, the fantasy went on, but I won't.

The truth is, I was teased about clapping my hands in unison with the pep squad and for actually singing the school song, and I'd gotten shoved back and forth by a couple of upper-classmen who decided to teach me a lesson about the Monarch High caste system. So I'd given up Janelle's bright eyes and shiny smile for reasons of personal safety, and hadn't attended a Monarch football game since. Hell, I didn't even *like* football.

But there I was, a senior who knew the ropes and didn't

remember the words to the school song. I clapped a few times, cheered Winnie on, and thought about screaming a few choice words at Timmy Spahn. Something along the lines of "Go jump into a snowdrift" or "Seen Greenberg lately?" But even with relative anonymity, I wasn't that brave.

Joe was in the stands with me; in fact, he's the reason I was faking enthusiasm and pretending to know intricacies of the game. He'd wanted to see Winnie play, and I had agreed to take him to a game. I guess it wasn't all *that* bad; there was a pleasant crispness to the air and Joe seemed to be enjoying the festivities. Still, I was a senior, supposedly at the top of the food chain, yet I was tentative with the surroundings, still unsure, and it bothered me that I even cared.

"That quarterback you like so much owes Winnie big time. Saved his butt the last two plays. No way he gets those passes off without Winnie," Joe said.

He had on the same cowboy boots, but wore new jeans and a new sweatshirt, part of the collection he'd bought at the Flat Iron Crossing Mall a few days earlier. Joe had lost more weight during the previous seven weeks and his old clothes, with bunched up waistlines and draping shirts, were just too big. It was hard for Joe to look in the mirror while we shopped, seeing an image that he wasn't used to, knowing the new clothes would be worn but a few months, or maybe weeks. At least the Cubbies cap, a familiar trademark those days, was pulled firmly on his head.

"And he doesn't even *like* the guy."

I had a tantalizing notion: Monarch up by a bunch and Winnie just happened to let a defensive end get a free shot at Timmy. Wishful thinking, but Winnie might have done that.

Go Coyotes!

I'd ended up calling Winnie two days after our backpacking trip and explaining the situation, at least the part about Joe dying from cancer (I still hadn't shared anything about Joe's family with anyone), and he'd tagged along to Joe's apartment a couple of times. Joe *did* like football, and seemed to get a kick out of listening to such a good-natured guy wrapped in such a massive body. And Winnie? Well, Winnie had a lot more on the ball than I ever imagined. He listened when Joe talked, made several intuitive observations about the paintings, and he peppered Joe with questions about the university. He even asked Joe how to fix a leaky faucet so he could do the job instead of having his mom call a plumber. Winnie was definitely on the good guy list.

The noise in the stadium grew and everyone around us stood, cheering and screaming. We stood, too, and saw two Monarch players streaking toward the opposing team's end zone. Timmy Spahn had the ball with Winnie leading the way, and both were going full speed at a single remaining defender. That defender must not have been too bright, or maybe it was brain-freeze. Either way, he just stood there, not moving an inch, while everyone in the stands hungrily anticipated the collision ten yards before it happened. Winnie delivered, absolutely flattened the guy, while the little shit-head quarterback with wavy blond hair scampered untouched into the end zone.

"You know what?" Joe yelled over the celebrating.

"What?"

"I'm *really* glad I picked you, and not Winnie, that day at Hideaway Lake." Joe nudged me with his shoulder and smiled. "Damn, that kid's like a freight train going eighty miles an hour."

JOE'S APARTMENT HAD CHANGED SOME. He was spending most of his time in the living room and, considering my room at home, I couldn't call it a mess. But for Joe? Let's just say it was comfortable. It was cluttered with pillows and blankets, and there always seemed to be a half-full glass of juice within easy reach. The coffee table in front of the couch served as a gathering place for two or three books (usually the latest bestsellers), reading glasses, a box of Kleenex, and a notepad with a pen clipped to its wiry spiral. When I'd asked about the notepad, Joe barked, "It's a to-do list." I never asked about it again.

The office went the other way; it was neater. Except for the computer, the desktop was bare, there were no loose papers or textbooks with protruding yellow stickies, and the bookshelves seemed organized. Joe wasn't spending much time there, but I used it almost every night to do homework.

Joe's bedroom was no longer a barracks. He bought a new mattress, one of those pillow-tops, and covered it with a navy and gray striped bedspread. He kept the blinds open during the day and had me hang several paintings and a few of my photographs. It wasn't a gallery, and I never did figure out the decorating scheme, but it was a whole lot better than before. Moreover, Joe was still sleeping—eight or nine hours every night in the bedroom and several daytime naps on the couch.

"Pretty good game," he said, fiddling with a slice of apple pie.

We were at the kitchen table, our usual spot just before Joe turned in, rehashing the day's events.

"It *was* a good game." I was glad Winnie had played so well with Joe watching. The Monarch Coyotes spanked the team from Lafayette 35-0, and I couldn't have cared less. But I didn't let Joe know my feelings. He'd had a great time, so that meant I did, too.

"Think he'll go to Boulder?"

"Maybe." I shrugged and sipped from a can of soda. "Depends on the scholarship offers. He still has another year, and he told me there are two or three college scouts at every game now. With another year left, I'm thinking he gets bigger and stronger and better, and that he can pick almost any school he wants."

Joe nodded and gently chewed. I suspected he'd manage two or three bites and a small glass of grape juice before calling it a night. His eyelids looked heavy, and the color in his face, invigorated by a few of hours of autumn air, had returned to a too-familiar shade of yellow. Joe had given me the physiological reason (the cancer had blocked the drainage of bile from his liver), but I really wasn't into the particulars of the disease. I just knew he looked sick.

"Anything going on tomorrow?" I asked.

Joe paused with a vacant look, then shook his head. He wanted to suggest a hike, or maybe a trip to Hideaway Lake, but he knew the physical strain would be too great. It had taken almost forty minutes for us to get from my Explorer to our seats in the stadium that night, and the outing had drained his energy for the next several days.

"The application from Northwestern came today. They want an essay. I get to choose from four topics and then write five hundred words. Wanna help?"

Attending Northwestern University was not a likely event; they're highly selective and don't advertise any sympathetic bent toward underachieving head cases. But its undergraduate journalism school is topnotch and that was an area that interested me. Nicki said she knew a professor in the department who was coordinating outside photography classes in downtown Chicago for Northwestern students. Supposedly, the professor was interested in establishing a photojournalism curriculum, and Nicki was going to write a letter of recommendation for me. I knew there wasn't much chance, but what the hell? Backup applications to Colorado State and the University of Northern Colorado were in the works, and they *had* to accept me.

Joe was alert again, back in the conversation. "Do they interview in Denver?"

"Next month. I can sign up, but the application is supposed to be done and sent in beforehand." I wasn't looking forward to any college interviews. Sitting across from the designated alumnus, smiling and nodding, asking only the right questions, reciting a perfectly practiced spiel that said, "Pick me! Pick me!" Right, I'd do *real* well.

"Nicki told me she thinks it would be a good fit, but she didn't know if you'd risk being rejected. Glad to hear you're applying." Joe eyed my muted reaction, then added, "I checked their website. Your SAT scores are good enough, Quinn."

Good SAT scores and a couple of F's still equaled "no fucking way," so I was ready to change the rejection topic.

"How about the essay? You up for a little creative writing session tomorrow?"

And I meant creative. Explaining plagiarism and attitudes and a lack of community service was going to be a tricky proposition, but none of that mattered to me. I knew I wouldn't be accepted; hell, I wouldn't make the first cut. But writing the essay wouldn't be a waste of time. It kept Joe involved. It kept him in the game.

MY FEET WERE PROPPED ON JOE'S DESK, and I occasionally swiveled the chair while I tested the absurdity of questions that couldn't be answered. Stuff like "Could God create a rock so heavy, even he couldn't lift it?" or "Is it ever completely quiet, like there's no sound whatsoever?" I didn't have a clue about the rock, but it seemed to me that quiet was a relative, and not an absolute term. Even deaf people have thoughts, and that inner voice, the one we all have, the one that's always talking, it precludes absolute silence. I wondered if you achieved absolute silence when you died.

I'd been playing those little mind games since Joe went to bed an hour earlier. They weren't satisfying but I guess they were okay company. They distracted me from other questions that didn't have answers either.

It had been almost seven weeks since the backpacking trip, and other than Joe's health, everything in my life was going well. School wasn't much of a challenge. I paid attention in class and did the homework ... period. It had become a habit and, to use the cliché, habits are hard to break. It was the point in my life when I figured out you can have *good* habits. And I was snapping pictures all the time: school, trips to the mall, even around the house. It was like I'd developed some kind of third eye that saw everyday life a little differently, or maybe it was just a bit twisted. Anyway, I was only shooting black and white. My third eye seemed to appreciate varying shades of gray.

My situation at home was fine, too. Of course that began when I'd first started going to Joe's apartment, but it's still worth mentioning. Mom, in particular, had really backed off, almost like she traded in the choke chain for a twenty-foot leash. I knew she worried how I was handling Joe's situation, and I think that had a lot to do with the way she treated me—not adding stress to my life, that sort of thing. She even brought home-baked pies to Joe's apartment, took him to lunch a couple of times, and got to know Joe pretty well.

They must have talked quite a bit because just a week earlier Mom had come into my room and told me how much she appreciated Joe's way, his wisdom, and then she tried to smile and hide her tears. When the words finally came, she apologized for throwing my camera bag that afternoon, and said she didn't have any excuses. When I told her it was okay, that I was sorry too, and that I appreciated what she was doing for Joe, Mom hugged me. In tears, she said she never wanted to lose me.

Oh yeah, losing Joe.

He wasn't doing well. The disease, the cancer, had progressed pretty much the way the doctors expected: headaches, loss of appetite, constipation, fatigue. Joe gutted through those first few weeks with nonprescription drugs, aspirin mostly, and experimented with relaxation techniques. He'd resisted taking stronger painkillers because he didn't want to feel out of it, afraid he would sleepwalk through his final days, but that eventually changed. The tumors had enlarged and multiplied, and they were constantly pressing against Joe's internal organs. The pain was constant, sometimes severe, so Joe began taking morphine tablets. They kept him comfortable, and a bit drowsy.

He was still getting around, but any activity longer than an hour exhausted him. Most of his outings related to the cancer: lab analysis of his blood, urine, and stools, CAT scans, weekly doctor appointments. I attended a few of those sessions and, surprise-surprise, he was everyone's friend. But the techs and nurses seemed both happy and sad to see him. I wondered if they saw the changes, the signs that caused me to take deep breaths to hide my concern. I envied how they seemed able to keep a manageable distance.

Joe and I had talked some about the quality of life issue, and he never regretted his decision to forego the chemo. There was an obvious pride that he hadn't yet needed assistance with transportation (he scheduled most of the medical appointments while I was in school), or help with his daily living activities. He still said that being incapacitated with chemo in exchange for an extra month or two made no sense; that being able to live life, no matter how long or short the time period, was what mattered. Every walk we took, every movie we watched, even the books he'd read while lying on the couch—Joe said they were gifts, and that he was grateful he could still enjoy them. I knew he included the Monarch football game, too.

I had wondered about his to-do list, that spiral notebook on the coffee table. He never talked about what he wrote and just left the damned thing unattended, almost like he was testing me, checking to see if I would honor his privacy. Well, I was interested, but not tempted. Not even a little bit. Besides, I had stumbled across something else more pressing. I found it wedged between two textbooks when I was doing my homework two nights earlier. I took it home that night and hid it underneath my dresser.

That was the other reason I was wasting time on unanswerable questions about heavy rocks and God and silence. They were keeping a tough decision at arm's length.

twenty-five

I remembered something from my sophomore year's physics class that had gotten me thinking. Newton's Third Law of Motion says that for every action there's an equal and opposite reaction. I always wondered whether Newton was Hindu, you know, the Karma thing, but I guess he was thinking in terms of an immediate effect; like bouncing a ball off the pavement or a car crashing into a brick wall. I don't know, maybe he did think longer term. Maybe he would have been able to tell me what was going to happen in a few hours or days. Maybe he would have warned me, told me that venturing a guess was too risky, that I hadn't accounted for all the variables to insure the desired outcome. His advice probably would have been simpler: Mind your own business.

But Sir Isaac Newton wasn't sitting in an Explorer on Ash Street in the Cherry Creek section of Denver. He wasn't glancing in the rearview mirror, halfway hoping a cop would pull up and tell him to scram, and he wasn't checking strained eyes that had yet to offer courage or inspiration. Nope, Newton wasn't parked in front of Jack Torrance's house. I was. I'd been there fifteen minutes and still hadn't decided whether pushing the doorbell, the button that would trigger an equal and opposite reaction I couldn't calculate, would make everything better or turn it to shit.

I'd faced off against the quandary before, replaying different scenarios in my mind. I had even mentioned the idea to Joe once, said enough time had passed that he should give it another try, or that if he didn't feel comfortable, I'd knock on Jack's door. Joe's reaction was immediate, his tone blunt. "No." Newton wouldn't have had much trouble gauging that reaction.

When I didn't back down and pushed harder, when I said that circumstances were different, that there wasn't enough time to keep playing a waiting game, that Jack deserved a chance to say goodbye—well, I didn't expect Joe's response. Instead of an unqualified and angry "Forget it," he closed his eyes and took a deep breath. And then he laughed, like he'd heard a surprise punch line, and said I'd come a long way in just a few months. He apologized for being so curt, said it was an example of his old behavior (and how Jack probably remembered him), then gave me his reasons.

Joe said he didn't want to use the illness as an excuse to see his son, and that barging into Jack's life would be selfish, that Jack already considered him dead. He said guilt was a weapon that would taint the reunion, a weapon he chose not to use. Joe didn't need to say much else; his eyes warned that the discussion was over. They reminded me that the tough guy, the never-ask-for-anything piece of Joe that intimidated and commanded respect, still lurked beneath the surface.

I understood what he said (those eyes made it hard to miss), but I'd also heard a softer than usual voice, and I saw a tired distance on his face. They nagged me with frustrating regularity until I let my mind wander. I could visualize Joe and Jack embracing, and I imagined their tears washing away years of bitterness and denial and regret. I saw Joe's smile, subtle and knowing, thanking me for bringing them together. I watched him being comforted in death by his family, his son's family. Those images were relentless.

Joe didn't need to hear Jack say "I forgive you," just "Hi, Dad."

I gripped the steering wheel and held in a breath. What if Jack slammed the door in my face? What if Joe found out and really got pissed? What if he never trusted me again?

Enough!

I clenched my eyes, blew out the air with all the what-ifs, and yanked the key from the ignition.

CHERRY CREEK IS OLD-MONEY DENVER where one-hundred-dred-year-old trees and thick hedges dictate pace and noise, and guard privacy. It's where brigades of Latino women ride buses to cook and clean and care for children between eight a.m. and five p.m.; it's where sixteenth birthdays are celebrated with gigantic bows wrapped around shiny new cars; it's where Junior Leaguers sip tea and write checks; it's where carloads of kids are dropped on Halloween night and picked up hours later; it's where Christmas decorations are hung by professionals and then judged. Cherry Creek is where the rich live who want to be close to downtown Denver.

Describing homes in the neighborhood is easier if you think in terms of three categories: teardown, new, and established. Teardowns, the real estate term for buying a house and then bulldozing it just to own the land, were becoming scarce. The choice lots had already been transformed, but a few sites still pockmarked Cherry Creek with clusters of pickup trucks and chainlink fences wrapped around new building materials. I suppose it was a double-edged sword for the neighbors; endure the mess and commotion, and a new, upscale home eventually appeared.

New houses jumped prices for everyone in the neighborhood. They were the largest and showiest. They incorporated the finest elements of architecture and art and design while flaunting imported marbles, exotic woods and crystal chandeliers. Like actresses wearing designer gowns to the Academy Awards, they were prestigiously not subtle.

The established houses were either too big or too expensive or too historical to tear down. Most were built in the 1920s and '30s, had been unobtrusively remodeled, and remained confident behind the years of knowing money. They were comfortably formal. They were elegant but discreet. They were the community adhesive that kept the new houses coming.

Jack lived in a new house which sat high and proud, and pushed deep from the street. Nestled between towering pines that had survived construction, it was a two-story red brick colonial with white pillars strategically (if not aesthetically) placed, and symmetric windows framed by white shutters. It was orderly, boastfully precise. I studied the fourteen-foot-tall front door while catching my breath from climbing three layers of steps, and decided that the fancy brass and intricate patterns of leaded glass were a fitting entry into a mansion.

Someone was home. I heard music blaring and a voice screaming for the volume to be turned down. I paused as I reached for the doorbell, trying to make out the song. I was pretty sure it was something by Saves the Day, but the constant thud of a pounding bass could have been disguising any one of several rock bands. Before I could start tapping my foot and bobbing my head, I saw a figure walk through the foyer and I figured it would be best if they didn't spot someone lingering on the front porch. I pressed the doorbell and muttered, "Please, God," under my breath.

I was tense, I was rigid, and I was ready. I wasn't going to back down from Jack Torrance.

"Yeah?" A girl about my age, dressed in a pale blue T-shirt and gray sweatpants, kept one hand on the doorknob and sized me up. Her long brown hair was tied high on her head in a ponytail, she was five-six, maybe five-seven, slender, and well developed. I didn't think I had raging hormones, but the T-shirt was tight, and I battled to focus on more mundane features. So, instead of meeting Jack Torrance with all the bravado I could muster, I was shifting weight from foot to foot, holding air in my chest to make it look bigger, and finger-brushing the hair out of my eyes.

"Uh, hi." *Real smooth there, Quinn.* "Uh, is this where Jack Torrance lives? I mean, I'm looking for Jack Torrance, and, well . . . "

She opened the door wider and motioned me into the foyer, then tilted her head back and yelled, "Dad, someone to see you."

There was an amused look when she faced me again, like she expected my clumsiness, like I was just another guy taken with her looks. She didn't speak. That would have made her too nice, almost perfect. She waited, knowing she was hot, and knowing I knew she was hot.

I was right, it was Saves the Day; one of their songs about dying that my mom went ballistic over. It was loud and coming from somewhere upstairs. Then it hit me that I was gawking at Joe's granddaughter. Who was this? Patricia? It had to be Patricia. Joe said she would be sixteen.

Now it was my turn to be smug. I knew who she was (well, kind of), but I was still mysterious, a stranger there to see her father. Maybe she thought I was a young attorney from his firm. Hey, maybe I needed legal advice about some pressing tax issue that couldn't wait until Monday. Sure, I could be rich and demanding, insisting that my attorney be available 24/7. That would have been impressive. Then reality tapped me on the shoulder and said, "She probably thinks you're the guy who mows the yard, fool."

My imagination was interrupted by approaching footsteps padding across the marbled foyer floor.

"Yes?"

I pulled my eyes from Patricia and faced a barefooted man dressed in khaki shorts and a long-sleeved white shirt folded back at the cuffs. I was startled by the resemblance to Joe. Jack Torrance was taller than his father, I guessed by three or four inches, and had a similar build: broad shoulders and a barrel chest, and heavy forearms with well-defined muscles. His hair, mostly gray with flecks of black, was rebelliously long for a middle-aged man and was combed straight back. It wasn't wrapped with a rubber band in the back, but it could have been. His eyes, dark and focused, could have become friendly.

"Mr. Torrance," I said, remembering one of my lines, "my name is Quinn Marshall. I apologize for interrupting your Sunday afternoon, and that I just came by unannounced, but I really need to talk to you."

Not bad. At least I hadn't tripped or anything.

"What do you want to see me about, Quinn?"

Jack didn't forgive the intrusion but his tone wasn't annoyed either. His wait-and-see attitude was carefully polite, though I suspected he would have been less tolerant if Patricia wasn't listening.

"It's a personal matter, sir. Could I please have just a minute of your time in private?" From the corner of my eye, I saw Patricia wrinkle a frown and I heard a faint grumble, but my attention, my energy, were focused on Jack Torrance.

Jack paused and pursed his lips with an irritated impatience. Probably thought I was selling magazine subscriptions or something. Or maybe he was waiting for me to ask if he believed in God before I launched into a "You can be saved" speech.

"Just tell me what you want," he said.

I glanced at Patricia, and then back to Jack and said, "I really think we should talk in private, Mr. Torrance."

"Say what's on your mind or leave." Focused eyes had become fierce.

I swallowed and took a deep breath. I knew what to say. I was prepared. It was the line I'd practiced over and over, and I had known there was a chance I'd be forced to say it in front of an audience. "It's about Joe Toscano." I locked my eyes to Jack's.

Jack must have been one hell of a poker player; his expression was frozen without a flinch. There was no look of surprise or shock, not even a chilling glare. He just turned to his daughter and said, "You'll have to excuse us, Trisha. Please go and turn your music down like I asked."

Trisha tightened her eyes on me while she wondered how I'd managed to survive this long with her father. Or maybe I *had* become mysterious. And I thought, for a moment, she wanted to know about Joe Toscano. Instead, she casually shrugged like she had better things to do, and that I shouldn't even think she was concerned with parental compliance. Her silent version of "whatever" was impressive as she turned and started up the stairs, her ponytail knowing just how to bounce.

Jack watched her climb the winding staircase and waited until we heard a door shut before redirecting his attention to me. His face was still expressionless but colder, his body stiff. "I don't know a Joe Toscano," he said flatly, "and I think you need to leave now."

He started toward the front door but he wasn't committed. I figured he was testing, waiting to see whether I'd give in.

My confidence inched higher so I stood in the middle of the foyer, waiting and watching for Jack's reaction when he realized I hadn't followed him to the door. I was breathing normally again but my heart was pounding against my chest. I tried to control my emotions by focusing on Joe.

Jack twisted the knob and pulled the heavy door open. His jaw tightened and his eyes narrowed when he saw that I hadn't moved. That's when I realized I was wrong, that he wasn't testing my commitment or playing mind games. He flat out didn't want me to say another word.

"You need to leave now." His tone was low and harsh, a final warning.

"Joe Toscano is your father, and it's very important that I talk to you." There they were, the magic words that certified my right to be there. I'd just blurted them out, but at least he now knew I was serious, that I had something important to say.

Jack's eyes blazed back at me. They said "Fuck you." He said, "Leave."

I panicked. I'd driven to Denver, sweated bullets outside Jack's house, and he was tossing me? Without a peep? How could I tell him about Joe's condition, that his father was dying, if he threw me out? Then I remembered the quizzical look on his daughter's face when I'd said Joe's name, and decided to take a long shot.

"I wonder what Trisha is going to say when she finds out she has a grandfather who lives twenty miles away?" I stood straight, staring through Jack. I wasn't bluffing.

I watched Jack's nostrils flare and could feel his anger surge. Threatening him in his own house? Bringing his daughter into the mix? I guess I would have been pretty pissed off, too. Jack's eyes narrowed as he calculated the odds with a reluctant deliberation.

"You've got five minutes," he finally said.

twenty-six

I always thought you could tell a lot about a man from the private space where he sorts things out. My piles and messes warned of an unruly teenager, one who resisted structure and authority, yet was prepared to accept change. It's why I used thumbtacks for pictures and posters. My dad's space was predictable, too; secure and quiet, a retreat wrapped in hobbies where he could bottle up in privacy or just get comfortable with a good book.

Jack Torrance's library was like a bout with schizophrenia.

Mostly it was an overdose of refinement with lots of leather and dark wood, and row after row of thick volumes that seemed color-coordinated and unread. I guess it was impressive; everything cost a ton of money, right down to the oil paintings and Waterford crystal, but it was cold, stuffy and vain. Pretty much what you'd expect from an attorney who lived in Cherry Creek.

Then there was his desk and the credenza behind it. They were out of the way, almost disconnected from the rest of the room as if a compromise had been reached, like there was an invisible sign that read: The Decorator Stopped Here. It was nice furniture, all right, but the area was cluttered, it was lived in. Stacks of papers and files, two leftover Diet Coke cans, and the newest Clancy thriller were scattered across the desk in no apparent order. An opened laptop sat on the right edge and was plugged into a phone jack three feet away, threatening to trip anyone walking by. A golf club leaned in the corner against the credenza; it was a putter, and there were two golf balls in a glass on the floor next to it. Both the credenza and the wall behind it were covered with photographs, family pictures, all of them. None were professionally taken, they weren't framed in expensive metal or cleverly arranged, and they projected a different image, a warm spirit that defied the decorator's correctness across the room. Looking at the pictures, at Joe's family, connecting their names and faces, imagining memories, gave my mission hope.

Jack directed me to one of two wing-backed chairs in front of the desk and then sat in the other. Between us, a small oval table held a glossy picture book about Tuscany and a stack of fancy coasters. I doubted if I would be offered anything needing a coaster. Jack crossed his legs and calmly folded his hands in his lap while I sat straight up and gripped the armrests, wondering when the clock started.

Jack ignored the tension with measured words. He was back in control. "How do you know my father?"

"We met about seven months ago," I said, trying to keep my voice from faltering. As much as I hated to admit it, I was intimidated. "He helped me with school, helped me get some problems squared away, and we're friends. We do stuff together."

Jack nodded. "Is he still in Boulder?"

"Yeah, same apartment." He remembered Boulder and that relaxed me a bit. At least he knew some of the story. Maybe he'd want more.

Jack paused and brushed an invisible piece of lint from the front of his shirt. He could have just as easily slapped a gavel against the desk and called the meeting to order. It was show time. His eyes met mine again. They were experienced, slowly and expertly reading my face. They warned that I was too young to be pitted against such an adversary.

"I closed the door to my study for a reason. This is a private conversation and I expect it to remain private. What's discussed, what you came to say, doesn't leave this room. I want your word."

"Okay."

Jack nodded. "Then tell me what's so important, Quinn."

I'd decided over a week ago that if I ever pulled it off, if I got in front of Jack Torrance, I wouldn't pussyfoot around. He didn't need to hear how his father had changed or how thirty years was too long to carry a grudge. Spilling my guts about university classes and paintings and Joe being my best friend, no matter how tempting and important, had to wait until Jack cared.

"Joe ... your dad ... has stage IV pancreatic cancer. He's dying."

Jack's lips moved slightly but he didn't speak.

"He's not taking any treatments, just drugs to control the pain. He's almost completely bedridden." I had hoped my description would tell Jack that his father had only a few weeks to live because I knew I couldn't say the words.

"I see."

Jack moved a hand to his mouth and pressed the fingers together, tapping them lightly against his lips. I couldn't tell whether I'd shocked him or if he was just considering options, thinking what to say or do next.

His eyes weren't as harsh when he looked back at me, but his voice was strangely confident. "And you're the messenger?"

"What?" I guess I'd expected a different question. Maybe something that said the information hadn't been so coldly processed.

"You said he's your friend. Did he send you?"

My words were heated. They came fast. "No! Joe doesn't know I'm here. He doesn't want you to feel sorry for him or see him just because he's dying. It's not like that!" Okay, so I'd blinked first. Fuck it. "Look Mr. Torrance, there's a lot you don't know about your father, unbelievable stuff, and you need to find out about it before it's too late. Your father's dying. Joe's going to die in a few weeks!"

Jack eyed me for the truth, yet was reluctant to challenge or interrogate me.

When he finally spoke, his tone was gentler. "I can see you care for him, and I appreciate how difficult this must be for you." He nodded his head with raised eyebrows, like he understood. "I'm sorry you're going to lose a friend, Quinn, really I am. But telling me my father's dying? He's been dead for thirty years."

"He's not dead, not yet!" I was on the verge of totally losing it. My hands were shaking, my brain was like a pinball machine on steroids, and my eyes wanted to fight back with tears. *My friend is not dead. He needs to see his son. Joe deserves better!*

"It's a complicated situation, Quinn. I know you don't understand, but there are reasons my father and I haven't spoken for all these years. It's not something I'll go into with you, but his death, his physical death, doesn't really change anything."

"I know everything!" I blurted.

"No, you don't." Jack's tone was patronizing.

"Yeah, I pretty much do."

Jack just sat there, so calm, so in control. That was about to change. I was pissed; my threatening tears and logical arguments had taken a back seat to rage.

"I know all about the Vietnam War and the draft, and that you ran away to Canada. I know Joe called you a coward and that you called him a murderer. I know lots of stuff. Like how you couldn't wait to get back into the United States with a pardon in hand, how you didn't have the decency to talk to Joe face to face at your office. You sent a secretary to do your dirty work. Am I leaving anything out?"

Jack was nicked. He wasn't changing color or anything, and he hadn't shifted in his chair, but there was a change. The wheels were definitely turning in a different direction.

I pressed forward. "So it's complicated, huh? How *complicated* is accepting an apology?"

"Is that what this is all about? He wants me to forgive him before he dies? Head off into the afterlife with a clear conscience? I suppose he's going to church, too."

I glared at Jack, not with anger, but with frustration. It didn't matter that I knew I was right, that Joe had changed and he wasn't anything close to what Jack remembered. But I couldn't ignore feelings or purge memories, I couldn't fast forward, and I couldn't go into the apology stuff. That wasn't why I was there.

"He changed, Mr. Torrance. He's different." My voice was barely above a whisper.

Jack wasn't angry, either. He was subdued. His body slid a bit in the chair, causing his shoulders to slump, and he stroked the bottom of his chin with the back of his hand. Weary eyes closed with a heavy breath. He wasn't jockeying for position or feeling me out; he was sorting.

I scanned the pictures surrounding Jack's private space and decided to change the emphasis. "Does your family know anything about Joe?"

"Abby knows everything. She knows he lives in Boulder." Jack slowly opened his eyes, then twisted his lips and shook his head. "The girls know that I protested the war and went to Canada. We've had long talks about that decision and what staying true to your beliefs means, what it can cost. But they don't know about my father. Not the real story. They know their grandmother divorced him before they were even born."

"Joe told me that people have to completely trust my word," I said. "This conversation stays private. It's between you and me." I didn't know if saying that made a difference, but it felt right, like we'd been running in place and had finally reached the starting point.

"Thanks," Jack said, then looked away from me.

"Don't you ever think about him? Wonder how he's doing?"

"Not really. I just want to forget." Jack stared forward and saw the past. "He's the meanest son-of-a-bitch I've ever known. Selfish, domineering, controlling ... I said 'yes sir' so many times... there was a duty roster taped to our refrigerator ... everything had to be checked off every day. No exceptions, no excuses. Everything had to be perfect. I polished bathroom fixtures with a toothbrush, I used toothpicks to dig tiny weeds from the cracks in our driveway. I was six years old ... we lived in base housing, for God's sake.

"Nothing was ever good enough. He could always find something wrong. And if I complained or talked back, he'd spank me and then double the duty roster. Told my mom he was toughening me up, getting me ready to face the real world. She tried to make it better for me but she didn't know how to tell him to stop, to let me be a kid, that I wasn't some grunt in basic training.

"Yeah, she loved him. But she hated him ... she was afraid of him. She cooked and cleaned and obeyed all his orders. My mom ... we'd do things together when he wasn't around. We'd go to movies or get an ice cream cone, and we'd laugh and talk. Not about him. There was an unwritten rule ... we didn't complain or say how unhappy we were, but we talked ... about books or current events or gardening. My mom always had a garden ... a place to escape.

"Well, I toughened up all right ... football, wrestling, track ... anything so I wouldn't have to come home until dinnertime ... then I'd have homework ... got bigger and stronger. My father could still whoop me, but I stopped crying ... so he stopped.

"We barely spoke at dinner ... other than that, we managed to stay out of each other's way. I followed the rules when I was around, but I wasn't around much ... made damn sure of that. Thought it would get better when I went to college, but I couldn't afford to go away ... my father refused to pay for college ... called it a waste.

"So I went to the community college a few miles away and

lived at home, but didn't play his game anymore ... grew my hair... wore ratty T-shirts and bell-bottomed jeans with holes ... had a jacket with a big peace sign on the back. I demonstrated, did sit-ins ... didn't do too well in school. Flunked out.

"I skipped the third grade so I didn't turn eighteen until after I flunked out that first semester. Got my draft notice, but I'd already decided ... I wasn't going in the military, I wasn't going to be like my father. I guess he told you about that night ... I was in Canada two days later."

I was horrified and captivated by Jack's story. I saw the anguish and felt pricks of pain from his words, his memories, and I imagined what I would have done, how I would have reacted. I knew Joe's history—he hadn't covered up or withheld anything—but hearing specifics, seeing the past through middle-aged eyes. It made me pause. I touched the side of my face where a bruise once attested to my first meeting with Joe, and I remembered the intensity and the fear. But I also remembered Joe's expression while he stood over me, when I was sure I was toast. It had cried with regret and humiliation.

Jack faced me with probing eyes, but they weren't digging. They were careful, almost protective. "You look as though I've shocked you, Quinn."

"A little."

"Sorry," he said, "but now you know why I don't care, why it doesn't matter."

"Joe's changed. You have to believe me that Joe changed a long time ago. He's not sorry just because he's dying. He tried to tell you everything, how he felt ... about what he'd done. He tried a long time ago. Your mom, Mary, she saw the changes. You know she did, don't you?"

Jack nodded. "He never knew it, but she fell in love with him again. Yeah, she told me."

"Well?"

Jack slowly shook his head and sucked on his lower lip.

"Maybe he has changed, Quinn. It's hard for me to imagine, but even if I believe you, my feelings *haven't* changed. He'll always be the man I could never please and the father who never loved me." Jack breathed deeply and held his eyes to mine. "I hope you get through the next few weeks okay, I really do. But I don't want to see him or talk to him. And I don't want to hear from you again."

I could have played amateur psychologist with "You have to have closure," or kept pleading and citing all the reasons. I'd have tried it if I thought it would have worked. But even though I didn't agree with Jack, he'd listened, he'd given me a fair shake, and it was time to go. The manila envelope in my lap dropped to the floor when I stood to leave, and as I bent over to pick it up, in that instant I found my voice.

"Mr. Torrance, we all do things that can't be changed or undone. We all have a past, and we make mistakes. Some of them ... well, they're pretty big." My best-effort smile fell flat when I handed over the envelope. "Here's a letter you chose not to read before. You should read it now."

twenty-seven

Joe was losing his battle. The cancer that hid, staying undetected and seemingly immobile, was no longer shy about when or where it attacked. It had become the homerun hitter glaring at the pitcher while he trotted the bases, the wide receiver spiking a football in the end zone, and the boxer standing over an opponent lying prone on the canvas. Cancer was a horrible winner.

I had deluded myself that, even without treatment, Joe was going to beat this thing; that one of those "amazing story" TV shows would pony up big time for Joe's tale, his miracle. That was when I couldn't see the changes, when Joe looked normal. Thinking back, I was pretty naïve that first month.

Then I tried to ignore the physical changes: the loose skin marred by purplish bruises and poked by never-ending needles, the sunken eyes with lids that rose and fell in tandem with cycles of morphine tablets, the dry mouth with dingy teeth and cracked lips that quivered when Joe spoke. I tried to ignore them, but it was hard. Physical deterioration was sprinting an unforgiving final lap.

Except for school and sleep, I stayed in the apartment with Joe. Mom had been cool about that. She wanted me home by ten on school nights, but let me crash on Joe's couch on weekends.

She even brought by casseroles and soup every few days, and sat with Joe. They talked or watched TV, and then Mom would check the refrigerator for needed items and funny-colored leftovers. I'd been uneasy with her visits at first, maybe even a little jealous, but she wasn't intrusive or pushy. And she didn't even ask about my homework or tests, like she knew I was trying hard with my classes, and that carrying forward the success of summer school had become a tribute of sorts. It was hard for me to admit that I appreciated what she was doing.

A dreaded companion arrived a few days after my talk with Jack; her name was Gwen. She was short and fat in an athletic way, and a bit too cheerful. She was a live-in nurse Joe hired in lieu of spending his last days in a hospital or hospice, and she slept in Joe's bedroom on that new pillow-top mattress. I didn't know what bugged Joe more: trading in the bed that had finally yielded sleep for a hospital version that took up most of the living room, or realizing he needed constant monitoring. Probably both.

Gwen was okay, I guess. She was busily efficient, laughed at Joe's jokes, and somehow knew to stay in the bedroom when I was around. Mostly, I liked that she was good with needles. It was rare when she didn't hit a vein on the first stick, and after a slew of hit-and-miss agency nurses who had haphazardly rotated schedules and patients and diseases, Gwen's precision was a welcome relief. She was expensive, seven hundred dollars a day that insurance didn't reimburse, which was initially a stumbling block.

Joe was leaving his estate to the University of Colorado, establishing a scholarship fund for art majors, and he didn't want to dilute the donation, saying the money could be better spent on people with lives still ahead of them. Even though Joe didn't want to be selfish, I think the idea of leaving the apartment, the books and pictures and paintings, was too much. After he finally made the choice, he told me there would still be money left to

fund the scholarship, but I knew that making the calculation, mul-
tiplying Gwen's rate by days and not months, was a raw reminder.

So my senior year wasn't about parties or lenient curfews, and
I didn't bother daydreaming much about freedom from my parents. Coasting down the home stretch wasn't happening; no
marathon television or computer sessions, no sleeping in until
my eyes refused to stay closed, no prowling the streets or
hanging out in search of the perfect female (or even a date).
Keeping up with school and spending free time with Joe had
become my priorities, and I was okay with that. It was my choice,
my decision.

"READY FOR TOMORROW?"

I looked up from my calculus problem and saw Joe smile while
he pushed himself higher against the back of the bed. It was a
Wednesday night, *West Wing* night, according to Joe, and he'd
been asleep for almost an hour.

"What's tomorrow?" I asked while glancing at the digital clock
on the table. Still twenty minutes until we turned on the TV to
hear President Bartlett and Toby and CJ crack the one-liners we
mere mortals thought of a day too late.

"There's no hope. What are you going to do when I'm gone?
Probably won't even know what day it is."

I laid my notebook and pencil on the foot of his bed and
wedged another pillow lengthwise behind his back. Joe had said
the extra pillow kept him from sliding while he watched TV even
though the front of the bed was raised at a steep angle. I tried
not to notice that Joe winced when I did this.

"God, has my mother been giving you lessons or what?" I
rested my hand on Joe's shoulder, letting him know I was done.

"Good woman, your mother. Don't know how she manages to

keep from getting a head full of gray hair chasing after you." Joe nodded, letting me know he was ready to lean back.

"It's called hair dye," I said, returning to my chair, and we both laughed.

"Your interview is tomorrow," Joe said in a muffled tone, like he didn't want to tell me what to do but was going to anyway.

"Yep. Nine-thirty."

Oh yeah, my appointment. The one that let me sleep in an extra hour and skip a half-day of school, the one in a conference room at Arapahoe High School, the one that squished me in between thirteen other hopefuls and dreamers, the one with Mr. Tom Rainey, Northwestern Class of '86 who scoured Colorado for the best and brightest. Yeah, I remembered that appointment.

"I've read that interviews count a lot, that these people sometimes get three or four free pass cards every year. It's like currency. If the interviewer recommends you, uses a free pass, it means the admissions office almost has to accept you." Joe wanted to go on, to tell me more about the process and what he knew, but there was an embarrassed pause. He knew he rambled. It was another reminder.

"Joe, I'm prepared. I'll do my best at the interview," I said, not backing away from hazy eyes that struggled to focus. "But this guy interviews a bunch of kids every year. Arapahoe is just one of his stops. Four passes with forty, maybe fifty applicants? Just don't be disappointed, okay?"

"I'm doing it again, aren't I?" Joe said.

His frown had become harder to distinguish, loose skin and all, but I saw it then. It was a puzzled, not angry look.

"Proud is the best word to describe my feelings, Quinn, not disappointed. I'm so proud of you. Hell, I'm acting like Northwestern's the only damn college in the country, and here I've been at the University of Colorado for twelve years. Think I was brainwashed growing up in Chicago?"

"It's okay." I smiled and lightly patted Joe's arm. Funny, but if

Mom or Dad had pushed Northwestern a year ago, if they'd connected the dots that led to a prestigious journalism school, I would have sabotaged the application at every turn. But now Northwestern seemed like a helluva place, and I found myself pushing the mute button on what-ifs quite a bit.

"How we doing for time?" Joe flicked his eyes at the television.

"Still got fifteen minutes."

"Good. I want to talk to you about something. That spiral notebook I kept on the coffee table—it's in the nightstand drawer. Will you get it for me?"

"Sure," I said, walking around the bed and pulling out the drawer. There it was, Joe's private journal, next to the Chapstick and Life Savers and Kleenex; hardly a fitting place of honor for the diary that had interrupted meals, closed books and ended conversations for the sake of an entry. I handed it to Joe, illogically proud I hadn't read a word.

"We haven't talked much about what happens after I die."

"No, we haven't," I said. *Now? And it's only going to take fifteen minutes?*

"I've already made arrangements with the funeral home. Riverside Mortuary. Everything's been paid. When the time comes, have someone call them. They have instructions."

"Okay."

"They're going to cremate my remains, and I want you to spread the ashes, Quinn. Somewhere in the mountains, somewhere you think is right. Take a long walk after I'm gone. You decide, okay?"

"Okay." I know I should have looked at Joe and held his gaze, but I couldn't.

"I don't want a memorial service."

"But—"

"They're a pain in the ass. Always thought they were a lot of trouble. People feel guilty if they can't come, cry when they *do* come. Not my style."

"But people ... your friends. They'll want to do something. How are they going to feel?"

"There are so many people I've known, so many friends. I thought about calling each of them, telling them I'm dying, and that I wanted to say goodbye. Didn't make sense. I'd be on the phone constantly, repeating everything over and over. So I thought about talking to just a few, the special friends, but that didn't sit right either."

"Okay, so a service would make sense."

"No memorial service." Joe grinned and tapped the spiral notebook. He shifted in the bed and tried to sit up straighter. "Memories," he said with livelier eyes. "These are my best memories, Quinn. I want you to distribute them."

"Sure, Joe, I can do that," I said too quickly.

"I'm not talking about just making copies of this and sending it to people," Joe warned. "Every page is a special recollection about someone, an experience, a moment we shared. I wrote down my favorite memory of them, how I want them to remember me. And you want to know something?"

"What?"

"When I wrote in this notebook, when I remembered the people in my life, it made me feel blessed, truly blessed. The people who shared my journey, so many wonderful experiences." Joe's watery eyes were content and his smile broadened. "Hard to feel sorry for myself when I remember how lucky I was."

I wondered what he'd written about me; whether there was more than one page, what our friendship had meant. I wanted to read it right then, before Joe died. I wanted to talk to him about *our* memories.

"I need a favor, Quinn. It won't be easy. In fact, it'll be damned hard."

I just nodded.

"There's an address book on the computer. After I die, I want you to mail my memories. You can stick in a preprinted card, say

I had cancer and the date and that there wasn't a service, but make sure to tell these people that they were special to me, that knowing them made a difference in my life. And then enclose the note I wrote for them."

An uncomfortable silence hung in the air, not because of Joe's request—of course I'd do it—but because I was sure the first person, the first page in Joe's notebook, would be Jack. I got stressed whenever I thought of that meeting and of my not telling Joe. I'd come close to admitting a worthy but failed cause, and I knew Joe would have chalked up my Pollyannaish attempt to immaturity, then let it go. That wasn't it. Being scolded for interfering hadn't kept me from coming clean. It was the pain that I knew would come from Joe learning his son had refused to see him.

"There are over forty entries. Think you can do it?"

"Yeah, sure," I said, coming back to the moment. In an instant I had decided I would read Joe's note to Jack and then determine whether Jack deserved to receive it. Mailing the rest? I was honored by the mission.

"The first page is to Gene Karatowski, a guy I knew in the Marines. He'll handle the legal paperwork for my estate. He knows what to do. Call him after I'm gone."

"Sure." It was all I could manage. I was hanging on, barely, and wanted this conversation to end. I'd been okay with the philosophical discussions we'd had about God and afterlife and all that, but the realities of death, combining decaying bodies and administrative details—it was overpowering.

Joe saw my vacant expression and slid the notebook toward me. "I'm done writing, Quinn. No regrets. I'm thankful for my seventy-five years."

I lifted the notebook and cradled it in my arms, silently vowing not to read any entries until after Joe passed. It was a bond I wouldn't break. Joe said no regrets. Okay, I'd honor that, too.

"Are you doing that funny math thing on me?" I said with a bit of sarcasm. "You're seventy-four."

Joe winked. "I think I can make another eight days. I'll be seventy-five next Thursday."

twenty-eight

It was three a.m. and I hadn't even attempted sleep. I was too busy juggling frustration and guilt. I wouldn't be well rested the next morning—okay, *that* morning—but so what? Who cared about clear eyes and engaging attitudes and insightful questions anyway? Like they would really make a difference, like a stupid interview would override everything else. My fuck-it attitude reemerged.

Unbelievable. My best friend, the guy I would have done anything for, the one I was spending every free moment with, the one who was dying; he would be having a birthday the following week, his *last* birthday. And I hadn't even had a clue.

The guilt landed pretty stiff jabs, but hey, I was a teenager. It was my job to be insensitive and self-centered, and then explain it away. But the frustration, my inability to come up with an appropriate celebration idea, or even a gift, a single gift? That was pounding away with relentless vigor. It became an exercise in futility, like running the hundred-yard dash with one of those X-ray vests strapped around my chest. Do I go ahead and run? Do I rip off the vest? Do I complain about an unfair race?

I floated a bunch of ideas. I even made a list of everything Joe liked and then brainstormed; wrote down everything that popped into my mind related to the list, made notes and scribbles, and then drew connecting lines, hoping some mystical picture would form, that an answer would be revealed. I should have unboxed the Ouija board instead. At least then I would have had an excuse.

What do you give someone who's dying, someone who might live another week, maybe two or three at the most? What can you buy that's meaningful or needed or wanted? Joe had to use it fast, and it couldn't have physical limitations, like hopping a plane to Chicago for a final visit (why hadn't we done that before?). And it couldn't be extravagant; he would have resented my spending too much money. A gift certificate to Marie Callender's? A book? How about a sweatshirt that fit better; I could order one from Northwestern. Or maybe another bottle of his favorite aftershave, a small bottle so not to waste any … a bottle of champagne to celebrate his life, except mixing alcohol with his regimen of drugs would have been a disaster … a bottle of milk to go with pie … a bottle of ink … a ship in a bottle … a bottle. See what I mean?

I wanted to give him something connected to his paintings; at least that way I'd have a shot at making it special. Canvas or paints or brushes were out, but maybe have some of his work framed? The paintings would have looked great, but if Joe had wanted them framed he would have done it a long time ago. Besides, I didn't know how I could get the paintings out of his apartment without his noticing, and then I didn't know which paintings to choose because I couldn't afford to frame them all. I thought about making a book of his paintings. I could use a digital camera and create a collection of his works, like in a scrapbook or stored on the computer. But why would he look at pictures of his paintings in a book or on a screen when he could see them in person?

I even thought about just giving him a card with some carefully crafted prose and calling it a day. He might have liked the no-frills approach, and he would have probably appreciated how hard it was to buy a gift for someone who's dying. Joe would have understood.

Right. Like I was really going to get just a card.

I kept coming back to a word I'd circled at least ten different times. Friendship. Somehow my gift to Joe had to be about our friendship. It had to show him what it had meant to me. He had to know that our friendship would live on and wouldn't waste away, that the laughter, the lessons, and the tears of our friendship would be remembered.

And then I knew.

Tapping my pencil against the desk had turned vigorous and I sat straight up. My breathing quickened and became louder while my mind raced through possibilities. It was something I'd give, not buy, and it would capture the essence of our friendship. It fit. I'd be giving Joe a part of me.

When would I do it? School hours were set, and I didn't want to sacrifice any time with Joe. But it was going to take time; if I did it right and didn't just slop through, it would take a lot of time, marathon sessions under normal circumstances.

Logic kept telling me there wasn't enough time, that I couldn't do it. But I knew I had to.

THIS WASN'T WORKING. SITTING ACROSS the conference table from Tom Rainey, wearing a 3-P smile (polite, passive, perfunctory), and compliantly nodding my head at words I pretended to hear. It was a colossal waste of time for both of us, but I had to give Rainey credit; he was pretty good at going through the motions.

We were ten minutes into my interview, the beauty contest I could have won but never should have entered, and we'd just about exhausted the niceties; the "Why would anyone leave the

Colorado Rockies" and "I can remember when Louisville had three thousand people" type stuff. But he'd read my file. He knew. And we were both ready for the real interview to begin.

Tom Rainey, Northwestern class of '86, an executive with a software company in Colorado Springs, the dispenser of go-to-the-front-of-the-line passes who needed to wear contact lenses and hit the gym before middle age got serious. That's who was strumming his fingers across my file, waiting for a reason, any reason, to dig deeper or just move on to the next candidate, a girl from Pueblo who was sitting in the reception area, wrapping too-short hair behind her ears every twenty seconds.

"I've read your file, Quinn, and it appears everything's here. Solid SAT's and a rousing letter of recommendation from Nicole Strandlund. And I like your essay. You're good with words."

"Thanks," I said, knowing a takeaway "but" was aimed right below my knees. I decided to preempt it. "I guess you don't get too many people with F's applying to Northwestern." My 3-P smile turned a bit aggressive.

Rainey tented his fingers and shrugged like the direct approach didn't faze him, like it was his preferred style. "Seven-forty math SAT and an F in Pre-Calc. Only fifteen students were selected for the honors course in Contemporary American History, but another F."

"I plagiarized a term paper," I said, pressing my lips and raising my eyebrows, confident I'd get a stronger reaction.

"So I see." Rainey opened my file and casually flipped the pages, like he was taking a final look, making sure he hadn't missed anything. His expression was noncommittal, his eyes steady. "So why *does* a student with F's apply to one of the most prestigious universities in the country, Quinn?" he said, looking back at me.

I took a deep breath and held it while staring at my file. I had a couple of measured answers ready; they played on sympathy, they were laced with excuses ... and they just didn't fit.

"Because I deserved those F's. The A's you see in Chemistry and Spanish were F's, too. I retook the classes in summer school."

Rainey narrowed his eyes on me. He was finally interested.

"I screwed off, I tried to get by, and I had a crappy attitude about pretty much everything. The proverbial teenage funk. So I'm applying to Northwestern because I *got* F's, because I know what it's like to make mistakes, because I learned about consequences, and because I saw how easy it was to get into trouble."

"I couldn't ask for a more candid answer."

"Like I said, I got A's in summer school, and I have A's in all my classes this semester." I thought of my talk with Joe and decided to throw in, "And maybe even more important, I know the material. I'm learning."

Tom Rainey took off his glasses and rubbed his eyes. When he replaced them, he seemed resolved and harder. "You should be commended, Quinn. Admitting mistakes and then squaring away priorities isn't easy for anyone, but especially for teenagers."

When he twitched his lips and swallowed, I knew what came next wouldn't be good news. "I have eighty kids from Colorado and Wyoming who have applied to Northwestern, just about every one of them has straight A's, and they have comparable SAT scores to yours. They're good kids, they played by the rules, they stayed focused and gave their best, day in and day out, all four years of high school. They didn't let life's bumps detour their goal."

How'd I know we'd end up here?

"And out of those eighty, maybe we accept ten. So, Quinn, with all due respect to your turnaround, how does Northwestern accept you? How do I explain to a student who did all the right things, who didn't take a year to goof off—how do I tell them that their spot at Northwestern was claimed by someone who earned F's and who plagiarized a paper?"

Rainey's expression wasn't severe; it was conciliatory. But it said "Game over."

"I think I'd be pretty pissed off if I was one of those kids," I said matter-of-factly. "Being that disciplined and determined? Yeah, I'd be pretty pissed off."

Rainey nodded his head in victory.

I said, "But do any of them blow it when they get away from their parents, when they're on their own?"

Rainey shrugged away the expected question. "History tells us that ten percent of the freshman class will not make it past the first year; maybe another twenty percent struggle with grades until they acclimate to the environment."

"And I've already been through that." My tone was hopeful, but borderline edgy.

Rainey allowed a point-well-taken look and said, "They played by the rules, so they get a chance, and hopefully they *don't* screw up. You already did."

I could only nod at my interviewer while my mind flashed back to regrets that came in small, crushing doses: remembering wasted hours lying on my bed listening to music, trashing my parents and anyone else who might have crossed me that day, assuming I was smarter than everyone else, being lazy when all I had to do was try. It was a seductive but unsatisfying game.

I stood and offered my hand. The interview? Not all that bad. I'd played it straight, didn't grovel or plead or make up some bullshit story, and I'd gotten a straightforward answer. Life goes on, right? But there was still an issue, something that I'd realized while I was making my case to Tom Rainey, and it seemed an appropriate remark to make.

"I don't know what you'd tell those other students you talked about," I said, "but I know what you could tell the admissions counselors at Northwestern."

Rainey had already opened the next file, the girl from Pueblo with uncooperative hair. "What's that?" he said, glancing at me.

"You could tell them that the world would be a pretty hopeless place if you never got a chance to fix a mistake. You could tell them I didn't give up."

twenty-nine

Laughter and sorrow don't seem like they should go together.

It was Thursday night in Joe's apartment, it was his seventy-fifth birthday, and everyone there knew Joe had little time left. They knew he was in constant pain, that the hourly intravenous infusion of Dilaudid was seven times stronger than the morphine tablets of just two weeks earlier, and that he could push an extra dose when the pain became too great. They knew he drifted in and out of consciousness, that lucid conversations became incoherent. They winced when Joe coughed, hoping a breath would follow. They stared at his disfiguration when they thought he wouldn't notice. And in between, they told funny stories and did some pretty silly things. The laughter in Joe's apartment was genuine and boisterous.

It wasn't a big party—besides Joe and Gwen, there were eight of us—but I have to admit, we were an enthusiastic bunch. I don't think Joe had expected such a get-together when he mentioned his birthday the previous week; actually I think he wanted a quiet evening alone with me and maybe a small cake with just a few candles, the ready-made grocery store type inscribed at the last minute. Maybe we would have talked and watched some television, nothing too excessive.

No, I hadn't planned this party.

Mom had gotten the ball rolling. I had to talk to her about my idea for Joe's present, and she'd decided then and there to bake a birthday cake. She asked if anyone else should know about Joe's birthday, who he'd feel comfortable having at his bedside. Like I said, I wasn't thinking in terms of a party, so I told her a cake would be appreciated, and just dropped it. Not Mom. She went to Joe's apartment with a fresh batch of chicken noodle soup the next day and flat-out asked him who he'd like to celebrate with. And Joe told her. So our band of merrymakers included me, Winnie, Mom and Dad, Nicki, Tony from an apartment upstairs, Julie from a used bookstore on Pearl Street, and Boyd Warthers, Joe's favorite art teacher.

Joe wore one of those cone-shaped party hats with the elastic string pinched under his chin. It was navy blue with red and white and gold stars, and looked absolutely ridiculous. He'd blow a noisemaker every once in awhile, drawing our attention. We saw a sick old man camouflaged by tubes and drip bags and monitors, taken hostage by a depressing hospital gown. But we also saw that hat and Joe's playful smile, and we couldn't help but laugh. Joe knew this, seemed to relish it, I think, so he tooted the horn whenever there was a lull in the action.

We'd already sung *Happy Birthday* and clapped when Joe blew out a single candle stuck in the middle of the cake. He must have been afraid of not having enough air because he blew hard enough that some spit landed next to the candle, and then pooled into a small blob. I thought Mom would be disgusted that her beautiful cake was ruined before anyone had a chance to eat it, but it didn't faze her. She clapped along with everyone else, then lifted the cake from the tray resting on Joe's lap and took it to the kitchen. I watched her, waiting to see if the party face would wash off once she was away from the group, but her demeanor didn't change. She simply dug out the tainted patch with a spatula, dumped it in the sink, and then cut pieces from the border and served them on plastic plates.

So we all had cake, everyone was helping themselves to soda or beer in the fridge, and there was an unofficial tour of Joe's art gallery. Professor Warthers seemed the most interested, and lingered with each piece a little longer than the rest of us. Maybe it was because we'd all seen the paintings before. Well, I assume Tony and Julie had seen them, but I would have guessed Joe's art teacher had, too. Maybe coming back to them was like rereading a book; taking a fresh perspective, discovering new details. Maybe it was how he wanted to remember Joe.

After Joe's paintings had been admired, the stories began: Joe browsing the shelves at Books Forever in search of bargains, Joe bringing a slice of peach pie to Tony to introduce himself and happening to mention the music was a little loud, Winnie's saga about fixing a leaky faucet and a comment that Joe should have told him to turn off the water source first.

Both Joe and Winnie retold the story of our first meeting at Hideaway Lake, each embellishing their version, spicing it up with exaggerations and loose interpretations. Winnie relived how we'd snuck up on Joe, like little kids playing a game of hide-and-seek, and how Joe was just painting away, serenading nature with off-key notes and chopped-up lyrics. Winnie said if there was one guy he never wanted to mess with, it was Joe, and that he was relieved when Joe chased me and not him.

That's when Joe took over. He told the group to take a good look at Winnie, then said, "Hey, I was stupid to get so upset by their interruption, but I'm not so stupid to pick a fight with that guy!"

Everyone roared.

Nicki got into the act when she described seeing my profile picture of Joe chewing on the paintbrush handle. She said that despite her concern with the confrontation at Hideaway Lake, she knew from the moment she saw the photograph that she wanted to meet Joe, to get to know him, that the picture oozed character, that it captured his spirit. And then she retrieved a package wrapped in bright yellow paper from the kitchen table and handed it to Joe. Nicki had enlarged my photo and framed it for a birthday gift. Joe nodded his approval and accepted Nicki's hug as everyone else took turns admiring the photograph.

A parade of birthday gifts followed. Bookstore Julie brought a first edition of a novel by one of Joe's favorite authors; Upstairs Tony created a certificate on his computer that was "good for one significant volume adjustment to any stereo equipment in my apartment"; and Professor Warthers brought a paint-by-numbers kit with a note saying not to go outside the lines. Joe gave lingering handshakes to each of them.

Winnie seemed especially pleased with his gift; it was a video-tape of the funniest moments in sports. He thought an immediate screening was a good idea, but Joe took a rain check, promising him they'd watch it over the weekend, to which Winnie replied, "Saturday morning, dude."

Mom and Dad ... well, they surprised me. Not because they each got Joe a gift; no, giving gifts sometimes came a little *too* easy in my family. I was surprised by what they gave.

Joe lit up when he opened Dad's gift. It was a baseball encased in clear protective plastic and signed by Joe's all-time favorite Chicago Cubs player, Ernie Banks. I don't know if Dad knew that—maybe I'd mentioned it—or if he just assumed any diehard Cubbie fan would love a ball autographed by Banks. Didn't matter. It was a great idea, and I doubted if it would ever leave Joe's sight.

Mom had this mischievous grin while Joe unwrapped, and then tried to figure out her gift. Winnie and I recognized it immediately; an MP3 player not inside its original packaging. While Winnie fitted the earphones over Joe's head and explained he could listen to music, Joe tried to be polite and said thank you, but you could tell he didn't think he'd have much use for some newfangled device that stored hundreds of songs. But a smile erupted on Joe's face when Winnie pushed the PLAY button.

"It's from *My Fair Lady*," he said too loudly while his head swayed back and forth.

Mom leaned over Joe, lifted the earphones, and told him she'd recorded thirty show tune albums. She gave him a typed list of every song on every album, wished him happy birthday, and kissed him on the cheek.

And then it was my turn.

WHEN I LEARNED THERE WAS GOING to be a party, I decided I wouldn't give my gift to Joe until after everyone else had left. I didn't mind sharing Joe's birthday; it felt good to ignore the constant strain of Joe's health by having people celebrate, even if only for a few hours. It was just that my gift was personal, between Joe and me, and no one else would have understood or appreciated it.

Mom and Dad knew about the gift because I had to get their permission to work on it. Well, not exactly to work on it, but to take time away from school so that I could finish.

My approach was honest and straightforward. I told them my idea, how long I thought it would take, and how much it meant to me. I explained that I didn't want to give up any time with Joe, and then updated them on my classes, showed them I was current, and in some cases even ahead with the assignments. I tabulated my grades for them—A's across the board. I promised I wouldn't fall behind, that I'd make up everything I missed. And then I asked to miss a week of school. It wouldn't have mattered if they'd said no—I would have skipped classes anyway—but I wanted to give them a chance to say yes.

Dad asked about my timeline, then tried to analyze it and

make it more efficient. I guess he thought spending forty hours on my idea was too much, that I could finish it in less time, and that school wouldn't have to be sacrificed. I told him forty hours was the minimum and that I didn't want to do the project unless I did my best work. He was impressed with my resolve.

That Mom didn't freak or have a knee-jerk reaction really surprised me. She asked whether I'd factored in missing a few days of school after Joe died. I was honest, said I knew that would be a tough time for me and that I didn't know how I'd react, but that I knew she and Dad would be there for me. Mom smiled like she heard the magic words, and asked what she could do to help. It was a pretty nice way of saying yes.

So I started the day after my interview with Tom Rainey, a Friday, and I finished the afternoon of Joe's birthday. I figured it had taken me sixty hours; I averaged ten hours for each of the five days of school I missed, plus some time I squeezed in on Saturday and Sunday. I'd never worked as hard on anything in my life.

"THEY SURE CLEARED OUT FAST," Joe said, taking off his party hat.

His eyes weren't as lively and his voice faltered a bit. He hadn't taken an extra push of painkiller since four o'clock that afternoon because he wanted to be part of the festivities, and in a responsive state regardless of the pain. But the excitement had worn off, and Joe was coming down fast. He was tired. He hurt.

"I didn't mean for that to happen. When Winnie asked what I got for your birthday, I figured it was okay to tell everyone it's something I wanted to share with you alone. Did you want the party to keep going?"

Joe grunted through a half-smile. "Nope. I needed to push my little yellow button a while ago. Just didn't want to be the one who told everyone to scram."

Joe's pain management was around the clock; a timing mechanism released a dose of Dilaudid into an intravenous drip every hour to keep a steady infusion rate. But there was also the yellow button, Joe's drug-on-demand option that delivered an extra dose when he decided the pain was too severe. It provided almost immediate relief, and usually made him fall asleep.

"It's okay if you want to sleep, Joe. I'm the only one left." I'd already worked out with Mom and Dad that I would spend the night with Joe, but that I'd go to school the next day. There would still be time to give him my gift later if he needed to dull the pain and rest.

"I can wait a few more minutes," he said, but I could tell that uncomfortable had become unbearable. Joe grimaced, making his eyes look like narrow slits, and he gripped the blanket like he was wringing the last drop of water from a sponge.

Joe had told me that the pain snuck up on him, that it began with a nagging throb, and that he felt guilty pushing the yellow button for just a nuisance. But we both knew it was the signal, a warning that the pain was about to get serious.

Gwen peeked from the bedroom, checking to see if it was a good time to take vitals or whatever nurse thing needed to be done. Joe waved her off.

"Yeah, I need a boost, Quinn, but my curiosity is stronger than the pain ... at least for a few more minutes." Joe swallowed and tried to suppress another wince. "So, what's so special that you had to kick everyone out?"

All of a sudden I felt anxious. I'd been so busy working, so determined. What if he didn't like it? What if I'd gone the wrong way?

"I didn't know what to give you," I said, walking to the kitchen table. My throat was dry and I was drained, all of my emotional and physical energy spent. I closed my eyes briefly, and then claimed the last present from the kitchen table, a high-gloss red package that Mom had decorated with white ribbon and a delicate bow. I returned with it to Joe's bedside.

"It was so hard. I didn't want to get you just anything. It had to be special. I mean the baseball and the book and the MP3 player are great, and I know you like them, but I had to give you something more." I turned my head away from Joe because my eyes were filled with tears. I knew we still had a few more days together, that we'd talk and laugh and cry a little more, but that moment, my gift . . . it was the real goodbye.

"Come sit with me, Quinn." Joe patted the side of his bed.

"I didn't know what to give you," I said again. The tears streamed down my cheeks and my lower lip quivered. I was stammering, almost babbling. "You mean so much to me, Joe. I had to figure out a way to tell you how much you mean to me." I sat on the bed still clutching the package against my chest, and wiped the wet from my cheeks with the back of my hand. I tried to collect myself, and took a few short and measured breaths.

When I finally dared to look at Joe, his eyes were clear and soothing.

"I've never had a better friend than you, Quinn."

And that's all it took. To be reminded, to be told that I mattered. I held Joe's eyes a few more seconds, knowing I'd never forget how I felt at that moment, then lowered the box from my chest and laid it on Joe's lap.

"Happy birthday, Joe."

Joe lifted his present, then arched an eyebrow at me. "Pretty fancy package."

"Mom."

"I like it," he said, ripping into the paper. "She doesn't reuse this stuff, does she?"

"Yeah, and she's really going to be pissed," I said, and we both laughed.

Joe opened the box when the wrapping was cleared and sifted

through the tissue paper inside until he found it. He removed an oversized manila envelope and flashed a quizzical look at me, like what he'd expected couldn't possibly fit inside, then smiled at the renewed suspense. And then he grimaced and closed his eyes. The pain that had been momentarily ignored shot through the moment, and there was a soft repetitive moan while Joe took deep breaths.

"Take the medication. It'll take a minute to kick in. You can still open the present," I said, thinking I shouldn't have drawn this out and that Joe shouldn't be suffering because of me.

Joe nodded and pressed the yellow button. He clenched his teeth and the muscles in his jaw tightened. Joe breathed in heavily, and blew it out through his mouth over and over. Relief would come soon, but he knew the pain would be excruciating until then.

Those were the hardest times for me, watching the strongest person I'd ever known fight back while I was powerless to do anything but steady my hand on his shoulder until the pain subsided.

"Okay," he said after two minutes of unyielding determination and a final sigh. "I'm okay now. Let's see what I got here."

Joe lifted the envelope flap and slid out the plastic binder. He turned it right-side up, read silently, and then aloud. *"Provocation or Protection: A Discussion of Japan's Attack on Pearl Harbor, by Quinnlan Marshall."* Joe glanced at me and then returned to my report. He flipped through the pages, twenty-nine including the bibliography and footnotes, and his face, racked with pain just seconds ago, was transfigured. In a near-whisper, he said, "You wrote the report."

All I could do was nod.

A burst of energy pierced through the disease and drugs, and gave Joe an unrestricted moment of clarity. He examined each of the pages, from back to front, skimming passages and picking out words, appreciating the crisp clean sheets, the precise margins, the exact grammar and punctuation. His touch was gentle, like he was handling an ancient manuscript, when he turned a page. He didn't read it then—couldn't, really—but he knew.

"I had to give you a part of me. I had to show you. You had to know that you made a difference." My tears had slowed to a trickle, and I didn't bother wiping them. They slid down my cheeks, slowly following the same path, before finally dripping onto my jeans.

I watched as he approached the front of the report, almost holding my breath, waiting for the moment when he'd read the words, my words that told Joe I loved him.

"What's this?" Joe cleared his throat and fixed his eyes to mine. "Don't think this qualifies as MLA format."

"A wise man once told me that learning was more important than subjective rules. Fuck MLA," I said, knowing the rest of my report precisely followed the guidelines.

Joe tried to smile. His eyes, now watery and wistful, returned to the second page of my report, and he read it aloud.

"A dedication: To the man who showed me I always have choices and that it's never too late; to the guide who taught me that true success is measured from within; to the friend who listened, then helped me understand my gifts and my place in the world."

Joe couldn't speak; he was crying, but not making any noise.

I bent over, gently lifted him from the pillow, and cradled him in my arms until he fell asleep.

thirty

Having regrets, owning up to mistakes and understanding their cost, happens to everyone. Just part of life, right? Except I'd always thought older people were more susceptible, a kind of mental game that tortured and teased fifty- and sixty-year-olds with images of what could have been: a woman left behind, a job you didn't take, a passed opportunity, a senseless risk. I'd always thought regrets took years, even decades, to sink in.

I wasn't even eighteen and I already had regrets. The one I couldn't shake was Jack Torrance. With everything Joe meant to me, knowing how desperately he wanted to see his son again ... well, I didn't pull it off. Joe died six days before Thanksgiving that year.

Oh, I had other regrets, too. I wasn't with Joe when he died because I was in school, and I never really said goodbye or told Joe that I loved him even though there had been plenty of opportunities. It was all just too hard.

Intellectually, I understood there was no way of knowing when Joe would pass away, and looking back, I admit to being secretly relieved at not having witnessed the final gasp when death claimed my friend. And deep down I knew we'd said goodbye. Not those exact words, but we'd talked. So those regrets were self-inflicted, and I'd get over, or at least be able to rationalize them.

Jack was a different story. He's the regret I would carry forever.

I had agreed not to bother him again, but I called him anyway, just three days before Joe died. I knew something was different, that Joe's condition had worsened. He was pretty much out of it, wasn't lucid more than a few minutes a day, and he had weird dreams when he would speak in different languages and talk to people I'd never heard of. But it was the smell that made me call Jack. It was distinctive, unlike anything I'd smelled before, unpleasant and rather pungent, but not foul. The smell of death made me forget my promise.

Jack's wife answered the phone, and when I explained who I was and why I was calling, she didn't even hesitate; she put Jack on the line. I expected to hear a click when I said my name again, but Jack didn't hang up. He just listened. Thinking back to the conversation, I really wasn't in control, not even close. I cried. I blurted out that Joe was dying, that he was barely conscious. I begged Jack to come. I think I even apologized for calling him again, that I knew I'd promised, but that I had to try one more time. He had to know this was Joe's last chance; that it was his last chance, too.

An unforgettable sense of bitterness swept over me when Jack said, "I don't want to see him, and I don't want you calling again." The click ending our conversation was sharp and emphatic, and it was the moment I quit trying. And I regretted it.

I never told Joe I'd made that call. Between drifting in and out of consciousness and struggling against the pain, I was afraid his hearing that my last-ditch effort had failed, that his son wasn't coming, would have killed him on the spot. And I never told him about meeting Jack or seeing his granddaughter or delivering a twenty-five-year-old letter on that Sunday afternoon. But I think he knew.

There was a page in the spiral notebook for me. Joe described the inspiration he felt while painting the rock formation at Hideaway Lake, and said he knew he was being given a second chance through me. He said the past couldn't be undone, but that a settled peace now soothed him, knowing that he'd learned from those mistakes so that he could help me. And there was a postscript. It said he might have misplaced the letter to Jack because it wasn't where he thought he'd put it, and that he wanted me to attach a note about his death and mail it to Jack if I came across it while the apartment was being cleared out.

Joe didn't misplace things. Everything in his life was orderly and disciplined, and his memory, even until the last few weeks, was crisp. I'm betting he looked for that letter, that maybe he was even going to resend it. Joe knew it was missing, and that I'd taken it. If that's the case, if what I feel is right, then Joe knew about my mission to Cherry Creek. He knew I'd tried and failed. And that's when he realized he wouldn't see Jack before he died. Even now, that thought saddens me.

There was a funeral—sort of. Gene Karatowski flew in from Phoenix the day after Joe died, followed through with the arrangements, and despite Joe's request, there was a small assembly at the funeral home the following Monday. Not much, really. Nothing religious, and there wasn't a visitation or even an obituary. Someone just made a few phone calls. Besides the folks from Joe's birthday party, maybe another twenty showed.

We gathered in a windowless room at the mortuary, sat in folding chairs with cushioned seats, and listened to soft music that was more depressing than comforting. I handed out prints of a couple pictures I'd taken of Joe and made sure people knew they could keep them, but there wasn't a program or even a printed synopsis of Joe's life. I guess no one had all the details, or everyone assumed Gene Karatowski, the guy Joe handpicked to handle his affairs, would pull that sort of thing together. He didn't.

So instead of reading biographical tidbits and reciting biblical verses, prayers or words of inspiration, our cadre of mourners stared solemnly and uncomfortably at a shiny blue urn containing Joe's ashes. It was centered on a white tableclothed stand and flanked on both sides by flowers, some professionally arranged and others picked from convenient gardens that morning.

Karatowski, a retired Marine who had served in Vietnam with Joe, was younger than I'd expected, fifty-five, maybe sixty years old. He was huge—probably what Winnie will look like at that age—but his size didn't help him take control of an awkward situation. Instead, a too-tight suit and a wide necktie falling six inches short of his belt accentuated a beer belly, and were appropriate visuals to his stammering and disjointed words. No one else tried or was able to take over when he floundered and, in the end, there were more handshakes than hugs, even fewer words.

All in all, the service was a pretty pathetic attempt at honoring Joe Toscano. It, too, joined my list of regrets.

I will give some credit; Karatowski was efficient at wrapping up the legalities of death. He went through all of Joe's papers and followed specific instructions like he was assembling a bicycle on Christmas Eve. Notification letters were typed and sent the day that death certificates were available, an inventory of Joe's possessions was prepared, and Karatowski met with Joe's landlord, who agreed to terminate the lease on December 31st. He'd contacted the University of Colorado and informed them of Joe's intent to establish a scholarship fund, and he told me that Joe had left his paintings, all of them, to me. And of course he made sure I knew that they needed to be removed from the apartment before the end of the year.

Gene Karatowski was efficient and coldly focused, which was probably why Joe selected him.

Joe's death collided head-on with our Thanksgiving, and no one seemed in the mood to celebrate, much less summon the energy for our normal Martha Stewart-type extravaganza. Mom roasted a turkey and baked pies, Dad stoked the fireplace and kept continuous football flashing across the television, and Elizabeth and I had managed to iron out a temporary truce. That was about it. Our dinner was simpler, more subdued than any I remembered. There was a reflective quiet surrounding that day; we allowed each other space but still knew we were together.

I suppose butting up against Thanksgiving was two-sided; it gave me a few more days away from school without falling behind. I'd already caught up with my classes after Joe's birthday, and the teachers hadn't thrown much work at us with the holiday and all. Good thing. I couldn't imagine making up homework or studying for tests. I was too tired.

Even though it wasn't like before, I spent hours in bed not wanting to move, not really able to, remembering my times with Joe, and crying tears of grief and loneliness and anger. I tried listening to music and fiddled with the computer. I even managed a couple of hot baths. It felt good to soak, to cover my head with a washcloth that dripped water instead of tears down my face.

Mostly though, I was numb. Like my whole body had been injected with Novocain and was moving in slow motion. A part of my brain said I needed to snap out of it; that my life would go on, that I had responsibilities and that I still cared.

Another part insisted I didn't.

thirty-one

"Up for a walk?" It was Mom, and she'd already tapped on my bedroom door and entered. Her tone was gentle but energetic.

"Not really," I mumbled. It was eleven in the morning, a Monday morning, to be exact, but my mom hadn't fussed about me missing another day of school when I said I didn't feel like going.

"Hey, you're already dressed, it stopped raining, and *you* need some fresh air." Mom's arms were crossed across her chest, but she was smiling. She wore a gray warm-up suit, ready for action, and apparently not going to take no for an answer. "Come on, Mr. Quinn, we're going for a walk."

"Mom, I really don't want—"

"We're going, and then we're going to have some lunch." Mom's feet, wrapped in unscuffed sneakers, were planted. I knew she wasn't going to raise her voice and that there wouldn't be any guilt trips or outbursts, but I also knew she wasn't moving until I agreed.

"Okay," I said, swinging my legs around. "Where are we going?" Actually, I had been thinking about some time on the backyard swing for a breather from a room that had gotten darker and smaller the last few days. Walking would be an okay substitute.

"Doesn't matter."

I grabbed a sweatshirt from my dresser, pulled it over my head, and followed her out the front door. Her steps were quick, almost bouncy, like she was warning me this wasn't going to be a casual stroll. I'd seen Mom in the kitchen like this, cruising between the oven and the stove and the sink and the table, always combining trips and tasks, pumped by an approaching deadline. She had that same energy, that same focus as she bounded to the sidewalk and waited for me.

"I've got a few things to say," Mom announced as she headed toward McCoy Street, "and I want to ask a few questions. Is that all right with you?"

"Yeah, I guess."

The late autumn air was heavy with humidity and the ground was still wet from an overnight rain that drizzled instead of poured. Withered yellow-brown and burgundy leaves that had shuffled between yards with yesterday's wind were now soft and soggy; their musky scent sweetened a sharp mixture of wet asphalt and smoldering firewood. An occasional burst of sunlight penetrated an army of rolling clouds, but couldn't change a gloomy gray sky. The weather was normal for that time of year. Kind of depressing, too.

"How do you think you're dealing with everything?" Mom turned her head to make eye contact, but didn't slow the pace, like she was a trainer working me through a first-time routine, making sure I was getting it.

"Not so good," I said. It hadn't been that long ago when admitting weakness, any shortcoming, to my mother would have been unthinkable. I didn't have the energy to put up barriers that morning.

"What are your thoughts about school?"

"I'll go tomorrow." Okay, we were back to familiar territory.

"Good. I think it's important for you go to school, but not for the reason you probably think." Mom took a left on Eagle Rock Lane and looked over her shoulder to make sure I kept pace. She swung her arms in long, exaggerated strokes, and her breathing hinted at being tested. "You need someplace to go, Quinn. You need a reason to get up in the morning, and you need a routine. Even if it's only going through the motions, even if you daydream through your classes ... " Mom laughed out loud. "Did I just say that? Well, try *not* to daydream in class, but even if you do, at least you're out of the house and you'll be taking steps in the right direction."

Mom was right. I never would have guessed that was why she thought I should go back to school. I think I even twisted a grin when she laughed about the daydreaming.

"It's about doing little things, daily things. And beside the fact that I need the exercise, the reason we're walking is it will help you. Being active, doing something physical ... it helps."

"I don't feel like doing this, Mom. I really don't." I wasn't convinced that following my mother around our neighborhood while she exercised, hands stuffed in my jeans and eyes locked on the pavement three feet ahead, was helping me.

Mom was unflappable. She wasn't about to turn around and didn't seem bothered by my uncooperative attitude. Petty arguments weren't on her agenda.

"It's been a long time since my parents died, but I remember how I felt, how tough it was just getting through the day. So I know how hard this is for you, Quinn. And I wish I could tell you there was a pill you could take, a silver bullet, something." Mom stopped at an intersection a little winded, but she tried not to show it. When she turned toward me, her eyes gently held mine. "But there isn't a magical pill or silver bullet. It's a day-to-day process. Baby steps."

"How long did it take you?"

Mom wiped her forehead and quizzed me without words.

"To get over your mom and dad."

She pressed her lips together with an inaudible sigh, and swallowed before speaking, like she was checking memories, making sure they were under control before answering. "You don't ever get over it, Quinn. Not completely."

If this was supposed to be a pep talk, I sure wasn't feeling very peppy yet.

"Things get better and your life will go on. The pain fades," Mom said slowly while shaking her head, "but I won't lie to you. The emotional loss and the hurt never completely go away. They won't be as intense, but there will always be moments, sometimes when you expect them, sometimes when you don't, when the sorrow and the sense of loss return. Christmas is always hard for me." Mom bit her lower lip. Her eyes, now clouding with emotion, momentarily avoided me. It took a few seconds before she pasted a brave smile. When she spoke again, her voice was solemn. "Joe's death will get easier with time, but it will always stay with you."

I saw my mother's face tighten, and she swallowed again. Her rhythm was broken, her words were revealing, and I was drawn to her honesty, a vulnerability I'd never witnessed. She was taking on grief, inviting back her pain to try to help me. It was genuine and unconditional, and I momentarily forgot the purpose of our walk.

"I'm sorry, Mom."

My mother slid her arm around my waist and gave me a quick hug, the kind that didn't embarrass me, even if someone saw. "Let's keep walking," she said.

Our pace was not as brisk, and a restoring quiet settled, absorbing our thoughts. Yet we were still connected, still sharing. I was thinking about my grandparents, people not much older than Mom and Dad when they were killed, people I never knew but may have resembled, and whose personalities I would surely recognize. I imagined a horrible car crash. I wondered who told Mom. She was a sophomore in college, a thousand miles from home, and I think she'd just returned to school from spring break when it happened. I didn't know whether she finished the term, or dropped her classes and just stayed home for awhile. She was an only child. Had she lived alone in the family house or stayed with relatives? I knew she finished college—she had a degree in

English—but where had she gone for holidays? She'd just said Christmas was particularly hard. Why hadn't I known that?

Maybe her parents had been control freaks, too (Mom had to have learned that from someone), but she wasn't controlling that morning, hadn't been for several months, like all she'd needed was someone to show her how a different approach worked. Losing her parents with such sudden severity; maybe her chokehold manner of childrearing had been about protection, not power.

Our perfect silence was interrupted by a crosswalk signal that beamed bright red and warned us not to walk. It was a good stopping point. It was time to head back.

"I'm going to get a bit philosophical on you," she said in a cheerier voice as we turned around.

"Don't go too deep."

"Right. You're the kid with the genius IQ, so I'll try to keep it simple." Mom laughed, but then she took a serious tone. "In a strange way, your pain is a good thing. If you think about it, I suppose you can say that the pain validates your friendship with Joe, that the depth of your love will also be the depth of your pain. If you didn't love him, if you didn't care, you wouldn't be grieving now. The pain tells you just how great a friend you had."

It didn't take much to see where she was coming from, and I knew the intellectual argument was valid (How do you know beauty unless you've seen ugly?), but I didn't have much use for philosophy right then. It didn't lessen the suffering, and no matter how you sliced it, intellect had taken a seemingly permanent backseat to emotions for me.

"So, I have a question for you," Mom said, almost like a challenge.

"Okay."

"Imagine that you had the power to take it all away ... the pain, the grief ... everything. Imagine that you could make that decision, that it was your call. The loneliness and emptiness you feel right now? Gone. Poof. They disappear." Mom paused while

I let the idea take hold before she continued. "But getting rid of the pain comes at a price. You have to decide that you never knew Joe, that the time you had together would be erased from your memory. You wouldn't have experienced anything with Joe."

I stopped walking and stared at a slimy puddle against the curb. I'd heard her words: dump the grief, pretend like Joe never happened, and for a split second, feeling better sounded pretty good, almost tempting. But the answer was too obvious. Give up my time with Joe? To never know him? Mom's challenge made me think back to a chance meeting at Lucky's, to fragmented memories of leftovers and life lessons. It was hard not to smile.

"So what's your decision? Knowing how bad it hurts right now, would you rather not have known Joe at all?"

My mind was straying to images I saw flashing across the murky water six inches below my feet. I answered her in a soft voice. "No. Joe means too much. Even with the pain, Joe means too much."

Mom touched my elbow and started us walking again. She rubbed her hand across my shoulders and said, "Sometimes it helps to remember why it hurts."

I thought how to respond, of what to say to someone who had been a relentless taskmaster but my biggest cheerleader; to someone who snapped at the inconsequential, yet braved fragile situations. My mother, the woman who'd thrown my cameras across the room, but spent hours downloading show tunes into an MP3 player.

"Mom, I'm glad you got to know Joe. I'm glad you were friends."

Mom smiled and then blew an uneasy breath. "I have one last question."

"Okay."

"How do you feel about Joe's memorial service, the way it was handled?"

"I think it sucked," I said, not caring that Mom disapproved of that word.

"Me, too."

thirty-two

I was standing in a corner of what used to be a vacant store-front on Second Street, just around the block from Nicki's studio. Its previous lives, in beginning order, were a drugstore, a restaurant, a video store, and a gift shop. The drugstore lasted forty-three years, through three generations of the Pryor family, until the first Walgreen's opened just off Highway 36 in the late eighties. A couple of Denver real estate types figured Jimmy Pryor panicked and was selling the store too cheap; they snatched it up and opened a Mexican restaurant. Good idea, bad food. The video store made money until Blockbuster came to town, and the gift shop ... well, Louisville isn't much of a tourist destination, and the T-shirts and mugs and painted plates didn't exactly fly off the shelves. It lasted fourteen months.

And now there had been another transformation. The place looked like an art gallery, but it was really a place for people to celebrate Joe Toscano's life.

We hadn't rented it, not exactly. Knowing the building had been empty for over a year, Nicki called the owner, told him we'd paint the walls, strip and wax the linoleum floor, change out light bulbs, and clean the restrooms—in exchange for holding our gathering on the second Saturday night in January. A good deal for both sides; his property was spic-and-span, ready to catch the eye of a fight-the-odds kind of tenant, and we got enough room (aided by the easels Nicki borrowed from the school's art room) to hang all of Joe's paintings and a bunch of my photographs of him.

I was wedged between Winnie and Dad, grateful for a bit of camouflage, and trying to keep from shaking any more hands. I wasn't being antisocial; it was actually kind of fun meeting everyone and connecting names with faces. But I was nervous.

In five minutes, at seven o'clock, I'd speak into a microphone and a whole lot of people I didn't know but had invited would be watching me, listening to the tall skinny kid while a whisper circulated the room: "That's Joe's friend. That's the kid who arranged all this."

I couldn't really take credit for putting this thing together. It was Mom's idea. When we both admitted being disappointed by the funeral home proceedings, she said holding a memorial service didn't have to occur right after someone died, that extenuating circumstances or conflicting schedules could be reasons for delaying a service and ... well, the idea of inviting Joe's friends to celebrate his life began to grow. Within twenty-four hours we had a plan, and started recruiting volunteers.

Mom knew I would be sending Joe's notes from the spiral notebook, and she found even more names in an address book that Joe must have used before he'd computerized. So I mailed invitations for that night's gathering along with the notes and a brief account of Joe's death. Nicki jumped on board and insisted that we needed to share Joe's paintings, that they should be displayed. She came up with the mini-makeover of the place. Even Winnie and his football buddies got into the act. Nightly crews of Monarch High's strongest and toughest whipped the facility into shape in less than two weeks. Even though my social status jumped a notch or two while I worked alongside Winnie's friends, I still wasn't one of them. That was okay by me. Seeing such different people working nights and weekends to make it all happen was pretty special.

But there needed to be a spokesman, a name and a face, and since I was the one sending Joe's notes, since Joe called me his best friend and everything, I'd decided to go for it. But at that moment my stomach was churning and threatening a spectacle, my hands were moist with perspiration, and I was self-conscious about wiping them before accepting the next stranger's greeting. Talking in front of a group of strangers? Public speaking? I would have rather worn a basketball jersey backward again.

I just never thought there would be so many people. No one did. I mailed forty-three notes for Joe, and sent another sixty invitations to people we'd found in his records. Many lived outside Denver and at least half were outside the state. We figured forty or fifty people would show, seventy tops if kids tagged along. But we'd already tripled the top estimate and more folks were pushing their way through the front door, thanks to an article in *The Denver Post*.

A reporter, Amy Granger, called me just before Christmas break, and said she'd been faxed a copy of my mailing. She wanted to know more about Joe, said she was intrigued by a local personality who'd lived such a diverse life, and asked to interview me. We met at Joe's apartment two days after Christmas. She scribbled page after page of notes; about Korea and Vietnam, about his days as a student, how we met and became friends, his paintings. She didn't have to ask many questions because I did a pretty decent job of nonstop talking.

She left saying she'd think about doing a piece, but I knew from the moment she entered Joe's apartment, when she saw the paintings, from the wonder in her eyes, that it was a done deal, that she just needed to wrestle a bit with the right angle to Joe's story.

Amy got her angle, and with the names I provided and some help from the University of Colorado, she interviewed professors and classmates, former neighbors, and even a few Marine buddies. I could tell she was excited, that Joe's story meant something to her each time she verified information with me. Her finished product was the feature story in the *Lifestyles* section of the previous Sunday's paper. Joe's picture, the one of him chewing the paintbrush handle, was on the first page under a headline that read: Local Renaissance Man to be Honored.

It was quite an account, a tribute really, covering two and a half pages that chronicled Joe's military career, how he'd begun painting while running a plumbing business, and a sampling of the classes he'd taken during his twelve years as a student at the University of Colorado. There were even two pictures of his paintings. When I read and then reread the article that Sunday morning, I was satisfied. I knew Joe Toscano's story had been told.

Amy was there that night, along with a photographer from the *Post*. We said a quick hello before each of us became busy with social niceties, but I saw her look my way a couple times. She gave me half-smiles and bobbed her head slightly; her gestures acknowledged a good thing was happening and that she was proud to be involved.

So I had set up a database, mail-merged a letter with the news about Joe and the invitation to this reception, I licked envelopes, peeled and stuck stamps, and e-mailed or phoned the people without snail-mail addresses. But Amy Granger's story had gathered those people, most of them at least, and had created an air of excitement. Amy was right. She was part of it.

There was an air of eager anticipation among the collection of colleagues and friends and strangers. They were chatting and mingling, admiring paintings, and remembering. Their voices, like in a packed Broadway theater right before the curtain went up, grew louder.

I wanted to quit worrying and just be happy that it was turning out so well; over three hundred people had come to honor Joe, to pay respects, or just learn more about the remarkable man they'd read about in Sunday's paper. But it was seven o'clock, and my nerves were out of control.

thirty-three

After three deep breaths and a clenched-eyes prayer, I stepped behind the podium and neatly placed my speech on the ledge.

I'd printed, in block style, my entire speech on 4x6 index cards, I'd edited and reviewed each sequentially numbered card, and practiced reading them over and over and over. I wanted to make eye contact with the audience and not appear nervous, so I looked up from the cards while I practiced, yet the odds still favored me succumbing to the pressure and gluing my eyes to the damned things.

When I tapped my finger against the microphone, lightly and inconspicuously, there wasn't any noise or echo. I flicked it a little harder, stressed and irritated—we'd checked the thing out an hour earlier—but still nothing. I took a couple of steps back, hoping no one had noticed, and thought through the options. Did I endure curious eyes while plugs and cords and connections were checked, or could I pull it off without the microphone?

Right. My mouth was hopelessly dry and my voice had cracked the last two times I'd spoken.

Then I saw Nicki squeeze between different groups, maneuvering her way toward me. Her smile was confident as she waved and nodded greetings through the crowd, but her pace was intentional, and warned she couldn't stop to chat. She kept glancing in my direction, letting me know she was on her way.

When she reached the podium, she gave me a hug and whispered, "You ready?"

I felt the warmth of her cheek against mine. She held it there, and I momentarily forgot my nervousness and hugged back. When we separated, still holding each other's forearms, I managed a here-goes-nothing smile.

She winked at me, then stepped to the podium and snapped a switch on the side of the microphone.

Oh yeah, it had to be turned on.

"Excuse me, ladies and gentlemen. If I may have your attention, we'd like to get started now." Her voice projected through the speakers we'd placed around the room.

A few people looked in our direction and the noise dropped a notch, but many conversations ignored her request.

"Excuse me. Ladies and gentlemen, I need your attention please." Nicki's voice was loud and firm and friendly. "Folks, please, we want to get started."

Lively chatter dissolved into catch-you-later buzzing as people spotted open chairs and calculated how to get to them. We'd rented eighty folding chairs, and it took less than a minute to fill them. Other guests searched out corners and empty walls to lean against. Many just stood in the back of the room.

"GOOD EVENING, MY NAME IS QUINN MARSHALL." My voice was creaky but discernable, and at least I hadn't forgotten the opening line. The last traces of conversation ceased and I felt the eyes, hundreds of them, trained on me. I didn't look back at them, not specifically at least. I looked above their heads and didn't focus on anyone or anything. It felt safer.

"Thank you all for coming." I fingered my note cards, knowing I'd be turning the first one over in two more sentences. I wanted to be prepared. I didn't want to fumble mid-sentence. "It's great to see such a turnout. I'm sure Joe would have appreciated the time and trouble it took for you to be here, especially those ... "

Ready, now flip the card and look at the audience. No problem. Don't read every single word. Card number two is in place.

" ... who've traveled so far ... " That wasn't right. I was supposed to say, "such great distances." It was time to read.

I turned the top card and lowered my eyes to pick up my place. And then my right hand—I'm pretty sure it was shaking—bumped the ledge of the podium. It wasn't like I'd smacked the thing; it was just a little tap. But a little tap was enough. All the cards, my perfectly printed and arranged speech, tumbled to the floor like cascading confetti, landing in a mess at my feet. I looked at the pile, hoping they'd all stayed together, praying I could just pick them up, swallow back the embarrassment, and start reading again.

That wasn't going to happen. My speech wasn't in a pile; it had scattered everywhere.

I stared at the floor. It seemed like minutes, not seconds. I didn't know whether to scoop up the cards and sort, or turn to Nicki and ask her to speak. I knew my face was red because my ears felt like they were on fire, and that I needed to look up and quit staring at the floor like a blundering fool. But I was frozen.

And everything had been going so well; the crowd, the newspaper story, Joe's paintings on the walls. I'd screwed it up. I'd screwed up the whole evening.

Do something!

Then I heard it, not really believing the sound. It was an explosion of laughter. Uncontrolled, loud, honest. It came from the back of the room, and I could make out a few copycats; snickers and chuckles not brave enough to let loose. I stared into the audience, people *I'd* invited there, people who were supposed to be understanding and sensitive, people who knew I'd lost Joe, and I couldn't imagine anyone thinking my predicament was funny. Identifying the culprit wasn't difficult. It was Winnie.

I clenched my teeth and blinked back tears. It was time to leave.

"Dude!" Winnie had stopped laughing, but his sloppy grin remained. "Quit lookin' at those stupid cards. You don't need 'em. You're, like, Joe's best friend, you knew him, you guys were tight." Winnie gave me an am-I-right shrug and then tossed a thumbs-up. "Those cards don't say nothin', dude. Just tell us about Joe."

Winnie's voice cut through the room's attentive silence. People had turned in their chairs or twisted their heads to see the exchange, of what came next. There was a smattering of handclapping. My eyes left Winnie and roamed the room. I saw people smiling and nodding, and turning back to me with looks of encouragement. The handclapping turned into applause, warm and energetic.

"If you can't tell, I'm really nervous," I said into the microphone.

The crowd laughed and clapped a little louder.

"And for those of you who don't know him yet, the big guy in the back is my friend Michael Wingate, but everyone calls him Winnie. He and Joe were friends, too."

I began to look at different people, engaging their eyes and acknowledging their smiles. A voice inside of me said, *Relax. You're here to talk about Joe, and you can do that.* It was like a switch had been flipped when I gave up control. I was still a mess on the outside, all frazzled and sweaty, but I felt strangely comfortable on the inside. I began speaking again, but had a sense they weren't my words, that I was merely a conduit.

"So thanks again for coming, especially those who have traveled. It's been seven weeks since Joe passed away, and there really wasn't much of a funeral service." I eyed Gene Karatowski standing against the wall to my left, and quickly added, "Joe didn't want a lot of hoopla at his funeral. He didn't even want an obituary. So there was a small ceremony, probably more than Joe would have wanted, and I was supposed to send out handwritten messages to a few people, and a short note about his death to some others." I was glad I remembered to say only a few people had received handwritten messages even though I'd mailed forty-three notes; it made them feel special and didn't slight everyone else.

"Like Winnie said, Joe and I were best friends. Except when I was in school, we were together almost all the time for the last five months of his life. And it bothered me, I mean it really tore me up inside, not to honor him or acknowledge his life after he died. He was too special to just forget.

"So tonight isn't a funeral or a memorial service, and it's not about saying prayers or singing hymns. It's a celebration. Tonight we celebrate Joe Toscano's life, his work, and his friends."

Another round of applause got louder and lasted nearly a minute.

"Before I forget—and I would forget because this is somewhere on one of those note cards—there are some people who should be thanked. You've already met Winnie. He and his friends from the Monarch High School football team painted this place, redid the floors and everything else that needed fixing. Thanks, guys."

There was a polite round of applause pumped up by hoots and hollers from the football players.

"My mom and dad spent a lot of time helping pull tonight off and they've been really supportive during a rough time for me." I couldn't help but be misty-eyed when I pointed to my parents. They were sitting in the third row holding hands and smiling, and I'd made them proud for reasons that counted. When over three hundred people applauded my parents, I clapped, too.

"For those who don't know that an award-winning photographer lives and teaches in Louisville, standing to my left is Nicole

Strandlund. She worked everything out so we could use this building, and she arranged for all of Joe's paintings to be framed. Oh yeah. And I'm supposed to let everyone know that Billy Levin over at Levin's Frame Shop provided the materials at cost."

Both Nicki and Billy waved at the applause.

"And finally, I'd like to thank Amy Granger from *The Denver Post*. I'm sure many of you are here tonight because of the story she wrote in Sunday's paper. Thank you, Amy, for sharing Joe's life with so many people, and for helping make tonight a success."

The crowd was still polite, but I noticed a few people shifting in chairs, crossing legs, and tapping rather than clapping their hands. It was time to move on.

"I have one last announcement before we start talking about Joe. All of the paintings in the room were painted by Joe Toscano, and all but one are for sale. Maybe that's not the right term. They're being auctioned. You don't need paddles with numbers on them or anything. We didn't want this to be a circus, you know, getting a guy in here with a gavel who talks fast, and all that."

The crowd's laughter interrupted me, and I smiled at the image of an auctioneer. *I got a hundred, now two, now two, gimme two, someone gimme two.*

"So it's a silent auction. Next to every painting is a card describing any information we know about it. Below the description is space to write your name and your bid. If someone outbids you, go back and write your name again, below theirs, and put in your new bid. At nine o'clock, the auction will end, and the highest bidder for each painting will win. And I should have said this earlier. Joe's entire estate is going to fund a scholarship at the University of Colorado, and all the money from tonight's auction will go toward that scholarship."

The crowd jumped back to life. People were whispering and pointing, checking with spouses and setting price targets. I decided to let the enthusiasm carry on a bit, and stepped back from the microphone and sipped water from a cup that Nicki handed me.

It's easier to admit now that I'd struggled with what to do with Joe's paintings. I didn't have enough room to hang them all, and I couldn't afford to rent a storage unit where they might be forgotten. I thought about donating them to the University of Colorado; even called Boyd Warthers about the possibility. He guessed the university would accept two or three, and said that he fancied a certain piece. Good to know, but it wasn't an effective solution. There were sixty-eight paintings.

When I asked Mom whether I should just give the one painting to Warthers, she said there were probably a lot of people, especially those attending tonight's event, who would want one of Joe's paintings, and that she might have a solution. So the silent auction was Mom's idea. She said it happened at charity events all the time. And she reminded me that distributing Joe's paintings to the people who knew him, to people who cared, would be a great way of keeping his memory alive.

I agreed.

I did face a tough decision about which paintings I wanted to keep. Joe left all of them to me, and there were several with special meaning. But not sharing Joe's passion, depleting the scholarship fund? That was too selfish, even for me. So I decided to keep only the painting of the rock formation at Hideaway Lake. It hung prominently on the far wall, and clearly stated, "This piece not being auctioned" under its description. I really wanted the hummingbird painting, too—it reminded me of the way Joe's eyes danced when he told stories—but I decided to bid on it like everyone else.

"So," I said deeply into the microphone, quieting the room, "an important part of Joe Toscano's life surrounds us on these walls. There's a piece of Joe in each painting. I hope you'll be generous, to the University of Colorado and to Joe's memory."

The crowd began buzzing again, but I needed to keep things moving.

"And now all of the announcements are over," I said, and then waited a few seconds for the group to settle. "When I sent the news and the invitation about tonight, I asked if you had stories about Joe. Several people answered back, and those present tonight will take a few minutes to share their memories. I'd also like to ask anyone else who wants to help us remember Joe, to honor him, to come up to the microphone after the last speaker."

My throat had become thick, and my heart began pounding, getting more aggressive with every beat. It wasn't about forgetting or stuttering; I was done with that. But I was the leadoff guy, the first to speak, to share. Sure, it was a friendly crowd, they were on my side and all, but talking about Joe, you know, the personal stuff?

I knew there was an out, that I could have skated with, "I still haven't come to terms with his death." But the thought of being nervous ... hell, of being afraid to tell people *my* story of Joe?

"I loved Joe Toscano," I said, and the first tear fell.

thirty-four

"You pulled it off, dude."

I was slumped in one of the front row chairs so my head rested on the metal back and my legs could stretch as far as they'd go. I didn't bother to turn. I was spent, totally drained. "Can't believe you laughed at me." I tried to keep a straight face but it wasn't working.

Winnie plopped next to me, reached his hands above his head, and then locked them around his neck. "Believe it. You were funny! Lookin' at those cards like you'd just lost a winning lottery ticket or something. Moanin' and groanin' without the noise. Man, I wish I had a video camera. Coulda sent a tape into one of those funniest video shows and made a bunch of money."

I rolled my head toward Winnie and prepared a comeback; something sharp and witty. "Asshole."

Winnie grinned. He had one foot stacked on top of the other and his eyes were closed while he pretended to ignore me.

"Yeah, and you probably laugh when Olympic ice skaters fall," I said, determined to get a response.

Winnie's grin widened, and he opened one eye. "Dude, *nobody* watches ice skating." He unhooked his hands and extended an upright fist for me to tap. "I mean it, though. You pulled it off. It was amazing, watchin' all those people, listenin' to their stories about Joe. I liked the funny ones the best, but I even got a little weepy with a couple of 'em." Winnie sat straighter in the chair and looked at me. "Joe was one helluva dude, Quinn. Lettin' people remember, hearing how he helped 'em ... that was tight."

"Thanks," I said, and exhaled a sigh of satisfaction. I never knew feeling tired could feel so good. I'd received a lot of praise, good job and all that kind of stuff, but this compliment felt the best. Winnie was my age, and that made a difference. "Hey, thanks for everything *you* did—even laughing at me. Got the audience good and warmed up."

"Told ya I was good at somethin' besides football."

We both laughed and looked around the room. A handful of people still lingered, exchanging phone numbers and business cards, sharing stories, getting reacquainted. But it was over. It was almost ten o'clock and our celebration of Joe Toscano's life was over.

Winnie was right; the stories people shared were amazing, they were inspiring, and they made me miss Joe even more. I knew that eleven people wanted to speak from the RSVPs and e-mails I'd received, but another sixteen shared memories, too. It took almost two hours even though it seemed like ten minutes.

I kicked off the proceedings, sweaty hands and all, by recalling seeing Joe on our doorstep almost three months after we'd met at Lucky's. I told everyone that I was the teenager from hell, rebelliously motivated, the kind who caused parents to question what they did wrong or what they could have done differently. I admitted failing four classes, that I'd started smoking cigarettes even though they made me sick (that got a laugh from everyone except Mom), and that I was ready to quit school and move out of the house. Life sucked, and there was Joe Toscano at my front door, making sure I was okay because he hadn't heard from me. It was an abridged version, but it took people to that point in my life. It helped them understand.

I recalled how Joe and I were almost inseparable from that

moment; that he'd paint while I studied, that we walked and ate leftovers and explored quirky stores, that we saw a rainbow touching the ground, how we talked about everything and about nothing. I told them that Joe never judged me or told me what to do, but that I learned things. I ended by saying that being accepted and liked for just being me was the greatest gift I'd ever received, and that Joe Toscano had given it to me.

Applause? Oh yeah.

Next up was Frank Miglini, Joe's best friend from high school, and at age seventy-six, the oldest storyteller. He looked at me when he reached the microphone, and grunted loud enough not to need it. "Cigarettes, huh? You're an angel compared to Joe and me when we was your age."

Frank told four stories about the mischief he and Joe instigated; each elicited successively louder laughter. My favorite was the time Joe and Frank were harassed for hanging around the train tracks in downtown Chicago. They decided that if they were going to be labeled hoodlums, they should at least live up to their reputation. Frank explained how they scouted railway track sites for two miles in every direction until they found the perfect spot; a steep hill, maybe sixty yards long, just past a station on the south side. He recalled how he and Joe meticulously planned their prank for a week. They charted the length and loads of the trains, figured which were likely to stop at the station, time schedules and intervals between trains. He said they decided on an exact time, and then greased that stretch of track with a combination of motor oil and lard. Frank told us they hid behind a nearby shed and waited.

The audience was laughing before he could finish the story.

"All of our planning paid off. Next train was eighty cars long and stopped at the station. It was big and slow and heavy. Couldn't get any speed going. Never had a chance." More laughter, but Frank Miglini kept a straight face. "Got to within twenty feet of the top of that hill, and then nuthin'. Started sliding backward. Engineer yellin' at the brakeman, brakeman cussin' out the engineer. Those poor bastards. Put the damn thing in reverse and tried again! Took three more runs at it before finally callin' it quits." Frank shook his head like an impatient teacher watching a student at the blackboard while the crowd roared.

And so it went. Story after story, memory after memory: fellow students Joe tutored, professors being told about Joe's attitude toward grades on the first day of class, thirty-somethings who'd lived in the same building a decade earlier and remembering how they could always count on an attentive ear and a piece of pie. The Marine Corps was well represented, too. There were three accounts of Joe's bravery and courage in battle; still others relived moments when Joe took them under his wing, showed them the ropes, or just offered encouragement. The stories alternated between gruff and sensitive, between innocent moments and life-changing events. They helped us laugh and made us cry.

"You two certainly look comfortable!" Nicki joined us but didn't sit.

"Just thinkin' about tonight. Pretty cool stuff," Winnie said.

Nicki nodded. "Way cool stuff." She paused, like she was remembering her favorite, and then handed me a slip of paper. "Thought you might be interested in this."

I took the paper and sat up straighter. And then my eyes opened wider. "Really?"

"I have a list of everything. The paintings, the bidders, and the final price. You can look at it later if you want to see where the pieces are going. But I thought you'd like to know the total."

The paper in my hand read $52,565.

"By the way," she said, "you didn't get the hummingbird. It was the highest priced piece."

I'd already known my bid wouldn't last. I maxed at four hundred dollars, and there were three names with higher bids after me when I stopped looking. "How much?" I asked.

"Six thousand dollars." Nicki spaced the words for emphasis

and wriggled her eyebrows at me. She was playing, but I also think she was making sure I was okay with letting it be sold. "And you know what else? Gene Karatowski was floored. He said that what we raised more than doubled the scholarship fund."

"How can that be? Joe had a military retirement, he sold a plumbing business. He had investments and stuff. He had money," I insisted. "He didn't have fifty thousand dollars?"

"Gene says Joe bought annuities with the money he got from the plumbing business. They paid a monthly income, just like his military pension, for as long as Joe lived, but they became worthless when Joe passed away. He said that Joe didn't spend all of his income, and he had some automatic monthly investment plan with a couple of mutual funds." Nicki shrugged and shook her head. "Gene said there was just over forty-six thousand dollars left after the funeral and medical expenses."

Any misgivings I'd had about giving up Joe's paintings just went out the window. Doubling the scholarship fund? Almost a hundred grand? I know pride is one of the seven deadly sins, but that didn't deter my feelings. I *was* proud of a decision to share Joe with so many, and knowing I had helped insure Joe's legacy at the University of Colorado. My pride wasn't arrogant; I was humbled by the power of giving.

It was a perfect end to a perfect evening.

Nicki snapped me out of the reverie. "And there's a guy who wants to talk to you. Said he hoped you had a minute."

thirty-five

Jack Torrance stood in a far corner pretending to admire a few paintings. He was wearing a navy blue blazer with a maroon turtleneck, gray dress slacks, shiny black loafers with tassels, and his hair was slicked back. He was dressed for a client's cocktail party, not a memorial service to which he wasn't invited.

I still hadn't told anyone about Jack. Maybe I wanted to avoid the frustration that would have accompanied explanations. Maybe I didn't want to admit failing. Mostly, I decided not everyone was entitled to all of Joe's past.

I approached Jack slowly, hoping to gain a few seconds, observing and steadying myself, not sure what to expect. How long had he been here? What did he want with me?

Why was he here?

Jack turned around when I got to within ten feet, cleared his throat and said, "Hello, Quinn. You've been a pretty busy young man." His voice, shaky and uneven, matched his smile. His eyes didn't match his clothes. They were a mess; puffy and red.

I shrugged. Not talking hadn't been used in awhile, but it was still an arrow in my quiver.

"Quite an event." Jack cleared his throat again, allowing just enough time for me to step into the conversation.

I didn't, and Jack seemed exposed in the awkward silence.

"Well, I just wanted to say, to tell you that you did a fantastic job here tonight. All the people, the stories ... really quite impressive. And the paintings." Jack's eyes drifted around the room at the remaining pieces, then came back to me a bit more confident. "Good job, Quinn. Joe would have been proud."

"How many stories about *your father* did you hear?"

"All of them."

He'd been here the whole time? Really? All of them?

"I found a comfortable column and ducked behind it every now and then. I didn't want to throw you off by being here," he said, answering the unasked question. "We just mingled afterward, sort of figured we'd bump into you sooner or later, but you had lots of hands to shake so we decided to wait around for awhile."

"We?"

"My wife and one of my daughters are here, too." Jack pointed across the room. I saw two ladies talking to Professor Warthers. I recognized Trisha, but not the other woman. She was middle-aged, tall and slender, and dressed in a white and black check-ered sweater and black pants. Her shoulder-length hair was dark and perfectly styled. "They heard all the stories, too," Jack added.

"Had you heard any of them before?" I asked. My voice was laced with superiority, my eyes steady and challenging.

"Some of the Marine stuff rang a bell." Jack raised his eyebrows and shook his head slowly, conceding the point. "But no, there was a lot about Joe I didn't know. You were right, Quinn— he changed."

I didn't know whether I should keep hammering the guy or walk off. Maybe I should have just told the prick to leave, that if the stories weren't good enough three months ago they sure as hell didn't mean anything now. I was angry and I wanted to scream, "Get out! Just get the fuck out!" but the voice inside my head kept chipping away at the hostility, breaking my stone-cold attitude into manageable pieces, counseling me to listen.

"Why are you here?" I asked.

Jack answered with reluctant deliberation. "I read the letter." He tried to smile but couldn't. He turned and faced the wall instead, still talking. "Wish I could say it was my idea, but it wasn't. After you called that night, right before Joe died? Well, Abby got pretty worked up. She told me that I was being given a last chance to see my father, that maybe we could resolve some things. She said I needed to face him and say goodbye. When I refused, told her to mind her own damn business and that I was handling it my own way, she called me a coward and stormed out of the room."

I winced at the last few words, and stepped toward Jack. His voice was reedy, hard to hear, and his head was tilted back so his hair hung on bunched-up shoulders that rose and fell with each breath. I felt the tension and stress. I couldn't imagine Jack's emotions.

"I still didn't read the letter. I wasn't going to allow thirty years of anger to be whitewashed with words."

"When did you read it?"

"Christmas Day." Jack turned from the wall. His eyes touched mine long enough to appreciate my interest, but were then withdrawn. "Abby did a fancy wrap job on a box, filled it with tissue, and put the letter inside. She wrote a note that said she loved me, that I was her hero, and that the letter represented a rare gift—forgiveness. You know, Quinn, as much as I wanted to rip that letter in pieces, to make it go away once and for all, the only thing I felt was the gentle love of my wife. She was asking me to trust her." Jack strained for several seconds, then said, "I read it in my study that afternoon."

I wasn't sure what to say or how to react. I still wanted to be angry, to pummel the guy with cruel words and administer an overdose of guilt, thinking payback would deaden my recurring pain. But I knew how it felt to lose Joe. I stepped closer and put my hand on Jack's shoulder.

"I'm not sure I can share the letter with you, Quinn, at least not yet."

Jack faced me and drew a breath. There were no tears staining his face or filling his eyes, but anguish was exposed like freshly-scraped skin still embedded with bits of gravel.

"I wouldn't have appreciated it when Mom first gave it to me—Joe wrote a lot of things I wouldn't have understood then. But I could have read it when he came by my office that day." Jack paused and swallowed back now threatening tears. "I should have read it before he died."

OUR CONSERVATION WASN'T INTERRUPTED by well-wishers or departing guests even though more than a few had glanced in our direction. It was like they saw an intense aura of familiarity that forbade intrusion, an invitation-only type of party. And that was okay by me. Jack and I were sorting through details and stories and timelines no one else would appreciate. Besides, Winnie and Mom and Dad and Nicki were handling the social niceties just fine.

It turned out that Jack told both his daughters about Joe a few days after Christmas, and had promised them he would try to track me down for more information. He assumed I was a high school student in Boulder, but he didn't remember my last name. Jack didn't get far describing a tall skinny kid named Quinn who knew Joe Toscano to a secretary at the wrong high school after Christmas break ended.

Even though Jack didn't know where Joe lived in Boulder (he'd thrown away the note with Joe's address and phone number), he got lucky with the phone number. Well, sort of. Joe was listed in the phone book but the line had already been disconnected. Jack worked his way through layers of phone company higher-ups, explaining the circumstances and asking for Joe's address, but Joe only listed his phone number; the address couldn't be released. Jack had just begun a death certificate search at the county records office when Amy Granger's story appeared in *The Denver Post*.

Jack said he wasn't a big believer in fate and destiny, but that the article was too coincidental. He and Abby decided that Sunday morning to attend Joe's memorial. They agreed that Jack should not announce his presence or try to speak, that they would strictly be observers, just blend in so they could hear the stories and see the paintings. And Jack said he'd wanted to talk to me.

So I promised Jack a visit. He said he had lots of questions, and wanted to hear more about my struggles as a teenager. And details, specific details about what Joe did and said, and why it worked. Seems Trisha had a bit of an attitude—maybe not as incorrigible or destructive as mine—that was causing some parental concern.

Right. I would have given up my cameras and a year of allowance to have a date with Trisha, and I was going to tell her father how to correct her behavior? Nope, that would never happen. I was willing to go to the house, talk about Joe, and bring copies of pictures I'd taken, but Jack was on his own with Trisha.

"I'M GOING TO INTERRUPT AND INTRODUCE your wife and one of your daughters, Mr. Torrance."

Jack and I turned simultaneously and saw Abby and Trisha standing next to us. Abby had a playful grin. Trisha was a step behind and seemed friendlier than the last time I saw her. It took Jack a second to realize what was happening, but that was too long.

"I'm Jack's wife, Abby." She poked Jack in the side and then stepped toward me with open arms. She hugged like she'd known me forever and kissed my now flushed-red cheek. "Thanks for bringing Joe's letter to the house," she said, releasing me. "Pretty gutsy move considering everything you knew."

"You're welcome." I hadn't mastered charming replies at that age.

"And this is our youngest daughter, Trisha."

"Hey," Trisha said with minor enthusiasm.

"Hi, Trisha. I'm Quinn." I thrust my hand past Abby and offered it to Joe's granddaughter, not knowing where the surge of confidence had come from or when it would abandon me. "We met before, at your house. Thanks for coming."

Yes! Yes! Yes!

"I remember you," she said, seemingly startled by my boldness. She arched an eyebrow, nodded her head and eyed me a little closer. "I'm glad I came. It's pretty cool what you did tonight, getting up in front of all those people, talking about personal stuff and all."

"Quinn's going to bring some pictures of Dad by the house. Maybe dinner?" Jack looked at me and then at his wife for confirmation. "And he has a list of other people who couldn't be here tonight if we want to contact them."

Abby's and my eyes met long enough to acknowledge the word that had slipped naturally through Jack's lips, the word that Joe, somewhere and somehow, must have heard.

"Sometime in the next couple of weeks, Quinn, okay?" Abby gave me a knowing look and winked. "But right now we're going to head home. Almost everyone's gone and we're keeping Quinn's parents from closing up. Come on, Jack. You guys can pick this up next time."

I scanned the room. Abby was right; the walls had been stripped of all but maybe ten paintings, and the room was empty except for Mom and Dad and Nicki.

Jack looked like a little kid who'd been told playground time was over and knew a few-more-minutes request wouldn't be granted. "Okay," he sighed, "so you're coming to the house for dinner sometime in the next two or three weeks, right?" Jack waited for my concurring nod, then swung an arm around his wife's shoulders and drew her near. It was a familiar and comfortable position for both.

"I'll call in a couple of days," I said, already hoping Trisha would be a part of the evening.

"Don't forget the painting, Jack. I already put the other two in the car." Abby gave her husband a final squeeze and touched Trisha's elbow as she walked toward the front door. "Thanks again, Quinn. I'm looking forward to seeing you soon."

"Bye." And my mind raced that three of Joe's paintings would be hanging in the Torrance house. *Which three? Where?*

Jack nodded for me to follow, and he walked from our corner to the back wall where two paintings still hung. He gingerly lifted one off the wall; it was the hummingbird. "Here," he said, handing me the painting.

"Oh." I was a little embarrassed about drifting from the conversation. "I'm sorry, do you need help to the car?" I accepted the painting and started to walk.

Jack laughed out loud. "No," he said, "you don't need to walk me to my car. This painting is for you, Quinn. It's a gift, something Abby and I want you to have."

I was frozen in midstep. I knew Jack and Abby had just paid six thousand dollars for the painting ... and they were giving it to me? I was torn between saying I couldn't possibly accept such an expensive gift and jumping up and down.

"I noticed you bid on it several times."

"It got kind of expensive," I said with a tentative tone, debating whether to confess knowing the amount of the winning bid.

I searched Jack's face for clues. I saw nothing but satisfied pleasure.

"I figured that was the case. I also heard that Dad left all his paintings to you, and that you donated them for tonight's auction.

Pretty generous, so don't even think about saying it's too expensive or some other such rubbish."

"I kept one of the paintings," I admitted, and pointed to the opposite wall.

"And you wanted this one, too. It's a gift, Quinn, and it doesn't even come close to being enough. And by the way, I planted myself in front of that sheet just to make sure no one tried to sneak in a last-minute bid." Jack angled around me to take a final look at the painting. "I loved the narrative about how Dad kept moving the feeder to capture the right light. Probably cursed that hummingbird more than a few times."

I stared at the painting, still a bit numb, still debating how to respond to Jack's generosity. Finally, I said, "Thanks." It was all I could manage and it didn't seem enough. I vowed to myself to make prints of every picture, good or bad, I'd ever taken of Joe. And I'd be there for dinner, however many times I was invited. I had an obligation to share more of Joe with the Torrance family. One I now looked forward to fulfilling.

Then I remembered . . . pictures and family.

Amy Granger had briefly mentioned Mary in her story, but I hadn't told her that Mary and Joe had a son. Apparently no one did; Jack wasn't in the article. Still, I had no idea who knew Mary or Jack, or if any of that night's stories would include them. I needed a contingency plan, one that dealt head-on with the possibility, so I had a reference to Joe's family ready just in case. Something that would show, but not tell. Since no one mentioned them, at least with the microphone or to me, I'd forgotten about it.

Until that moment.

"I have something for you, too," I said. My chest filled and I strutted to the podium, not waiting to see if Jack followed. I knelt and grabbed the box, my contingency plan, from a shelf under it. "Here," I said, handing it to Jack. "This is for you."

Jack was amused by the notion of a gift for him. "What's this?"

He placed the box on top of the podium and shook off the lid, then looked back at me for permission with lively and curious eyes. When I nodded, he lifted my surprise from the box and slowly opened the double-frame.

Jack stood perfectly still while he swallowed back tears.

The two pictures Joe took from Mary's house twelve years earlier were now side by side, bordered by silver-plated metal and covered with a thin sheet of glass: Joe and Mary on their wedding day, and Joe with five-year-old Jack sitting on his shoulders waving a Chicago Cubs pennant.

thirty-six

It's been over four years since Joe Toscano died.

I graduated from college last week and for the first time since I can remember, I'm not managing a schedule of studying and tests and term papers. I'm done, accepted the diploma and flipped the tassel, and will begin a job with *The Chicago Sun-Times* next month. Working for a newspaper isn't new for me; I interned at *The Denver Post* for the last four summers, thanks to Amy Granger.

Amy's follow-up article on Joe created quite a stir, and the editor was inundated with mail applauding a story about the good side of teenagers. Amy suggested they hire me, let me learn the ropes, observe the inner workings of a daily newspaper, and get a taste of real-life journalism. Even though I could have made more money bagging groceries with Winnie, I jumped at the chance. The opportunity to tag alongside a photographer and even snap a few shots of my own, to hear story ideas and decide how certain photographs reinforce the text was too great a temptation. Plus, it gave me a head start with my upcoming college classes.

Oh yeah. I was accepted at Northwestern University and graduated from its Medill School of Journalism. Pretty amazing considering my interview with Tom Rainey. Maybe I was so far out of the box that he took a chance, like pro football teams that draft track stars for their speed even though they've never played football. Sounds good, but absent knowing the reasoning behind the admissions board's decision, I doubt it was anything so intriguing. It was probably because of Mr. McCormack.

I was surprised—okay, shocked—by my admission letter, but there was no one home to share my whooping and hollering. I raced to Nicki's studio, showed her the letter, and we both gorged on ice cream. That's when I learned that Mr. McCormack had written a recommendation letter for me.

It turns out that Joe phoned Nicki the day after his birthday and asked her to bring Mr. McCormack to his apartment as soon as possible. "No explanations—just do it" was how Nicki described the call. Well, Nicki brought Mr. McCormack by that afternoon, and Joe bulled through the formalities, said he didn't have time for niceties. Joe recapped his understanding of the plagiarism incident, congratulated McCormack on being fair and on drawing lines that came with consequences, and then explained his theory about quitting. After McCormack agreed with everything, Joe handed him my paper on Pearl Harbor.

Nicki remembered that Mr. McCormack was a bit defensive at first, said it was too late to change a grade, and that I shouldn't expect any kind of favoritism just because I'd finally done the work. When Joe didn't respond, just lay in bed with that icy stare of his, Mr. McCormack became uncomfortable. Then he asked what Joe wanted.

Nicki said Joe was Joe; concise words and straight to the point.

"Quinn didn't write this paper for you, he wrote it for me. It's an A+ caliber paper at the college level, and you are being pre-sented with a unique opportunity, Mr. McCormack. You started the stream of F's, but that isn't the reason Quinn won't be accepted to Northwestern. No, Quinn owns that and he knows it.

But you can be the reason he *is* accepted. Read the paper. Decide when a student, one of your students, is worth fighting for."

Mr. McCormack just nodded, trying to hide his obvious intimidation. That Joe was dying of cancer, lying in a hospital bed and connected to a host of medical gadgets, didn't seem to matter. Nicki said that Joe's eyes stayed locked until Mr. McCormack finally slid my paper in the side pocket of his top-coat. And then, without recognizing victory or defeat, Joe suggested they munch on leftover birthday cake, and he showed Mr. McCormack a baseball signed by Ernie Banks.

Nicki said I wasn't supposed to know this, but Mr. McCormack not only read my paper, he fired off a three-page recommendation letter to the admissions people at Northwestern, and showed her a copy. His letter explained the plagiarism and his response to the infraction, and then chronicled the sequence of events through my senior year. He compared that point in my life to the challenges faced by special consideration applicants, and he urged the admissions board to consider perseverance with intensely difficult circumstances, as part of my application. He even included a copy of my paper, explained it was a birthday present and how it was written with passion, and not motivated by a grade. Nicki said Mr. McCormack's letter was pretty passionate itself.

I'd like to think my time with Tom Rainey had some pull, that foregoing bullshit answers and shooting straight with him made the difference. And maybe that interview was important, maybe Rainey's comments did sway a crucial vote. But my gut tells me that's not the way it went down. My gut says that Mr. McCormack, my self-conceived nemesis and the preferred target of my hostilities, was responsible for my acceptance at Northwestern. It turned out he was quite a teacher, but my lessons had nothing to do with deciphering Japanese code or FDR's intentions.

So, yeah, I'm twenty-two and doing okay. Actually better than okay. I don't hide my intellect, I don't guard my priorities or passions from judgment, and even though I'm comfortable being alone, I've decided not to be lonely. I'll even admit that every now and then, when the mood strikes, when I'm absolutely sure no one can hear, I break into a rousing chorus from *The Sound of Music*.

Unfortunately though, Mom was right about one thing—I've never gotten over losing Joe.

It's scary admitting an intimacy with Death. Death is harsh and cruel and unforgiving; there are no do-overs. Death is the ever-present reminder of bittersweet memories and the never-answered plea for just one more moment together. It's the pain, even after four years, that hasn't gone away. The stark reality is I can't hang out with Joe, and it depresses me to think of the conversations we'll never have. Yet, that's what Death has taught me; to not take anything or anyone for granted, to see day-to-day beauty, and to appreciate. Death taught me about the fragility of life.

Even though I've pretty much worked through the grieving process, the denial and anger and acceptance stuff, I don't think Jack Torrance has. I visit them when I'm back in Denver, and have gotten to know the family quite well. Jack and I talk, we've taken a few hikes to Hideaway Lake (we spread Joe's ashes during one trip), and in a strange way, his words and mannerisms remind me of Joe.

It's felt good helping Jack get to know his father by retelling stories and filling in some of the gaps. Still, it's painfully obvious that guilt continues to be a pretty big stumbling block for him. Even though he talks with Abby and has gone for professional help, I suspect that lugging around that kind of baggage has taken a toll. Seems like such a waste—woulda, coulda, shoulda—because the truth is, you can't go back and change what's already happened.

Life doesn't come with erasers, just more paper.

acknowledgments

I am grateful to so many for helping me bring
A Dedication to life.

To Sam, Joan, and George; thanks for inspiring me
and for sharing the daily challenges of writing.

To my mother and brother, Virginia Zaiss and Rick Zaiss;
thanks for always believing in me.

To Joanne Jackson; thanks for reading, rereading,
editing, and re-editing the manuscript while
beating me at golf and Scrabble.

To Angela Prusia; thanks for taking time away
from your own writing to provide insightful
comments and criticisms.

To my readers; thanks for giving me a chance.
I hope you laughed and cried, and now love life
a little more.

Thank you all.